Patriarch

Soul of the Witch Saga - Book 6
C. Marie Bowen

Pixler Publications

Patriarch
Soul of the Witch Saga – Book 6
by C. Marie Bowen

This book was previously published as *Coven Moon, Book 3*.
ISBN-13: 978-1-945215-285 – Paperback

ISBN-13: 978-1-945215-278– EPUB

Cover Design by C. Marie Bowen

Published by Pixler Publications

Discover other titles by C. Marie Bowen at www.cmariebowen.com

Contents

1. Harbor Delight   1
    Ayden MacKenna

2. Balm to Cure   9
    Margaret Prescott

3. September News   15
    Isaac Coleman

4. Disruptions   17
    Ayden MacKenna

5. All Hallows'   26
    Ayden Mackenna

6. Fire and Spirit   38
    Ayden Mackenna

7. Yuletide Gathering   46
    Margaret Prescott

8. Snow and Blood   49
    Ayden MacKenna

9. Possession   54
    Ayden MacKenna

10. Tea and Surprises   61
    Margaret Prescott

11. Dinner and Disappointment   70
     Ayden MacKenna

12. Sail away   72
     Ayden MacKenna

13. Coming Home   80
     Margaret Prescott

14. Family Fractured   84
     Lisbeth Coleman

15. Traveling Companions   87
     Melvyn MacKenna

16. Family Found   94
     Ayden MacKenna

17. Circle of Trust   99
     Margaret Prescott

18. Rumors and Stories   103
     Melvyn MacKenna

19. Word from Glasgow.   110
     Ayden MacKenna

20. Measured and Fitted   121
     Melvyn MacKenna

21. Arrivals   129
     Margaret Prescott

22. Truth Revealed   135
     Ayden MacKenna

23. Aftermath   143
     Jason Harris

24. Unfinished Reckonings   146
     Ayden MacKenna

25. Borrowed Shelter   154
   Melvyn MacKenna

26. Missing Shadows   156
   Ayden MacKenna

27. Everything Else   161
   Margaret Prescott

28. After The Storm   164
   Jason Harris

29. The Fracture Between   169
   Alyse James

30. Held on Suspicion   174
   Margaret Prescott

31. News from the Sea   186
   Margaret Prescott

32. Cold Inheritance   192
   Ayden MacKenna

33. What Slips Away   195
   Isaac Coleman

34. The Net Tightens   197
   Ayden MacKenna

35. Under Glass and Feathers   202
   Amy Harris

36. Ash and fury   204
   Ayden MacKenna

37. Bonds and Whispers   211
   Amy Harris

38. A Name from the Past   214
   Alyse James

39. The House of Watching Wings   216
    Ayden MacKenna

40. Fire and Feathers   219
    Amy Harris

41. The Fall and The Rise   222
    Jason Harris

42. The Shape of Return   226
    Margaret Prescott

43. The Garden Vow   235
    Alyse James

44. With Quiet Promise   239
    Ayden MacKenna

45. Loose Ends   243
    Ayden MacKenna

Sneak Peek at Aubrielle's Call   250

Also by   251

About the Author   252

Chapter 1

Harbor Delight

Ayden MacKenna

Boston, September 1874

Ayden stepped from Revere's Tavern and paused on the narrow walkway. Although the day had been seasonably pleasant, the sun's recent departure took with it the day's warmth. East, across the harbor, darkness obscured the horizon while high clouds changed from pink to orange to purple overhead.

He gave a nod to the ever-present coven companions who still shadowed his every move.

Let's give them something new.

Instead of heading uphill into the city or south along the harbor, he turned and strolled north, adjacent to the pier.

Ayden didn't recognize the men who followed him tonight. They weren't the ones who had jumped him the night of the Boston fire with their friend Gordy, nor had he seen these individuals come into the tavern these last few weeks.

Perhaps they wore a glamour like Jason's friend, Lisbeth.

The skill required to create glamours had to be as complex as the skills needed to perform in-depth healing. Anyone could throw a fireball, even those not particularly skilled with *Fire*, but healing took both *Fire* and *Earth* and more than a scant knowledge of the human body. Ayden's mother spent years as a healer—a midwife—but only strong enough to ease pain and slow blood loss during birth.

A glamour would take a great deal of *earth-skill*, Ayden imagined. Then again, he honestly had no idea how Lisbeth changed her form so convincingly.

When Jason had recognized Lisbeth in Revere's the night of the fire, she appeared to Ayden as a large, broad-shouldered man. Remembering that encounter, he realized he could not describe the face she wore. She had worn a hat; that much was certain. She'd pulled it low on her forehead and fled after Jason called her name. But did the face have a beard? What had been the hair color? There was more to creating a glamour than simply changing what other people saw—it also appeared to muddle what they remembered.

A convenient skill. I'd like to speak with this Lisbeth about it.

He glanced back at his unwanted companions, noting their features, then looked forward, setting their faces to memory.

If I can remember their face, I'll assume it is indeed theirs and not a skill-crafted visage.

At the curve in the harbor road, several dozen angry men had gathered in the street. Shaking their fists, they yelled obscenities and threats toward a three-story building across from the pier.

Although Ayden rarely walked this direction, he knew of this place—a brothel that catered to diverse sexual tastes and the occasional outlandish perversion. Men would sometimes come into Revere's to eat and sometimes gamble but, at the end of the evening, they'd often take their winnings up the street to Harbor's Delight—or Har-De's—as a few locals dubbed it.

Ayden slowed.

Mob mentality chilled him. He'd seen a man torn apart by an angry crowd in India for stealing a loaf of day-old bread for his family.

He knew of no *mind-magic* that would calm an angry throng, then or now.

One of the outraged men approached the closed entrance. "Come out and face a real man," he yelled, then nodded back at his friends, who shouted and urged him on. He downed a gulp from the half-pint whiskey bottle in his hand then threw it at the door. Glass shattered, and the spectators roared their approval. "Ya filthy sodomites—come out, or we'll burn you out!" He kicked the entry until the wood splintered, and the door flew open. Instead of rushing inside, the man retreated to the safety of the angry crowd.

The coven members who followed Ayden moved forward, their interest piqued by the powder keg of violence before them. They stood, captivated, two feet behind Ayden.

"This is turning uglier by the minute," Ayden said over his shoulder to his watchers.

"Don't talk to us," one of them murmured, his attention on the scene unfolding before them.

A match flared within the crowd, and then a lighted kerosene lantern was hurled toward the broken door. The lamp struck the casement and burst into flames.

The angry mob cheered.

Where are the harbor patrols?

Movement on the third floor caught Ayden's attention.

Robert Prescott stepped onto the balcony, surveyed the angry mob in the street while he tucked in his shirt, and then returned to the room.

"Damn." Ayden turned to the men behind him. "There's a man in there I need to get out unharmed." He looked from one man's glare to the other. "You can watch if you want, but lift one single finger to interfere, and I will kill you without hesitation or remorse. *Do you understand me?*" Mind-magic drove home the warning. *Do not test me.*

Both men paled and took an involuntary step back.

Ayden didn't wait for their response.

First, the Fire.

He took control of the flames in the doorway, stretching them across the entry as a barrier and containing the spread.

No one comes in.

The brothel sat on an oversized lot. Unruly bushes and saplings grew along the side and back of the establishment.

As Ayden darted into the high weeds and made for the back door, gunshots sounded in the street.

Surely, Robert understands the danger and will try to escape.

Ayden paused at the corner of the building and looked toward the back door.

Three partially dressed women escaped down the back steps and ran into the tall brush behind the establishment.

Ayden suspected a trail led across the overgrown lot behind Harbor's Delight to the street on the other side.

A man with a long rifle emerged, scanned the area, and lifted his weapon toward Ayden.

"I have a friend upstairs." Ayden lifted his hands and stepped into the small yard. "I mean to see him escape unharmed."

The rifleman lowered his weapon slightly. "Name your friend."

"Prescott," Ayden responded.

Behind Ayden, one of the coven thugs hollered, "He went this way," to the overexcited crowd.

Anger flared inside Ayden. His eyes closed for a moment as he reached for his two unwanted companions.

Only one of the followers remained, leading the group of angry men through the bushes to the back door and Ayden.

Ayden raised one hand and clenched his fist. Water flowed from between his fingers, down his arm, and onto the ground. "A promise made."

"Everyone out." The guard yelled over his shoulder into the building, dropping to a crouch as gunfire erupted from alongside the building.

There was no cover other than the overgrown brush behind the tavern. Ayden ran across the exposed yard, crouched behind a bush in the weeds, and watched the back door.

Several men escaped the building and sprinted across the yard into the foliage along the path. Then Robert stood in the doorway. He spoke to the man with the rifle, nodded, and raced out the door.

"Robert!" Ayden rose to intercept him as they both ran for the narrow trail.

A flurry of angry shouts and gunfire erupted from the side of the house.

A molten fist struck Ayden in the back and threw him forward onto the ground.

"Ayden, what in God's name are you doing here?" Robert gripped him and urged him to his feet. "Come." He pulled Ayden's arm across his shoulder, taking his weight, and lifted him forward onto the narrow path.

Behind them, the rifleman on the back step gave cover fire as he ran to the path.

Ayden's shirt and pant leg were already slick with blood, and the material clung to his skin. "I've been shot."

"I saw that." Robert exited the trail and hurried across a cobblestone street and then down a path between two buildings. "Unfortunately, that will have to wait for the moment. Are you in much pain?"

"Some. I'll manage."

Robert released Ayden beside a door as he fumbled through his pocket. "I have the key here somewhere. Ah!" Robert unlocked the door, pushed it wide, and then gripped Ayden's jacket. "Inside, quickly."

The rifleman raced behind them between the buildings, and followed them in. "What a disaster." He closed the door and then set the rifle beside it.

Robert bolted the door and directed Ayden toward the back through aisles of cargo crates. "How did this happen?" He pushed open the office door and pointed to a sofa along the wall. "Have a seat, I'll find bandages." He paused as the other man entered the office. "Halstead, this is Ayden MacKenna—a friend of Margaret's." Robert gave Halstead's shoulder a pat as he hurried out of the office. "Ayden, this is Halstead Coffrey, an old friend of mine."

Halstead offered his hand to Ayden. "Call me Hal."

"Nice to meet you, Hal." Ayden tried to lift his right arm to take Hal's hand, but the pain in his side prevented it.

Hal withdrew his hand and stepped back, nodding toward Ayden's injury. "I almost shot you myself." He helped himself to the liquor on the sideboard, poured a drink, and handed it to Ayden. "How bad is it?" He motioned toward Ayden's side, then returned to the open cabinet and poured himself a drink.

Ayden downed the shot and set the glass on the side table. "I'm not sure how to answer since I've never been shot before." Ayden chuckled and then winced. "I'm not dead, so there's that. I'm fairly certain the slug passed through." He unbuttoned his shirt with his left hand, but the wound was high on his right side, beneath his arm, and it hurt too much to twist out of his shirt.

Robert returned with the bandages and placed a pile of folded cloth strips on the low table in front of Ayden. "I'll bandage this as best I can, but we must take you to Margaret."

"No." Ayden rolled his good shoulder as Robert pulled the sleeve of his jacket and shirt past his elbow and then off his left hand. "What can she do?"

"It isn't what Margaret can or can't do." Robert removed the jacket from the injured side and then pulled the bloody shirt from Ayden's wound. "Sorry."

Ayden winced as the stuck cloth tore away. He looked down at his side and felt hot bile crawl up his throat. "Goddess. Margaret can't fix this."

"She can sew a straight seam, which is more than either Hal, or I can do." Robert lowered his voice, "But it isn't Margaret per se; it's the salve Amy left us." His voice dropped to a whisper, "It works like... *like magic.*" He held Ayden's gaze.

Ayden's brows rose in understanding. "Even so, Revere's is much closer. I don't think I can manage the trip to Beacon Hill and back tonight."

Robert wiped the blood from Ayden's back and side. "Hal, under the side-board, there's a bottle of grain alcohol. Pour a bit on these pads."

Hal came to the settee, looked at Ayden's gunshot wound, and shuddered. "Jesus." He took the pads and returned quickly, handing them to Robert. "I'm going to step out." He downed the rest of his drink, set the glass on the table, and left the room.

"No stomach for blood?" Ayden asked.

Robert shook his head. "Not precisely. Hal is averse to other people's pain."

"He was going to shoot me."

"He didn't know you then. It's difficult to explain." Robert stared at Ayden. "Are you ready?"

"Yes." Ayden ground his teeth as the alcohol burned into his raw flesh. "Enough!" Ayden finally shouted.

Robert removed the alcohol-drenched pad and replaced it with absorbent gauze. "I'm blaming this entirely on you, of course. Running into a maddened crowd, getting shot, refusing to go to Margaret for treatment." He wrapped long strips of linen around Ayden's chest, then tied the ends together. "What were you doing there anyway?"

"I happened to walk in that direction when I left Revere's. I saw the angry crowd and then you on the balcony. I thought to help you escape."

"I appreciate the sentiment, and I'm sorry you were injured on my account." Robert's gaze kept returning to the amulet Ayden wore on a chain around his neck. "That's a very unusual pendant. Where did you find something like that?"

Ayden lifted the stone. "It was a gift I received while in India."

"The color flares with a life of its own."

"Not unlike fine fire opals, although this stone, whatever it is, is not an opal."

Robert nodded and gathered the bloody scraps of material, tossing them into a tall trash bin. "I wonder if there would be a market for jewelry like that in Boston."

Ayden gripped the jewel in his fist. "This is one of a kind, I believe."

Hal returned with a white garment folded over his arm. "I found a shirt that should fit." He shook it out, held it up, and tossed the clothing to Robert. "I don't think it's one of yours."

"No." Robert examined the shirt. "Where did you find this?"

"In a big basket at the back of the closet."

"A costume?" Robert speculated.

Hal shrugged, picked up his empty glass, and carried it to the sideboard to refill his drink. "It was the only one wide enough at the shoulders." He turned and gazed at Ayden's bare torso. "But it will be too large at the waist."

"That doesn't matter." Robert helped Ayden get the shirt on over his bandages, then picked up his jacket as Ayden buttoned the shirt. "And now the coat."

Ayden grimaced as he came to his feet. His head felt light, and his knees weak, as though the single shot of whiskey had gone to his head. Blood already soaked Robert's carefully applied bandages.

Robert acted as valet and slipped the jacket onto his arms and shoulders. "I'll see you home."

"That's not necessary. Revere's is only a couple blocks away."

"Nevertheless." Robert pulled on his jacket. "I'll hail a cab from there and head up the hill."

Ayden paused at the door. "Nice to have met you, Hal."

"Goodnight, Ayden." Hal lifted his glass. "Goodnight, Robert."

"Lock up behind us," Robert reminded him, then led Ayden to the warehouse door.

Outside, the night had turned chill, and a mist seeped across the town from the harbor.

"Hal lives there?" Ayden asked as they headed south along the empty street.

"He does. There's a living space above the office. I'd charge him rent, but honestly, having someone there at night is one less guard I must pay."

"Does he work at Harbor's Delight?"

"He provides security several nights a week, or he did. I have a feeling that mob may have torn Har-De's to the ground."

The connection between Robert, Hal, and Harbor's Delight made no sense to Ayden. He was having trouble keeping pace with Robert physically, and his thoughts were wrapped in a hazy gauze. His side burned and throbbed, and he could sense blood seeping from the bandages down his leg and into his boot.

I can stop the bleeding once I'm alone—I think—but I need to rest before I try.

"Is this your door?"

Ayden nodded and pulled the key from his pocket.

Robert unlocked the door, gathered Ayden in his grip, and helped him into the room. "The chair or the bed?"

"Bed."

"Do you want me to help you undress?"

"No. Just let me be." Ayden struggled to keep his eyes open.

"I'm going to wedge this towel next to you to staunch the bleeding."

An uncomfortable wad was shoved against his side, but he didn't complain; he didn't have the energy.

"Ayden, try to stay awake. I'm going to get Margaret."

Chapter 2

Balm to Cure

Margaret Prescott

"Margaret!" Robert's voice echoed up the stairs as the front door flew open and banged against the entry wall.

Margaret shut her book and came to her feet. "What's wrong?" She looked down the stairs at her distraught husband. "Where's your hat?"

Robert ran a hand through his hair. "I'm not sure. What does it matter?" He started toward the back of the house, then stopped and looked up at Margaret. "Ayden's been shot. I need Amy's best salve and bandages. I need Wrigley to hitch up the carriage—" He spun and headed to the back of the house.

"Robert, slow down." Margaret tossed the book onto the window seat of the reading nook and hurried after him, thankful she hadn't undressed for the evening. "Where is Ayden?"

"At Revere's, in his room." Robert stalked through the kitchen and out the door. "Wrigley!"

"Robert, stop. I need more information. How badly is he injured?" She followed him down the back steps and into the yard.

Robert raised his fist to pound on Wrigley's door when it was snatched open. "I hear ye. Like as not the whole hill heard you too."

"I'm sorry, but this is an emergency. Ayden's been shot, and I need to take some of Amy's salve to him." When Wrigley didn't move, Robert raised his voice. "Right now, man. This is life and death." He waved his hand in the air, stomped to the carriage house door, and jerked it open. "Never mind, I'll rig it myself."

Margaret and Wrigley stared at each other in stunned silence for a moment. Margaret couldn't remember the last time she'd seen Robert this upset. "I'll gather bandages and the salve. I have it in the house." She spun on her heel and ran up the back steps into the kitchen. "Don't let him leave without me."

"What's the matter?" Peg stood in the opening between the kitchen and the dining room.

"Ayden MacKenna's been injured. Run upstairs and gather a basket full of sterile bandages. I'll need pads to staunch blood, long binding strips, and anything else you think I might need for a bullet wound. Hurry."

Peg ran for the stairs.

Margaret opened the remedy cupboard and reached over several packets and vials until she felt the mason jars with Amy's liniment. Careful not to knock the other items from the cabinet, she withdrew two jars, one at a time.

Peg returned to the kitchen with a large, hinged picnic basket over her arm. She lifted the lid to display sterilized bandages, a hooked needle with silk thread, and a vial of alcohol. "Will this do?" She flicked her wrist to light all the lamps in the kitchen and then sat the basket on the table for Margaret's inspection.

"Perfect." Margaret slipped the two jars into the basket and then lifted the container.

"I'll carry the bandages; you get your coat." Peg took the handbasket from Margaret's grip and headed outside.

Margaret pulled one of the gardening jackets from the wall and slipped it on as she followed Peg into the yard.

Behind the carriage house, Wrigley tightened the girth and checked the breast collar and breeching. "Good boy, Hob. Easy now." He climbed onto the high seat and arranged the reins.

"We have to wait for Margaret," Robert said as he opened the door.

"I'm here." She handed the basket to Robert, took his other hand, and climbed into the vehicle. "Peg, can you close everything up?"

"Yes, ma'am," Peggy called.

Robert pulled the door closed and shouted out the open window to Wrigley, "Let's go!"

It wasn't long before the transport pulled to an abrupt stop in front of Revere's Tavern.

Robert opened the vehicle door, jumped down, lifted the basket from the seat, and then helped Margaret to the ground. "The door to his room is this way." Robert indicated the narrow alleyway beside the tavern. "There won't be room to turn," he called to Wrigley.

"I'll back the carriage in."

"You can do that?"

Margaret yanked his jacket sleeve, "Take me to Ayden."

Robert nodded and took Margaret's arm. "You're wearing the gardening jacket?"

"The whole time. You just now noticed?"

At a door beside a darkened window, Robert pulled a key from his pocket and stepped inside. "I left a candle burning. I haven't been gone that long. Ayden, are you in here?"

When Ayden made no answer, Margaret flicked her wrist, and both a candle on the dresser and the kerosene lamp beside the bed sprang to light."

"Good Lord, Margaret. You startle me when you do that."

"Sorry." Margaret crossed the small room to the bed and dropped to her knees. "Ayden? Can you hear me?" She shed her jacket and then caught her breath at the amount of blood soaked into the towel wadded beside him.

"Is he... dead?" Robert queried hesitantly.

When Robert spoke, Ayden rolled his head, murmured something unintelligible, and struggled to open his eyes.

Wrigley entered the room, closed the alley door, and walked to the foot of the bed. "What are you waiting for? Turn him over and apply the salve. You don't need his permission."

"He's coming around. Ayden?" Margaret shook his shoulder gently. "I'm here to take care of your wound."

"Wrigley, take his feet and help me turn him." Robert slid his arms beneath Ayden's back. "The damage is on his right side."

When they lifted, Ayden's eyes opened, and he exclaimed with pain, "Ah!"

"Yup. That woke him up." Wrigley pulled off Ayden's boots. Blood dripped from his right boot and his sock was soaked with red. Wrigley glanced up and met Margaret's worried gaze.

"He's lost a lot of blood." Margaret tossed the blood-soaked towel from the bed behind her and reached for the basket.

I hope Peg packed the larger scissors.

Ayden murmured, "I dreamed of you."

Margaret looked over at Ayden and brushed his hair from his forehead, laying her palm across his brow. "You have a fever." His skin was hot and dry to the touch.

"Fire dancers burn my soul."

"And you're delirious."

His half-lidded gaze followed her as she worked, cutting away his borrowed shirt. "You're so beautiful."

"Hush, Ayden. Robert, hand me the alcohol." When she looked back, Ayden's eyes closed again.

"This is going to sting, but I must clean it before I stitch the wound. Ayden?" No response.

"You best take a good grip on him, Rob, before she pours the spirits on that bloody mess. He's like to cock up and smack her a good one." Wrigley gripped both ankles.

Ayden struggled against the pressure on his shoulders and legs.

Margaret placed the soaked pad of alcohol on the wound, and an agonized scream tore from Ayden's throat.

Margaret choked back a sob but held the pad in place as she murmured, "I'm sorry, Ayden. I'm so sorry. Almost done. I'm sorry."

Ayden muttered to Wrigley at the foot of his bed, "I'm awake now. I won't strike her."

"I still have to stitch the wound," Margaret leaned forward, then sat back with a sigh. "But I need more light."

"Robert, through the door behind you." Ayden tipped his head back to view Robert. "Follow the aisle—Harry behind the bar—he'll get what you need."

Robert nodded, sniffed, and wiped his face.

"This wasn't your fault," Ayden said, then closed his eyes again, his face gray.

"Your fault?" Margaret stared at her husband.

"I'll get more light." Robert shook his head at Margaret and mouthed, "Not my fault," then left the room.

In moments, Harry surged into the room. "What have you done now, Mac?" The lamp he carried brightened the room. He stopped beside the bed, rubbed his mouth, and started aghast at Ayden's bloody side.

Robert followed with a lamp as well and held it above the bed.

"Very good. I'll be quick." Margaret drew the ragged edges of Ayden's torn skin together and pressed the sharp tip of her hooked needle through them.

Ayden flinched but held still, eyes closed, his face ashen.

Margaret finished the tiny stitches, then sat back on her heels. "I need to see where the bullet went in. Wrigley, can you help Ayden roll onto his other side?"

"I can roll," Ayden assured her.

"Nevertheless." Margaret tipped her head at Wrigley to help, and the older man steadied Ayden's shoulder and helped him roll.

"The back is not as bad," Margaret murmured. Her hand shook as she reached for another alcohol-drenched cloth. She'd never seen someone lose so much blood and live.

"He's out again," Wrigley told her.

Margaret nodded and cleaned the entrance wound. "This isn't bleeding as much. The opening is small and should close well on its own. Amy's salve and a bandage is all this needs." She dipped two fingers into the light green salve and applied it to both the stitches on his back and the hole in front.

Blood continued to ooze through the stitches, and she bit her bottom lip to stop it from quivering.

I can't lose him again; dear Goddess, be merciful.

The folded pads covering the wounds would need to be strapped in place.

Together, Robert and Wrigley lifted Ayden's shoulders from the bed, and Margaret, with Harry's help, passed long strips of binding cloth beneath him several times.

When Margaret was satisfied the bandages would remain in place, she nodded to the men.

With care, they eased Ayden down on his left side.

"The ointment will make him sleep. Hard." She looked at Harry. "He won't be any use to you for a few days. If he wakes, offer him water or weak tea."

"I will." Harry nodded. "How did he get shot?"

"You heard about the ruckus down at Harbor's Delight..." Robert asked as he followed Harry out of Ayden's room.

"I want to stay with him," Margaret confessed to Wrigley.

"I know you do, but you know you can't. It's a shame we don't know a healer who could mend this."

"Amy would have been more help than I've been tonight." She pushed a strand of hair out of her face with the back of her wrist, then brushed a tear from her cheek.

"Maybe. But she couldn't care for him like you have. That must count for something." Wrigley came around the bed and held out his hand to Margaret. "Let me help you up."

She took his hand and then shook her head. "I can't feel my legs."

Wrigley wrapped his arm around her and helped her to her feet. "I've got you. Just hold on until the feeling comes back."

Margaret nodded as her legs began to tingle. She gazed down at Ayden. "What if the salve doesn't work?" Laying on his left side, he faced away from her. "Has he stopped breathing?"

"He's breathing." Wrigley helped Margaret to the single chair in the room. "Keep wiggling your toes."

"Should we have called a physician?" She wiped another tear. *What is wrong with me?*

"And what would they have done? The same as what you've done, probably less. Or worse, try to bleed the poor man. No. You've done well."

Robert returned to the room and looked from Margaret's tear-filled eyes to Ayden. "Is he...?"

"He's fine. Sleeping or unconscious from blood loss. We've done all we can," Wrigley picked up Margaret's gardening coat. "We should go and let your daughter's salve do its work."

"We don't know if it will work at all!" Margaret grabbed the handkerchief Robert offered and covered her face.

"It works on horses, small animals, and me. It helped heal that nasty cut from the leather knife." Wrigley offered, holding out the tiny scar on his hand.

"That was small compared to this." Margaret stood and approached Ayden's bed. "I should stay."

"Harry will look in on him, and I daresay, there are any number of ladies asking after his health. He'll be fine." Robert stepped past Margaret and locked the outside door. He picked up the basket from the bedside. "Is this everything?"

"Yes." Margaret took her coat from Wrigley and put it on. "I'd feel better if Peg came to check on him. At least she's skilled." With one last look at Ayden, she followed Robert from the room.

Chapter 3

September News

Isaac Coleman

Isaac Coleman shook the pages of the Boston Globe, folded it in half, and continued to read an article on recent renovations in the neighboring City of Chelsea. The article failed to hold his attention nor keep his mind from the recent quarrel with his wife.

The sharp sound of breaking glass echoed down the stairs. Apparently, Helena remained in a difficult mood.

"Such a shame," he muttered at the ceiling, then refocused on the article. His thoughts, however, wouldn't let go.

How had the James family gone these twenty years, broken my family apart?

How had a single man, returned from Goddess knows where, caused such an uproar among my congregation?

The current debacle began when that pig farmer, what was his name? Ah, yes, Gordon Carmichael stepped forward during a coven meeting and announced Ayden MacKenna had returned from the grave.

Several in his congregation remembered the MacKenna family, which, of course, recalled the James family—witches of the first order who terrified Carmichael, Milton Kohler, and the like.

Both families had departed long before Coleman moved his stables and his family from Savannah to Boston. Still, Carmichael's fear that MacKenna would somehow draw the James family back to Boston terrified the man.

A terror that only I should instill in my coven. After all, fear equals power.

It made sense to have MacKenna followed. To make sure he and the last remaining member of the James family, a Brahmin like himself, Mrs. Margaret Prescott, never ran afoul of each other.

How was he to know Gordon and his friends would confront MacKenna and burn down half the city?

Damn them all.

And now his wife, bitter at having their daughter participate in the defense of the very fabric of their lives, hid in their room, breaking her lovely and expensive bottles and mirrors because her darling Lisbeth patrolled the street disguised as a man.

A soft tap at the door ignited Isaac's pent fury, and he crumpled the paper and ground his teeth. "Yes?"

"Sorry to disturb you, sir. There's a man at the side gate. He asked to speak with you and gave me this." The manservant moved closer to Isaac and held out a folded piece of paper.

"You want me to reach for it?" Isaac's lip curled back as he snarled.

"No, sir." The servant placed the note in his employer's hand and stepped back quickly. "He said he would wait for a response."

The coven leader flipped open the note and scanned the scrawled message, then folded the missive and ran his nail along the crease several times before he spoke. "Did he say anything else? Be precise."

"Only that they lost sight of their... quarry after it went to ground, sir."

"Did he say how long ago he lost sight of his objective?"

"No. He only said earlier this evening, sir. He didn't give a time."

"I see." Isaac slipped the note into his jacket pocket and rose to his feet. "Tell the man he may return home. I've no need for him for the rest of this evening."

The manservant nodded and hurried toward the door.

"Also, tell the coachman I'll need the carriage in an hour."

"Very good, sir."

This madness has taken over my life. Tonight—yes, tonight—I will put an end to it.

Chapter 4

Disruptions

Ayden MacKenna

Heat pressed down on him.

The fire-dancers must be nearby.

He couldn't see them in the darkness, but their heat burned his skin and pierced his side.

Rakesh? Is this your doing?

"Thank you for letting me in to check on him, Mr. Tull."

"Call me Harry, Miss Johnson."

"Please, call me Peg."

I don't recognize the woman's voice, but Harry—I know Harry. Where am I?

Ayden struggled to open his eyes. But his eyelids refused to separate, as though they were bonded shut.

Has Rakesh blinded me?

"Look, I think he's waking up," Harry said. "Ayden, are you awake?"

A cool compress chilled his brow, and he shivered.

Ice-maidens. He'd heard the tales but never seen one.

"He still has a fever." The woman spoke, but her voice grew faint. "I'll change the bandages and apply more salve...." The voice faded away.

Emptiness overwhelmed him, and he sank into unconsciousness.

Sound returned first.

A footstep's soft shuffle sounded nearby, then the hard edge of a wooden chair scraped across the floor.

"I can tell you're awake," a man's voice, cold and annoyed, pronounced each syllable distinctly. "Open your damned eyes, witch. Let's see how impressive you are now."

Ayden rolled his head toward the voice and struggled to open his eyes. He gasped as a sudden cold splash drenched his face, but the water moistened his eyes and softened the rheum enough to allow him to part the lids and lashes. Through blurry vision, Ayden viewed his visitor.

Tall, thin, and white-haired like his daughter, the leader of the Boston coven sat on Ayden's only chair near his bedside. Dressed in a fine, cream-colored woolen suit, Isaac Coleman leaned forward; gloved hands rested on the head of his silver cane. He pushed back the brim of his top hat with the tip of one finger. "I thought a dowsing might get your attention."

Ayden's unused voice cracked when he spoke, "What do you want?" He coughed and struggled to sit upright.

"I want to know why you tried to kill one of my coven members."

"Tried?" Ayden swung his feet from the bed to the floor and hoped his head would stop spinning.

"Oh, I'm sorry. You thought you'd completed the deed? Did something interrupt you? A bullet, perhaps?" Coleman lifted his cane to poke Ayden's bandaged side with the sharp metal tip.

Ayden caught the gold inlaid stick with one hand and stopped it from advancing. He took a deep breath, gauging the damage to his side against the healthy man across from him, and smiled. "If you thought coming here, to what—intimidate me—kill me—would be easy, you've made a terrible mistake."

Isaac's lips pulled back with a snarl, and he thrust the cane again with considerably more force and a tinge of desperation.

Ayden tightened his grip, and the stick didn't move.

The coven leader jerked to his feet, knocking the chair to the floor. "Release my cane this instant!"

Ayden rose from the bed, holding the end of Isaac's walking stick in his fist. "Why should I?" He pulled the cane towards him, yanking Coleman close, and lowered his voice. "I warned your man not to interfere. They knew the price of their actions. Now I'm telling you—take your leave at once and think twice before entering my home uninvited. I might not be so forgiving the next time." He flattened the walking stick across Coleman's chest before shoving him and the stick toward the door.

The coven leader caught his balance, straightened his spine, and then his jacket. "You don't frighten me, Ayden MacKenna. You're a tall tale told to frighten young children, and I am not a child." He waved his hand, and the outside door swung violently open and crashed against the wall.

Wrigley stumbled back from the opening; his hand still raised in a fist to knock on the door. "Dear Lady, have mercy." His other hand came up, and an *earth-ward* shimmered between him and Isaac Coleman. "What are *you* doing here, of all places?"

Ayden followed Isaac to the door. "This uninvited guest was just leaving."

Coleman sniffed toward the Prescott driver with contempt and brushed at his fine jacket. "Know your place," he muttered, then strolled between the vehicle and the side of the building. He turned onto the street and glanced back briefly before he sauntered out of sight.

"What the devil did that bastard want?" Wrigley reached up and unbuckled a small case from the back of the carriage.

"I think he hoped I was near death, and if that were the case, to gloat and maybe help me along to that end."

"Had he seen you three days ago, he would have been more satisfied." Wrigley stepped into Ayden's small room and looked around. "Where's Margaret?"

"Margaret's here?"

"Well, clearly she's not, or I wouldn't have asked." He placed the case on the floor. "I dropped her and Peg off at the front of the tavern."

Ayden locked the outside door behind Wrigley, crossed the room, then came to an abrupt stop.

What am I thinking?

Shirtless and bandaged, he still wore the bloody trousers from the night of the Har-De's riot.

Did Wrigley say it had been three days?

Ayden turned to his dresser and pulled out the first shirt he found. "See what's keeping them. I'll change and follow you." He glanced back, but Wrigley had already gone. The room's door to the stockroom stood open.

Ayden peeked beneath the front bandage, frowned with confusion, and then unwrapped the binding. The flesh around the stitches had healed smoothly, and the puckered seam, with small, even stitches, was sealed completely. He felt his back, then pulled the shaving mirror from the wall and held it behind him while craning his neck to see. The bullet wound had left a scar, small, round, and white. Even the scab had fallen away.

How is this possible in just three days?

Ayden pulled on clean trousers and a shirt, then slipped on his shoes and took his jacket from a hook by the door. He rushed through the back room as he buttoned and tucked in his shirt.

He should have heard voices—Glenda, the waitress, calling an order to Li Qiang—Harry's laughter while chatting with a patron at the bar—but only silence greeted him as he entered the main room.

The tables were half filled, not unusual for the early hour. In the center of the tavern, Harry spoke with a familiar face.

That's the man who threw the lantern at Harbor's Delight.

Behind him, four of his followers nodded at everything their brave lantern-hurling leader said.

Margaret and Peg waited behind the group, unable or unwilling to pass them.

Near their usual corner table in the back, the two coven watchers stood to view the developments in the center of the tavern.

Ayden's glance moved around the room and up the staircase.

Molly gripped the rail as she stared down into the tavern. The only prostitute with a room at Revere's, she kept to her exclusive clients and never solicited the main room.

Still, she could be the spark that sets this blaze out of control.

His gaze captured Molly's, and he tipped his head toward her room.

Hide in your room.

Her eyes widened with surprise upon seeing him, then she nodded and disappeared through the door at the top of the stairs.

Wrigley waited just inside the main room. He leaned toward Ayden and whispered, "Are these the fellas that burned up that place down the block?"

"Some of them.

"They don't seem very happy with Revere's either." He jutted his chin towards the women. "Do you want me to get Peg and Margaret out of here?"

"I don't think so." Ayden's gaze locked with Margaret's. "The ladies presence makes this place even more respectable. Perhaps...."

"I've got just the thing." Wrigley hurried away and circled the room, moving around the men toward Peg and Margaret.

Harry's voice rose with ire, "As I explained before, if you want a meal, an ale, or a friendly game of Whist, feel free to have a seat." Harry took a deep breath and forced a smile as he struggled to regain his patience. "However, if you're looking for anything else, you'll need to go elsewhere."

"That wasn't my understanding," the leader of the small mob sneered.

"Unfortunately, you've been misinformed." Harry held out his arm to an empty table. "Please, have a seat. Today's menu was on the board as you entered and is also on the wall behind the bar. I would be glad to have our waitress come to your table and take your order."

Wrigley whispered in Margaret's ear, and a grin appeared on her face.

"Excuse me, gentlemen," Margaret announced in her mother's refined Boston Brahmin accent. Confidently loud and aristocratic, her voice carried throughout the tavern, and all eyes turned to Margaret. She sniffed down her nose at the suddenly confused men gathered around Harry and brushed at her skirt as she stepped between them and approached the barkeep. "I hate to interrupt your *very entertaining* discussion, but my niece and I would like to be seated." She glanced over her shoulder at the dumbfounded men, looked them up and down, sniffed with disdain again, and then looked back at Harry. "*Now,* please, and away from this riff-raff."

Harry nodded and moved away from the men. "I do apologize for your wait, Mrs. Prescott. Please, follow me." He led Margaret, Peg, and Wrigley to a table near the bar and held Margaret's chair.

With considerable flourish, she divested herself of her coat, hat, and gloves, handing them to Wrigley. "Perhaps there is a place in back you can put these until after our meal? Hmm?" She flicked her hand in a "go away" motion at Wrigley and gathered her skirt.

Harry pushed in her chair as she sat. "I'll send Glenda right over."

"Do wait until our entire party is seated, young man." She nodded her dismissal at Harry. "I do so hate to be bothered twice."

Ayden couldn't take his gaze from Margaret. Even her mannerisms mimicked those of her mother. Before his eyes, she had become the refined and demanding Chantal James in every aspect except her appearance.

If she could cast a glamour like Lisbeth, she would fool even me.

"I'll put these in your room," Wrigley commented as he passed Ayden.

"Thank you." Ayden ran a hand through his hair with the hope he appeared presentable.

The men who had been threatening Revere's left quickly. Their bravado was no match for Margaret's upper-crust snobbery.

Ayden chuckled and crossed the room to Margaret's table. "Very well done, Mrs. Prescott."

"I learned arrogance at my mother's knee." Margaret grinned, her gaze searched Ayden's face first, and then his injured side. "Are you really as well as you seem?"

Ayden pulled out a chair and sat beside Margaret. "I believe so. It's as though I've been healed. Did you become—" he looked at Peg, "or are you the healer?"

"Neither of us heal," Margaret said as Peg shook her head. "But Amy had a way with herbs and plants. She made a miraculous balm when the horse influenza broke out, then modified it into a liniment for people."

"Robert did mention her salve after I was injured. He said it worked like magic." Ayden raised an eyebrow.

"And so it does." Margaret acknowledged Wrigley's return with a warm smile. "Thank you for playing along so well."

"Your mother would be proud." Wrigley sat across from Ayden. "I put their coats in your room," he said to Ayden. "You need a better lock on your back door."

"One impervious to magical intrusion." Ayden signaled to Glenda they were ready to order.

"Did someone break in?" Margaret asked.

"Isaac Coleman, the scoundrel. He dashed water in my face and threatened me."

"Of course, he thought you were on your deathbed, the lout, or he wouldn't have had the gumption." Wrigley chuckled as he pounded his fist on the table with delight.

Ayden laughed. "He did appear rather surprised when I stood up."

"I'm sure the Coleman coven are not happy with us having dinner together." Margaret tipped her head toward the watchers. Only one remained, sipping a tall ale, his attention focused on their table.

"Honestly, I've had about enough of Coleman and his gang of witches. Besides us, who remains from Brown's coven?"

"So many have passed or moved away," Peg whispered, her head bowed.

"In Boston? Garrett is the only one that comes to mind," Wrigley said.

"Five would be enough to call corners and set large wards, but to take on Isaac's group..." Ayden shrugged. "I don't think it is enough."

"Take them on? Do you mean to fight them in the streets?" Margaret shook her head. "That is unacceptable."

"If they mean us harm, which they do, what else would you suggest?" Ayden asked.

The table fell silent.

The unacceptable is all that remains.

Glenda stopped at the table and took their drink and food orders. On Ayden's recommendation, they all ordered Li Qiang's spicy soup to eat with freshly baked bread served with each meal.

The missing watcher returned during the meal, but Ayden made no comment.

After dinner, the four returned to Ayden's small room so Margaret could inspect his injury.

"Undress from the waist up, and let me see the wounds," Margaret instructed.

"I'll go talk with Harry," Peg announced and left the room.

"I'll just step out with Peg." Wrigley headed for the door.

"No," Margaret stopped him. "Since Robert is so concerned with propriety, you'd best stay as a chaperone. Lord knows what I might do with a half-naked man."

"I don't think it's just *any* half-naked man your husband is concerned with," Wrigley replied with a chuckle and a wink at Ayden. "But I'll stay so you can't take advantage of poor Mr. MacKenna's delicate state."

"I didn't realize Robert is concerned about your coming here." Ayden hung up his jacket and unbuttoned his shirt.

"Robert doesn't care a fig about what might or might not go on between you and me." Margaret felt the smooth, unscarred flesh around the stitches on Ayden's side. "His only concern is what other people *might think*. The gossip on Beacon Hill is horrible. Not only does it destroy reputations, but businesses and marriages as well."

"So what you actually do is less important to your husband than a possible lack of discretion." Ayden turned as Margaret pulled his shirttail from his trousers to look at the entrance wound. "Were I your husband, I might not be so forgiving."

"Indeed? Well, I don't disagree with Robert's reasons." Margaret's gentle hand applied pressure, and she turned her gaze up to his. "Does that hurt? Can you feel my hand?"

"No, and yes." He smiled as their gazes held. "It feels nice."

"All right, then, with that, I'd best go find Peg." The door closed as Wrigley left the room.

Margaret chuckled. "I shouldn't laugh. Poor Wrigley."

Ayden rebuttoned his shirt. "He's a very poor chaperone, although I do believe he would swear he never left the room."

"Don't be fooled. He's right outside the door." Margaret gathered her and Peg's coats and lifted the medical basket. "Amy's salve worked better than expected." Sadness shadowed her eyes. "I wish she were here to see just how well it succeeded."

"Your daughter is amazing. I miss her and Jason, too." Ayden pulled his jacket on and took the basket from her hands. "Have you heard from them?"

"Yes. Amy wrote to us this summer. They arrived safely and are settling in. She's trying to adjust to the altitude and dry air."

"Don't be sad. You'll see her again." Ayden held out his arm to Margaret.

She stepped into his embrace, nodded, and sniffed, then turned her face into his shoulder. "I never realized how much I would miss her until she had gone."

"I know." He held her basket in one hand and cradled her close to his chest with the other, then softly kissed her hair. "I know she misses you as well."

Margaret stepped back and brushed the tears from her face. "I know, and I apologize. I'd forgotten what it's like to miss someone this much."

"Believe me. I understand."

"The holiday season will feel empty without her here." Margaret smiled and shrugged. "But we will all become used to it."

"Revere's hosts a Thanksgiving dinner. Li Qiang goes all out. You should bring Robert and Peg and Wrigley, of course." Ayden opened the door.

"Thank you. I'll speak with Robert and the others about your invitation."

Wrigley straightened as Ayden and Margaret entered the stockroom. "I was just coming to check on the two of you."

Ayden exchanged smiles with Margaret. "I believe Margaret is ready to go home now."

"Yes. If you would bring the carriage 'round front, I'll collect Peg, and we'll be right out."

Wrigley nodded and walked past them into Ayden's room. "Don't forget to ward this door. You never know what type of vermin will waltz right in." He chuckled, then went outside.

"He's right," Margaret said over her shoulder as they walked toward the main room. "As soon as we leave, put a ward on your door."

As promised, Peg waited at the bar chatting to Harry when he had a free moment. The tavern had filled with regulars from the dock and the sailors from ships in port. Harry filled Glenda's tray with beverages as she ferried the drinks to the tables.

"I'll let you know about Thanksgiving, but whether we can join you or not, I insist you spend Christmas Eve with us."

Chapter 5
All Hallows'

Ayden Mackenna

Ayden rolled over in bed and glanced toward the dim morning light creeping through his window. With a wave of his hand, he strengthened the fire in his coal stove. After a moment, he flicked his wrist, and the stove door swung open, then he rolled his head to the side and watched the flames.

Samhain is tomorrow.

The yearly holiday he most looked forward to as a child had become pale and pointless.

He couldn't even remember what he'd done last year.

Two years ago, he spent the night alone, a refugee adrift in a once familiar land. As he'd done so many times, he had turned to the fire for comfort and watched Jason and Amy waltz across a ballroom floor.

And before that?

The long years in India bled together. Magi Rakesh never bothered with celebrations unless a profit could be made.

The Zoroastrians they often lived with had numerous holy days and celebrations, many of which they dedicated to divine entities such as fire, earth, and water. Although he did not worship their creator, Ahura Mazda, Ayden felt a kinship with many Zoroastrian beliefs. But they did not celebrate Samhain.

Further back then. Samhain celebrations with Garrett's coven.

Those were the festivities he remembered the most. A carnival atmosphere—friends and family gathered—toasts, meals, and prayers shared by a close-knit community.

As his thoughts wandered, his memories reflected in the fire. Finally, he watched Garrett Brown speak with kind-hearted enthusiasm to the coven gathered in the big barn. Of course, he couldn't hear the coven leader's voice, but that didn't matter. He knew the gist of what Garrett would say.

I haven't seen Garrett since Jason and Amy's wedding, a year ago last August!

Although they both agreed to stay in touch, time had slipped away.

I should find out what Garrett is doing for Samhain.

Although the tavern opened for lunch at eleven, he wouldn't need to help behind the bar until the dinner rush.

Before he found other chores to manage this morning, he dressed and left his room through the stockroom door. The exit to the alley had wards in place to prevent intrusion, and he didn't want to bother removing and replacing them.

In the main room, Harry wiped glasses and readied the bar for the lunchtime rush. "Are you going out?"

"Yes. I want to check on an old friend." Ayden tucked his scarf into his overcoat and set his top hat on his head. "Are we doing anything special tomorrow night?"

"Tomorrow?" Harry's look of bewilderment passed, and he raised his eyebrows. "For All Saints' Eve?" He shrugged. "We're not too far from the Irish Wards." He set down the glass he'd polished and picked up the next. "What do you suggest?"

"A bonfire would be out of the question." Ayden pulled on his gloves. "And it's far too cold to bob for apples outside." He grinned at Harry. "Have you ever carved a gourd?"

"Carved one?"

"You make a hole in the top, empty the seeds, then carve a face in the shell, and put a short candle inside."

"MacKenna, you've lost your mind."

Ayden chuckled. "Have Glenda pick up several good sized pumpkins at the market before tomorrow tonight, and we'll set something up. Oh, and ask Li Qiang if he has a recipe for colcannon."

Harry laughed and waved his dishcloth at Ayden as he left the tavern. "I'm sure he does, but you know he'll put his own twist to mashed potatoes and cabbage."

"I'm counting on it."

Outside, the icy wind off the harbor grasped his hat, and he settled it more firmly on his head.

Across the street, his watchers rubbed their hands and stomped their feet to stay warm in the morning chill. He'd almost feel sorry for them if they didn't follow their twisted leader mindlessly.

Ayden waved to get their attention, pointed up the hill toward the business district, then turned his collar to the wind and headed to the courthouse in search of Garrett.

The rubble and destruction from the Boston fire had long since been cleared away. In its place, new buildings of stone rose beside now vacant lots. Construction boomed, and Ayden crossed the street at least four times to stay out of their way.

Once past the work areas, street vendors selling perogies' and bottled drinks waited for the workers to pause for lunch or take a break.

Ayden hurried past the food carts and continued up the street toward the courthouse. His pace slowed when the intense sensation of being watched brought the tiny hairs on his neck to attention. He peered over his shoulder to check the men who followed him.

The coven lackeys stood side by side at a food cart and spoke intensely with the vendor, paying Ayden no mind.

If not those two, then who?

Ayden threw his senses wide and immediately came up against a barrier. He spun toward the obstruction and found an old woman beside a vendor cart.

She wore a bright-colored scarf wrapped around her gray hair and tied beneath her chin. The woman must have been well over sixty, perhaps seventy. The sides of her pushcart stood open to the morning air. Silver chains of numerous lengths draped from hooks, while what appeared to be bracelets, pendants, and rings sparkled in the morning light.

Her gaze found him, and she tipped her head in greeting, her expression grim as though her worst suspicions were confirmed. She clutched a thick wool shawl around her shoulders and stepped from the shade of the building back into the relative warmth of the sunshine that shone on her trinket cart, turning her back to Ayden.

How odd.

Perplexed but no longer alarmed, Ayden climbed the steps to the courthouse entrance.

Inside, several courtrooms were in session with their doors closed. Ayden strolled to the end of the hallway and glanced in both directions. On his left were more closed doors; to the right, three stood open. He turned right.

Inside the second room, Ayden found his quarry.

Judge Garrett Brown hunched over a large desk, his forehead resting on the heel of his hand as he read the brief before him.

Ayden tapped on the open door. "Excuse me—"

"I'm not taking petitions today," Judge Brown said without looking up. "You should speak to the bailiff."

"I'm sorry, Judge, he got right past me." The bailiff gripped Ayden's arm. "If you'd come this way, sir."

"Of course." Ayden stepped back from the judge's chambers. "I didn't mean to bother you, Garrett. I only wanted to invite you to the tavern tomorrow for Samhain."

Judge Brown's head rose, and he blinked at the men in the doorway. "Ayden! I didn't realize it was you." He tossed his glasses onto the papers, stood, and came around the desk. "Ed, it's fine. I know this man." He held out his arm. "Please, come in, Ayden. Ed, could you close the door? Thank you."

Garrett extended his arm toward the leather guest chair. "I don't have much time to visit this morning. I have a hearing in less than an hour. Please, sit. Sit." Garrett relaxed onto the second chair and smiled as Ayden took his seat.

Although he'd spoken with Garrett at Jason and Amy's wedding, he'd half expected the clan leader to look like the man who filled his childhood memories. Where he once had a full head of thinning brown hair, he now boasted a fringe of gray-brown hair around his head with a shiny bald pate in the middle. His wire-rimmed glasses remained the same, but his stature seemed smaller.

A child's perspective, perhaps.

"Are you still in touch with Margaret?" Garrett asked.

"I am." Ayden smiled and released his jacket button. "Her husband and I are becoming quite good friends, if you can imagine such a thing."

"I'm not surprised." Garrett chuckled. "Barrister Hall told me Margaret's daughter and new husband moved west. To Colorado, was it?"

"Yes. Jason has an uncle there, I believe, and a cousin."

"Well, I wish them well."

"As do I." Ayden nodded. "It has been far too long, old friend. I apologize for not finding you sooner. I have questions to ask and stories to tell you."

"I understand. I was determined to find you after the wedding, but there are only so many hours...." Garrett pulled out his pocket watch. "And I've limited time today. You mentioned Samhain?"

"I did. We're having a small celebration at Revere's Tavern. It is nothing religious, only a fall festival. I came by to invite you. As I said, I have questions."

"I'd be delighted to raise a pint to the Goddess with you." Garrett came to his feet. "What time?"

"Around sunset. I'll buy you dinner." Ayden rose and held out his hand to Judge Brown.

Garrett shook his hand and smiled. "I look forward to it."

The bailiff caught his attention outside Garrett's chamber and escorted him to the exit. "I'm sorry I accosted you in the judge's chamber. I didn't realize you were an acquaintance of Judge Brown's."

"No apology is necessary. I shouldn't have intruded as I did." The men shook hands, and Ayden stepped outside into the brisk fall sunshine and adjusted his hat.

Construction workers crowded around the food vendors down the street, and the coven watchdogs were nowhere in sight. The trinket vendor who stared at him so intently earlier had also taken her leave.

He slipped the top button on his coat through the hole, tightened his scarf, and then pulled his warm leather gloves on his hands. The sensation of *not* being observed amused him, and he grinned as he hurried down the courthouse steps toward Revere's.

Glenda purchased two dozen small gourds, some pumpkin, and some squash and had them delivered, along with Li Qiang's cabbage and potatoes the next morning.

Ayden and Harry constructed a billboard sign inviting customers to come inside for an All Hallow's Eve meal and carving contest. Ayden carved a pumpkin and left it on a table near the window with the other gourds, small carving knives, spoons, and a large bowl.

By sunset, sailors and dock workers filled the tables. They raised a pint and enjoyed Li Qiang's spicy twist on colcannon.

Ayden had reserved the small table in the back near the bar and smiled with delight when Judge Garrett Brown crossed Revere's threshold.

Ayden nodded to Harry as he removed his apron and walked around the bar to shake hands with the judge. "Happy Samhain."

"And to you." Judge Brown smiled at Ayden and nodded to Harry, who watched from behind the bar.

"What will you have?" Harry called with a welcoming grin.

"Ale for me," Garrett replied.

Ayden held out his arm toward the table in the corner. "One for me as well, Harry."

Garrett hung his coat and hat on the wall hook behind the table, then settled into his chair. "Your tavern is much nicer than I'd thought it would be, I'm delighted to say. Most of the dockside taverns are less well maintained."

"I agree. The owner, Marion Tull, used to live above the tavern with his wife. He insisted Revere's be the type of place a man could take a lady for supper."

"Very nice." Garrett tipped his head to Glenda as she delivered their drinks. "Thank you."

"Two Samhain specials?" she asked.

"And that is?" Garrett queried.

"Half a roasted chicken with the cook's special cabbage and mash." Glenda grinned at the men.

"Yes, please," Garrett replied.

"Make that two." Ayden took a deep drink of his ale as Glenda left the table. "So, Judge Garrett Brown. I never knew you had an interest in law."

"Really?" The older man smiled. "Even with all the law books I had in the farm office." He chuckled and held up his hand to forestall Ayden's defense. "Well, I do. I always have. After Chantal sold the farm, I came to Boston and took the bar exam. That would have been nearly twenty-five years ago. I enjoyed working as a barrister for a time, then had the opportunity to become a judge."

"I'm glad for you." Ayden turned his mug on the table, then looked at his old coven leader. "Do you still correspond with Chantal?"

"Oh, heavens no. I did manage the sale of Sully's properties. There are still a few along the Carolina coast that the James family owns, but her boys have taken over those duties. I haven't heard from Chantal in a good ten years, probably more."

"I'm surprised they left Boston, what with Margaret with child. You'd think she'd want a hand in raising her granddaughter."

"I agree. They left town around the time Margaret gave birth, as I remember." Garrett took a drink and returned his mug to the table, a faraway look in his eyes. "Those were strange times. I was still at the farm. A cholera epidemic spread through Boston, mostly on the north end." He met Ayden's stare and shook his head. "That's when we lost your mother and the young Johnson couple. Your father came to me after she'd passed. Everything he owned was piled in an old wagon with your brother, Melvyn, was it? They spent a night at the farm before they headed south."

Ayden sat up. "Did he tell you where they were going?"

Garrett shook his head. "No. I thought they might return to New Haven. I even wrote to Cousin Lou, but he hadn't seen them."

"I'd like to find them," Ayden murmured.

"I'll write my cousin again. It couldn't hurt."

Glenda brought dinner to their table, and the conversation paused.

Li Qiang, a masterful cook, had provided his usual outstanding twist to local fare, making a simple cabbage and mash dish into a spicy and flavorful experience.

"This is marvelous!" Garrett exclaimed as he captured the last bit of potatoes on a piece of chicken. "Are the meals always so outstanding?"

Ayden nodded as he pushed his plate away. "Yes. That's not to say some of his offerings are a bit too well-seasoned for my taste, but overall, he is nothing short of a master chef. Don't tell him I said so."

From the corner of his eye, Ayden spotted two new watchers entering the tavern. He leaned forward and spoke softly to Garrett, "Do you know the coven leader in Boston?"

Garrett shook his head. "No. Not really. I had no interest in continuing the coven after Chantal sold the farm. I don't believe any of our old members belong to it."

"At least two do. Gordon and Milton. They were my age or thereabouts. I forget their last names."

"Carmichael and Kohler, as I recall. But why do you ask about the new leader?"

"He's had his men harass me to the point of magical violence. Then he showed up at Margaret's husband's birthday party uninvited, refused to come in, and warned Margaret, Wrigley, and I not to start a rival coven. He came to my room at the tavern one night after I'd been injured and threatened me directly."

"You jest?"

"No. Unfortunately, I do not. To make matters worse, he has me followed." Ayden tipped his head toward the tavern door. "The two gentlemen in dark coats waiting for a table are part of his coven. There are always two, and they shadow me everywhere I go. He even has Margaret's house watched."

"It sounds as though he is extremely insecure."

Garrett's comment caught Ayden by surprise, and he swallowed the sip of ale he'd just taken quickly so as not to choke as he laughed. "I would have to agree. I should have warned you about them before I invited you to sup with me. Now Coleman will be even more on edge."

"Oh, I don't know. I doubt those fellows over there even know who I am."

Glenda set two new mugs of ale on their table and put the empty mugs on her tray. "Harry wants to know when you'll start the carving contest." She smiled at both men, then moved on to the next table.

Ayden stood. "If you'll excuse me, I have a few duties to perform."

"I'll finish my drink and watch the show from here." Garrett raised his mug.

Ayden picked up his ale and crossed the room to the carving station. At the front of the tavern, he turned to face the room. "Could I have your attention for a moment?"

The tavern slowly quieted as Ayden paced before the table. "Perhaps you are wondering about the pumpkins on this table?" He nodded at those who shouted or raised their drinks. "As you may know, tonight we celebrate Samhain or All Hallow's Eve."

A scattering of applause sounded in the room.

"Halloween." He paused and gazed around the room. "A night of divination and séances, but also a harvest festival to mark the end of the farmer's growing season. In honor of this annual celebration, we offer you a carving competition." He held out his arm to the pumpkins arranged on the table. From where he stood, he noticed a dozen or more smaller ones stacked in a washtub behind the table.

"Does anyone have experience in carving pumpkins?"

Two hands rose.

"There is room for you both to demonstrate your skill and enter your creation into our pumpkin carving contest. The winner will receive their Samhain Supper at Revere's Tavern tonight for free!"

The contestants, both dock workers by their clothing, chuckled as they stood and approached the pumpkin-carving table.

"There are your knives, spoons to scoop, and the bowl for the seeds. Take all the time you need. Begin whenever you wish." Ayden turned to the tavern. "Let's give our first contestants a big round of applause."

As the men began carving their gourds, Ayden wove through the tables and returned to Garrett.

"A toast then." Garrett raised his mug as Ayden took his seat. "To the God and Goddess of all things, to beginnings and endings, and the chaos in between."

"To our Lord and Lady. *Sláinte.*" Ayden tapped his mug to Garrett's, then took a long draw on his ale. "It's good to spend time with you, old friend. We must do this more often."

"I agree."

They watched the contestants in silence for a while.

Both men were making significant progress. In short order, one held up a gutted and carved pumpkin for display. The pumpkin's toothy smile echoed the artist's childish grin.

"How are you going to determine a winner?" Garrett queried.

"I will have the audience vote by clapping."

The other contestant finished and held his carving above his head — the outline of a cat with an arched back.

"That is talent." Ayden proclaimed and clapped with the rest of the audience.

"They're both winners in my book. Look, more contestants."

Two customers hurried to take their place behind the pumpkin carving table.

Glenda directed the previous contestants to put their pumpkins on a bench along the wall as they returned to their tables. She placed candles inside both pumpkins and lit them with a flame at the end of a long straw.

"Do you have enough pumpkins?" Garrett wondered aloud.

"More than enough. We will be long sick of pumpkin pies and pumpkin bread before they are gone, I assure you."

"I believe you told me earlier that the owner used to live upstairs. Who lives there now?"

"It's empty. When Marion and his wife moved, he told me I would be welcome to move into the apartment; I just never have. It feels like it should be Harry's."

"The bartender? He's their son?"

"Yes. Harry Tull. I told him he should move in up there, but he refused. He rents a small house not far from here. He says he prefers not to be here when he's off work."

"Can't say as I blame him." Garrett lifted his empty mug to Glenda, and she nodded. "He doesn't want to be the tavern owner eventually?"

"He says he doesn't, but he's young. He could change his mind."

Garrett nodded. "Thank you, my dear," he said to Glenda as she brought him another ale.

They watched several more contestants, remarking on their creative minds and laughing at some participants' foolishness.

Garrett drained his mug, waved off Glenda, and smiled at Ayden. "Thank you for inviting me. I've had a nice time. We should get together again—soon."

"I agree. Thanksgiving?"

"I have plans. I am taking the train to New Haven to see my cousin. I'll ask about your brother again while I'm there."

"I appreciate that." Ayden finished his ale, stood when Garrett rose, and took the ex-coven leader's hand. "Then let's consider Christmas."

"Christmas, indeed. A yuletide gathering would be wonderful." He put on his coat and hat, tipped the brim to Ayden, and then made his way through the tables to the door.

Two more men finished carving pumpkins, and the no new contestants took their place.

Ayden crossed the tavern and stood beside the carving station. "Any other contestants?"

"Who's the winner?" one of the participants called, and laughter filled the room.

Once the amusement died, Ayden stepped to the row of carved pumpkins. "All of you will vote for the winner." He moved two of the pumpkins to the carving table. "Clap for the best of these two, and that pumpkin will move on to the next round."

Ayden held his hand over a pumpkin with three semi-round holes, and a scattering of applause sounded. He moved to one with a toothy grin, and loud applause rang out.

He held up the losing pumpkin. "Do you want to take your pumpkin home with you? If so, come get it. Otherwise, we will leave it over here." He placed it near the door.

It took several rounds of applause to get to the final two pumpkins. It came down to the cat with the arched back and a profile of a witch. The applause and shouts were loud for both.

"I declare this a tie! We have two winners." Ayden exclaimed. "If the contestants for these carvings would come up, Glenda will make sure to adjust your dinner tab."

The man who carved the cat stood and hurried to get his pumpkin, but the carver of the witch did not.

"Come on now, don't be shy. Come up and get your winnings!"

In back, one of the coven members who watched Ayden tonight stood up.

A witch carving. I should have guessed.

"Is this your pumpkin?" Ayden called, bemused. "It's all right. Come claim it, and Glenda will adjust your dinner tab."

The man walked slowly to the table. His counterpart laughed loudly, finding the situation hilarious.

Ayden looked at the man's face. He turned away to pick up the pumpkin and tried to recall his features.

Nothing.

Ayden smiled as he handed the man his carving. "Congratulations again. You are incredibly talented with a knife."

The man nodded, took his pumpkin, and hurried away.

Once more, when the man turned away, Ayden could not remember his face.

He's wearing a glamour, but why?

Lisbeth had told Jason she could no longer go to the tavern, so either that had changed, or this was another person with the skill to cast a false face charm.

The man returned to his table and nodded pleasantly when Glenda took their order.

"Now, if you have a pumpkin on your table, Glenda will bring the carver one free drink of their choice, so please claim your pumpkins and have a happy Samhain."

Before long, the pumpkins found their way to tables, and the happy participants claimed their drinks. Soon after, the crowd began to thin.

"Make sure Li Qiang gets his pick of the remaining pumpkins," Ayden told Harry.

Harry wiped a cloth across the top as the jovial crowd meandered toward the exit. "There are only a few uncarved. You had good participation for something so strange."

"It's not strange." Ayden laughed.

"If you say so." Harry chuckled. "But rest assured; I'll take them to the kitchen before I leave."

"Thank you, Harry. Happy Halloween."

Chapter 6

Fire and Spirit

Ayden Mackenna

In his room, Ayden relaxed on the bed and stared at the stove's flames as they warmed the small room. He removed his shoes, lay back on his bed, and watched the fire ripple and swell.

Often, during Samhain festivals on Garrett's farm, a few coven members would perform a séance and attempt to reach across the thinning veil to speak with the dead. Ayden had never participated for fear he would find the ghoulish face of the dead slave-catcher awaiting him.

In the silence of his room, his thoughts turned to his mother.

After a few moments, her face took shape and resolved, just as he remembered it.

As he watched a scene from his memory play out, his eyelids fluttered closed. "I'm sorry, Mother."

Ayden.

A voice from the flames shocked him awake. He swung his feet to the floor and stared hard at the fire. "Mother?"

His mother's face wavered and changed, resolving into a woman with a colorful scarf clutched around her shoulders. She breathed deeply with her eyes closed. Abruptly, she straightened and opened her eyes. You are the vitch named Ayden MacKenna. Son of Lyam and Rachael. The woman in the flame waited for a response.

Visions don't speak. They make no sound whatsoever, so what is this?

In disbelief, Ayden nodded. "I am the son of Lyam and Rachael. Who are you?"

The woman smiled cautiously. *I startled you. Forgive me. I needed to approach a being of such radiant power as yourself vith great care and caution, if possible, from a distance.*

She paused as though she considered her words with great care. *I pray you are not as vicked as the* thrall *at your chest and your unbridled power suggests. To speak with you may be imprudent, but my curiosity and a spirit familiar to you compels me.* She bowed, breaking eye contact.

When she straightened and opened her eyes, her wary smile remained. *I am Miera Barbaneagra.*

Her name meant nothing. An Eastern European accent colored her words, but her English was precise. The images around and behind her continued to strengthen and clear. She stood before a workbench littered with bits of twisted silver and small stones.

The trinket vendor? How is this possible?

Ayden's mind spun. He reached toward the flame, but his hand trembled, and instead, he rested his palm on his knee.

"Miera, you say. Can I call you Miera?"

The woman dipped her head slightly. *You may.*

"You're the trinket vendor I saw yesterday near the courthouse."

You remember me.

"How...." Ayden paused to clear his throat. "How are your words able to reach me through the flame?"

How? Confusion furrowed her brow, and her long, thin fingers tapped her pressed lips. *A spirit known to you stands before me. Her great vish is for you to know of her love for you. As I meditated on her vish, I saw you asleep. I admit, I hesitated, fearful of incurring your wrath, but in the end, I called your name.*

Miera's head swung slowly from side to side. *My meditation allows me to see vhat the spirit vishes me to see. When I saw you asleep in my mind, your mother bid me to call out to you, and I did. However, in this case, I believe our communication to be your magic, sorcerer, not my own.*

"My magic?" He blinked at the vision in the fire and gathered his wits. "Are you in a meditative trance now, *not* looking into a fire?

That is correct.

"And my mother is with you?"

Yes. Your mother stands beside me, and her heart yearns with in supplication. I am spirit-gifted, as are you. Spirits find me to gain both solace and rest. Your mother's need to assure you of her love keeps her bound in this place.

Miera turned her head as though listening to the distance. *Your mother says she lost you too soon. She thought you dead.* The trinket vendor lowered her chin and stared solemnly into Ayden's eyes. *Her spirit must move from this realm to find peace.*

The tightness in his throat made it difficult to speak. "What can I do?"

Can you not speak with her?

Ayden shook his head. "My spirit-gift does not work the same as yours."

Ah. That is too bad. Miera's shoulders slumped, but then her head came up. *Perhaps I can still help. Although, we vould need physical contact between us for you to see your mother's spirit.*

"Of course. Anything you need. Should I come to you? Tomorrow?"

No. I am not comfortable with you knowing where I live. I vill come to you.

"Revere's Tavern, along the wharf. You can come into the tavern and ask for me, or if you come in the morning, come to the back door and knock. I will answer."

Until tomorrow. Miera bowed her head. *Peace be vith you.* Her visage faded until only the fire remained.

When the knock on his outside door came the next morning, Ayden rose from his small desk in the corner and ran a hand through his hair. He couldn't remember the last time he'd felt so anxious about meeting someone.

With a wave, he dismissed the wards and opened the door.

Small in stature, Miera Barbaneagra tipped her head back to meet Ayden gaze. "Good morning, Mr. MacKenna. I hope I'm not late."

"You're right on time, and please, call me Ayden." He stepped back, opening the door wide. "Please, come in."

She hesitated for a moment, took a deep breath, squared her shoulders, and then dipped her head to Ayden and entered his room.

Ayden offered her the chair and sat across from her on the bed. "I know this is uncomfortable for you, but I assure you I'm not a dangerous man. I won't harm you."

She pressed her lips. "And the spirit chained around your neck? Is he un-harmed?"

Ayden withdrew the amulet. "I honestly don't know. This stone was a gift from a priest in India. He said it was unbelievably valuable. Too valuable for a servant such as I."

"You? A servant?"

"In India, yes. Magically indentured for twenty years, I was little more than a slave. But I've put that behind me." He lifted the flashing red stone bound in wire. "Caz, come forth."

A flicker, the size of a spark, jumped from the stone to Ayden's hand. There, it grew to the size of a candle flame. "We have company, Caz. I believe Miss Miera would like to meet you."

Miera's eyes widened with disbelief, and her mouth hung slack as she stared at the tiny elemental. "Is it... vhat is it?"

"It's a tiny fire elemental." Ayden held up his finger, and Caz scampered to the tip, hopping from one foot to the other in constant animation. "Across the vast Indian desert, larger elementals roam free."

"Amazing." Miera held up her finger. "May I? Does it burn?"

"He feels warm, but your skin won't blister. Be careful not to drop him." Ayden touched his fingertip to Miera's.

Caz danced across to her first knuckle, kicking up one ashen limb then the other."

"How do you get him back in the amulet?"

"Caz, return."

With a wave, the flame and cinder elemental hopped on the stone and disappeared inside. Red flashes bounced around the stone as Ayden tucked it beneath his shirt.

"Your tiny elemental has a soul, you know. That's how I knew it vas there. I felt his spirit. I never dreamed he was like that."

"What did you imagine it was?"

"I didn't know." Miera shrugged. "A soul ripped from the body of your enemy, worn around the victor's neck as a trophy perhaps." She lifted her chin. "I apologize for misjudging the situation."

Ayden chuckled and raised one brow. "A soul worn as a trophy. No wonder you were afraid to approach me."

"Had I known...."

"Should I release him? Caz, I mean. And how would I do that?"

Miera shook her head. Her steady gaze never left Ayden's. "If its kind dwells in a faraway land, it would be cruel to release him in this one. You would take away his haven, his tiny home. His spirit is not troubled, and he takes great pleasure in being near you. I believe he may be bonded to you of his own accord."

"I don't know what to say."

"Be at ease, Mr. Ayden." Miera patted his hand. "Your mother assures me you would never do something like what I imagined. I believe your elemental friend is safe."

"My mother."

"Yes."

"Is she here? Now?" Ayden involuntarily glanced around the room.

"She is. She wrings her hands both with anxiety and anticipation." Miera's assessing stare dug deep into Ayden's eyes. "Before I reveal her spirit, I must warn you not to be fearful or upset her in any way. Let her speak. Reassure her and encourage her to move on."

Ayden took a deep breath. "All right."

Miera held out her hand—long, thin fingers aged with veins and dark with discoloration. "When you're ready, take my hand."

Ayden ran his palms down his trouser legs. "I'm ready." He gently gripped her cool, dry fingers.

Behind Miera, a form coalesced, similar to the visions he watched in the flames.

"Is that? Is that her?" Ayden whispered with what breath remained in his lungs.

Miera never shifted her gaze from Ayden's face. "It is. Give her a moment. She is hesitant as well."

Ayden's chin came up as her face resolved. She hadn't aged since he last saw her. Realization dawned that she had been younger than he was now when he'd disappeared from her life.

"Mother?" His throat tightened, and he fought a sudden burning in his eyes. "Mama?"

"Ayden." The mist around her disappeared when she said his name, and she stepped forward to stand beside Miera. "You're alive, and you've come home." Although her outline had firmed, her form remained ghostly, semi-transparent.

"I wanted to come sooner, but I—"

"Careful," Miera murmured.

Ayden swallowed and nodded, then took a deep breath. "I love you, Mama."

Her head tipped back, and ghostly tears fell from her closed eyes and streaked down her face. "I love you, too." She opened her eyes and glanced at the surroundings. "You know, I can't find your father. He was with me at the house, and so was little Melvyn, but I haven't seen them in such a long time." Her voice trembled as she wrapped her arms around her waist.

"Ask her to look for a hallway," Miera whispered. "Perhaps she can find a light to guide her."

"Mother, do you see a hallway or a lighted passage?"

"No!" Rachael turned. "I see nothing like that—wait."

Behind Miera, a supernatural doorway opened, its passage extending far beyond the room into a blue swirling mist.

Rachael stared at the opening, her outline tense. "Someone is coming."

Ayden began to rise, but Miera gripped his hand with both of hers. "Be still. Watch."

Down the passage walked a lone figure. His stride tickled a memory in Ayden that remained just out of reach.

"Lyam," Rachael uttered. She stepped forward, then paused, hesitant to commit, as though unsure if her eyes deceived her.

The figure continued toward her but stopped a good distance from the end of the passageway. "I've waited for you, sweetheart." Lyam held out his arms, open and welcoming. "Won't you come home?"

Still gripping her stomach with both arms, she looked over her shoulder at Ayden. "But I've only just found you," she whispered.

"Father needs you." Ayden wiped his sleeve across his cheek and swallowed the lump in his throat. When he spoke, his voice sounded hoarse, "I'll be along, presently."

Rachael nodded. She glanced briefly at Miera, then squared her shoulders and proceeded down the hallway to Lyam.

Lyam hugged her like Ayden remembered he used to, and then arm in arm, they continued into the passage. The vision evaporated from the bottom up like smoke rising into the sky and was gone.

Ayden dropped Miera's hand and stared at the floor. "I've witnessed a miracle. Lord and Lady, bless my vision, for I have seen the miracle of your love."

Miera chuckled softly. "It's *spirit-magic*. You have it. I see it in the emanation surrounding you."

"I don't see spirits. My Goddess, I've never seen anything like that. No, my *spirit-gift* is visions of the future and memories of the past. They appear to me in fire. It's what my people call pyromancy. An unusual gift for one of us, those with elemental magic."

Miera blinked and shook her head. "Elemental magic?"

Ayden smiled and raised one hand. Above his fingers appeared a fist-sized flame. "*Fire*," he commented and held up his other hand. "*Water*." A similar-sized globe of water rotated above his fingers.

Miera sat back and gripped the edge of the wooden chair—her eyes wide with a mixture of amazement and fear.

"*Air*, in the form of a breeze." A gentle gust swirled around the room, lifting Miera's gray hair. "The remaining element is *Earth*. A simple demonstration is easier outside."

"No need," Miera replied quickly. "You control the elements. You are indeed a powerful sorcerer."

"There are a dozen or more *elementalists* that live in this area. Many of them belong to a coven and do the bidding of one man." Ayden rubbed his palms together and leaned forward. "I only mention this because he has his men follow me. They will undoubtedly know of your visit to me, and I do not want them to bother you." He met her gaze to convey his sincerity. "If you are visited by or bothered in any way by these men, you must let me know—through the fire."

"I'm cautious by nature and experience, but I will let you know."

"If they ask about your visit with me, you can tell them I purchased a necklace—an amulet."

"Don't vorry so much about me. I vill be fine." Miera rose slowly to her feet. "It has been my pleasure to meet and visit with you. I'm glad you had a visit with your mother before you sent her on to her rest."

"I am, too." He rose when she did and followed her to the door. "I learned my father has also passed."

"Was he the man who met your mother?"

"Yes."

"Well, it is best to know and not vonder."

"I still haven't located my younger brother. He was little more than a babe when I was taken."

Miera paused outside the door and looked up at Ayden with a knowing smile. "Well, there might be something we can do about that as well, but not today." She waved her hand as she turned and walked away.

Movement down the alley caught his eye.

A lone man stepped from the shadows near the building and hurried in the other direction.

Chapter 7

Yuletide Gathering

Margaret Prescott

Margaret paused at the sitting room window, pulled on her evening gloves, and smoothed the folds along her wrist. Her gaze again returned to the window. Outside, the blustery winter wind pushed the falling snow into new drifts against Wrigley's recently cleared front steps.

Beside her, Robert's Christmas tree glittered, bedecked with wrapped candy ornaments, popcorn strands, and bright red ribbons. Evergreen boughs woven with strings of bright red cranberries graced each room's mantle, and sprigs of mistletoe dangled above every doorway. Despite the festive holiday decorations throughout the house, a tiny mote of emptiness nestled in her heart.

Decorating the tree without Amy this year broke her heart. Robert tried to lighten her mood by making jokes and singing Christmas songs. To some extent, his efforts were successful, but she still missed her daughter. The one bright spot in this otherwise dismal holiday season was this evening and the extended family dinner she and Robert had planned.

The corners of Margaret's lips lifted in a slow smile. *Tonight, I'll see Ayden.* Movement on the street caught her attention.

A carriage stopped in front of the house, and two men climbed from the cab. The taller of the two reached up to pay the heavily bundled Hansom driver and then followed his companion to her front door.

Margaret straightened the bell of her skirt, then touched her hair as she left the sitting room and hurried to the entry.

As she stood beside the closed front door, her nervous stomach fluttered. She hadn't seen Ayden since before Halloween, after his injury healed.

Oh, for goodness' sake!

The knock sounded, and she waited, counting quietly to ten.

"Are they early? "Robert called from the railing above as he worked the collar button on his shirt.

"Just a bit, you have time."

Ten.

Margaret pulled open the door and immediately found Ayden's smile. "Hello. Please, come in."

The shorter man stepped over the threshold and smiled at Margaret as he stomped the snow from his boots on the entry rug. "Blessed Yule, young Margaret," Garrett said and chuckled.

Margaret's eyes widened, and she gasped, "Garrett! Ayden wrote he would bring a guest but failed to mention who."

"I hope it's not a problem." Garrett stepped close and kissed Margaret's cheek.

Behind him, Ayden entered and closed the door against the cold.

"Not at all," Margaret assured him. "This is a wonderful surprise."

"Here, let me take your coats." Peg hurried forward, dressed in her new deep blue velvet gown. She helped Ayden shed his coat, hung it in the coat closet, then took his hat and set it on the shelf. "Mr. Brown, may I take your coat?"

Garrett folded his coat over Peg's outstretched arm. "It's good to see you again, young lady."

"Thank you." Peg smiled as she accepted Garrett's top hat. "It is nice to see you too, Mr. Brown. Our cook informed me that dinner should be ready shortly."

"When did you get a cook?" Ayden asked as he followed Margaret into the sitting room.

"We hired her for Thanksgiving. It worked so well that I asked her to cook for us again tonight."

"Tired of Peg's cooking?" Ayden winked at Peg as she settled on the settee.

"Not at all," Margaret replied. "I want Peg and Wrigley to enjoy holiday dinners with Robert and me. There was simply no point in Peg cooking a feast for just two when I can hire Mrs. Bengston to cook for all four of us."

"Or tonight for seven," Robert quipped from the doorway.

"Dinner is about ready," the aforementioned cook's voice sounded from the dining room. "If your guests would like to take their seats."

"We're still waiting for one guest," Robert replied to Mrs. Bengston, then checked his watch. "I told Hal dinner would be at seven."

"Perhaps the weather delayed him." Ayden glanced out the window.

"Or perhaps he lost track of time," Garrett suggested, though his voice lacked conviction.

"No." Robert shook his head and joined Ayden at the window. "Something's amiss. It's not like Hal to be late."

"Perhaps we should go find him," Ayden suggested.

Robert nodded, "Garrett, are you up for braving the storm with us?"

Garrett walked to the entry closet, withdrew Ayden's long coat, and tossed it to the tall man. "Absolutely. Your friend wouldn't want us to leave him outside in this weather."

"Please be careful." Unease settled in Margaret's stomach, and she took Peg's hand. "We'll wait here."

Wrigley paused outside the dining room as he tugged at his jacket. He paused and stared at the men donning their winter jackets. "What's this then?"

"They're going to find Hal," Peg informed her uncle.

Mrs. Bengston's voice rang out again from the Kitchen. "Dinner is ready whenever you are."

"Keep it warm, Mrs. Bengston." Robert turned to Margaret. "We'll be back soon, hopefully with Hal."

Chapter 8

Snow and Blood

Ayden MacKenna

The three men donned coats and scarves and prepared to face the biting cold.

As Ayden stepped outside, the wind whipped around him, and stinging sleet peppered his face. The storm had driven even the strongest souls indoors, leaving the streets deserted of the familiar coven watchers.

They trudged through the snow-covered streets. The wind forced them to shield their eyes and hold their hats as they scanned the surroundings for any sign of Hal. The relentless cold seeped through their layers of clothing, but their determination pushed them forward.

Ayden glanced over every mound of snow, threw his senses ahead and on each side along their path as they traced the most likely route from the warehouse to Robert and Margaret's house.

"Would he have walked on a night like this?" Garrett questioned as they turned and headed into the Commons.

"No, I doubt it," Robert replied. "Then again, if he couldn't secure a cab...." His voice trailed off as they turned another corner.

After what felt like hours, Ayden sensed a figure bent beneath a drift beside a large oak tree near the park's edge. He squinted against the blowing snow and pointed. "Hal!" he shouted.

The mound of snow shifted and revealed Hal's bruised face, pale and shivering. "Ayden?"

Robert raced ahead. "Thank goodness we found you." Robert embraced Hal and pulled him to his feet. "Can you walk?"

Hal nodded, then sagged against Robert. "I think there were three of them."

Ayden caught Hal before he slipped from Robert's grasp and lifted Hal's arm around his neck to take Hal's weight. "We've got you."

With Hal secured between them, they returned to the house. The wind and snow made the journey slow and arduous. Finally, they reached the warmth of the entrance, where Margaret, Peg, and Wrigley waited anxiously.

Margaret rushed forward to help as they guided Hal inside. "Thank the Goddess," she breathed. "Is he badly injured?"

"I'm not sure. We came straight home," Robert replied, then hesitated. "Upstairs or the sitting room?"

Margaret pointed to the sitting room.

Ayden settled Hal on the settee and stepped back.

Hal had taken a terrible beating. He'd been hit several times in the face, his right eye swollen and dark, his lip split, with blood trailing from his nose. The hair on the back of his head was matted and darkened with more than melted snow. Blood oozed over his white collar.

Robert knelt before Hal, holding his hands. "Hal?"

Hal's uninjured eye opened. "I'm here. I'm fine, really, just so bloody cold." His body shook convulsively, and his open eye slowly closed.

Ayden glanced at the fireplace, and the flame rose slowly. A gentle breath of warm air from the fire settled around the settee.

"Robert, you need to move." Margaret edged her husband over and took his place before Hal. She ran her hand across Hal's forehead and dabbed her handkerchief at his eye, nose, and lip. "The bleeding has mostly stopped, thanks to the cold."

Peg placed a basket of bandages and ointments on the sofa beside Hal. "I wasn't sure what you'd need."

"This is fine. Help me with the back of his head."

Margaret and Peg worked quickly and efficiently, cleaning and bandaging Hal's wounds with gentle care. Hal winced occasionally but did not complain, his strength evident despite his injuries. The room was hushed, the only sounds being the crackle of the fire and the soft murmur of the women tending to Hal.

Once Hal was comfortable, Ayden looked around at the concerned faces. "Perhaps we should proceed with dinner," he suggested softly. "Hal needs rest and warmth, and the festivities might offer some distraction."

Margaret, hovering close to Hal, nodded in agreement. "I believe you're right, Ayden. We can keep an eye on him while we enjoy Mrs. Bengston's fine cooking." She smiled at Hal. "Would you like a tray to eat here, or would you prefer to join us in the dining room?"

"I'd like to try the dining room, please." Hal smiled up at Margaret.

Robert clasped Ayden's shoulder. "Help me move Hal."

"Just help me to my feet. I can get there on my own now that I've warmed."

Ayden gripped Hal's arm and assisted him to his feet.

Once upright, Hal leaned heavily on Robert, and Ayden followed them into the dining room.

In the center of the table was a roasted turkey beside a large platter of braised winter squash and sweet potatoes. Another large serving platter, filled with sliced, boiled ham, offered a choice of meats.

Each place setting already held a bowl of steaming clam chowder, ready for the diners to begin their meal. On the sideboard, a stack of rolls, sweet bread, various sauces, and pickled vegetables lent a spicy fragrance to the delicious aroma.

"This is *very* nice," Ayden said appreciatively. "Simply outstanding."

Robert helped Hal to his seat, then sat beside him rather than at the head of the table. "Ayden," he gestured to the open chair. "If you don't mind. I'll sit her and assist Hal."

Wrigley held Margaret's chair at the opposite end of the table from Ayden, then seated Peg before he took his seat beside her. Garrett sat across from Wrigley on the other side of Hal.

"Ayden, if you would say the blessing?" Margaret prompted.

Surprised, Ayden nodded. "Of course."

This honor is usually reserved for the head of the household.

Ayden glanced at Robert, but he had already bowed his head.

Ayden cleared his throat. "Lord and Lady, we give thanks for this Yuletide feast and the joy of gathered loved ones. May you bless us with peace and joy as you return light and warmth to this world."

"Amen," Hal whispered.

With heads bowed and the blessing concluded, the diners lifted their spoons and began to savor the clam chowder. The rich aroma of the turkey and ham mingled with the scent of the rolls and sweet bread, creating a warm and inviting atmosphere in the room. Conversation flowed easily, with the diners commenting on the delicious food and sharing laughter.

Mrs. Bengston hovered around the table, offering platters from the sideboard to the diners.

After their initial hunger was satisfied, Robert set his spoon down and looked to the head of the table. "Ayden, do you have any thoughts about who might have assaulted Hal?"

Ayden paused, his fork halfway to his mouth, and glanced at Hal, who nodded slightly, encouraging him to speak. Ayden lowered his utensil. "I've thought about it," he began, "The attack was too well-timed to be random."

Margaret leaned forward, her expression serious. "Do you think it was someone from Isaac Coleman's group?"

Ayden shook his head slowly. "I don't know, to be honest. What reason would they have to harm Hal?"

Hal shrugged. "I don't know an Isaac Coleman."

"Could it have been a few of those fanatics you spoke to me about?" Garrett suggested, his brow furrowed in thought.

"It's possible," Ayden agreed. "We need to consider both possibilities and keep our eyes open."

The discussion continued as they enjoyed the feast, each person contributing their thoughts and theories. Despite the shadow of the attack, the warmth of the gathering and the delicious food provided a sense of comfort and unity.

As the dinner wound down, Hal began to look weary.

Robert wiped his mouth and set his napkin aside. "Hal, let me help you upstairs to lie down," he offered gently.

Hal nodded, grateful for the assistance.

Robert supported Hal as they made their way to the front stairs, leaving the others to enjoy their tea and coffee. Wrigley, Garrett, and Peg engaged in light-hearted conversation, the warmth of the evening meal still lingering in the air.

Margaret and Ayden followed Robert and Hal toward the sitting room.

Ayden paused in the doorway beneath one of the many mistletoe decorations. He glanced up with a grin and then gazed down into Margaret's eyes, a soft smile on his lips. With a gentle tilt of his head, he leaned in, and their lips met in a tender kiss.

When Ayden lifted his head, he saw Robert and Hal watching from the stairs.

Robert gave a satisfied nod as if granting his silent approval.

Hal kissed Robert's neck with a contented smile before they continued their way upstairs.

"I'm not sure what to make of this," Ayden murmured.

"Don't think about it too much," Margaret replied. "Blessed Yule, my dear." She tipped her head back and leaned in for another.

After their kiss, Ayden encircled Margaret with his arms and rested his chin on her head. "I've missed you more than I can put into words."

Margaret nodded but remained silent.

"Ayden?" Peg's voice called from the dining room. "I have a question for you."

Ayden released Margaret, and they returned to the dining room. "Yes?"

"I thought Harry might have joined us for dinner tonight."

"Oh. Well, I did invite him," Ayden explained, "But he went to spend Christmas with his parents, Marion and Dolly, in South Carolina. After Marion's brother passed away, Marion inherited his brother's hotel and now is considering selling Revere's. Mr. Tull gave up hope that Harry would develop an interest in the restaurant-tavern trade and has encouraged me to make him an offer."

"Is that so?" Margaret said. "You should do it."

"Ah, well, I don't have that kind of capital, at least not yet."

"I could lend you the money, Ayden." Margaret encouraged. "I think it would be an excellent investment."

Ayden shook his head. "I couldn't do that."

"But…"

"Absolutely not." Ayden looked back at Peg. "If the storm doesn't delay Harry, I expect he'll return to work on Monday."

Chapter 9

Possession

Ayden MacKenna

Ayden stepped down from the cab and handed the driver a folded bill.

The evening air, lush with the scent of roses, drifted through the Commons. The walkways were alive with strolling couples and small groups of people enjoying the end of a lovely day.

If he hadn't been in a rush to make his evening walk past Margaret's home, he might have enjoyed a stroll up the hill.

Perhaps I'll enjoy the walk home.

Ayden made this trek almost nightly. Once around the Common to spot his shadows, then out of the park and down the street to where Margaret lived.

Since the Christmas attack on Halstead and their small group's inability to confirm if the assault had been part of the dockside fanatics or Coleman's coven, a growing unease took root deep in Ayden's heart.

He'd seen no sign of the fanatic gang since March when six of them strode into Revere's looking for trouble but settled for supper.

Ayden tipped his top hat to a couple who greeted him, then continued around the promenade. Along the north end of the park, he took the path to the gate, continued down the avenue, and then crossed to Margaret's side of the street before he turned.

Several strollers had abandoned the crush along the promenade. Instead, they chose to pace along the darker side of the road, making it easy to spot the motionless coven men who observed Robert and Margaret's home. There were two standing watch this evening.

As Ayden approached the Prescott home, a subtle movement near a bush caught his eye. Before he could identify the creature, a billow of fog rose from the ground before him, and his forward motion took him into the mist. A brief inhalation and his perspective changed.

No longer in control of his body, it stumbled, then straightened.

Panic seized Ayden as his hand lifted and turned front to back before his eyes, as though for inspection without his will.

Confusion clouded his thoughts. Trapped inside his body, a spectator to whatever controlled him, he watched as the view from his eyes changed. His body turned and hurried back the way he had come. He plowed into the couple behind him, shoving the pair out of his way.

"Hey, now!"

A chorus of chittering laughter erupted inside his head as his body began to run. On the verge of blacking out from sheer panic, he heard a woman's soft voice.

"There's nothing you can do. The demon has you."

"Demon?"

The woman's familiar voice continued to whisper against the backdrop of the giggling multitude.

"The Prophecy of the Twins is set in motion. Hell's spawn hunts them and will take whatever bodily transport it can find. Unfortunately, this is how you shall meet your end."

"Chantal!" Recognition jolted him. He'd heard her hated voice in his nightmares for most of his life. *"What have you done to me now?"*

The swarm ignored their hushed conversation as his body picked up speed. He ran southwest along the Charles River, past shuttered businesses, toward the edge of town.

Chantal remained quiet for a time, then cautiously asked, *"How do you know me?"*

"Are your crimes so vast you confuse your victims?"

She responded after another pause, drowned in the cackle of mindless minions. *"So—Ayden MacKenna found his way home. I hoped that Magi could keep you for a year but feared your return within a fortnight. How long did that madman hold you?"*

"You don't know? You placed my blood on a twenty-year Earth-bound slavery contract." His rage overrode his fear. *"Don't pretend as if you didn't know."*

"I overestimated your ability to gain your freedom."

"Or underestimated Magi Rakesh."

After a few seconds of silence, Ayden asked, *"So how are you here, inside my head?"*

"We're both inside the demon's head. He's simply using your body until it fails."

"And then?"

"And then, I believe you will die. Your mind will become still, and your soul will move on. I, however, shall remain here."

"Why is that?"

"He crushed the life from my body and took my soul hostage for my elemental skills. He hunts the twins, as was foretold."

"The demon thought they were at Margaret's?"

"He did. And now he knows they have gone west to reunite with Amy."

"In Colorado."

"Where I pray, he will be defeated, and the prophecy put to rest, once and for all."

Buildings became fewer along the river road as Ayden's lungs wheezed and his heart pounded like a drum. His feet stumbled, and he fell to one knee, then rose and continued.

He tripped once more before his chest hit the ground, and he didn't rise. Instead, in the direction his face landed, he watched a large black crow caw loudly and then take flight.

"Chantal?" he panted, his throat parched, his lungs and legs on fire.

Only silence responded. Ayden was alone, too weak to move.

Nausea overwhelmed him, and he vomited until his stomach emptied, and only dry heaves shook his frame.

"Easy now, I've got you."

Ayden peered up through watering eyes at a stranger. At first, he thought it was a man who helped him, but after he blinked, he realized it was a woman in a man's coat and hat.

"Can you sit? What happened? I saw you turn and run at the Prescott's. I had a devil of a time catching up."

A devil of a time...

Her words might have amused him at any other moment, but what he'd just experienced altered his perception of the world.

And he was still so sick.

He put his hand to the ground, turned his head, and heaved again. His head pounded like it might explode, and his chest and legs burned and cramped.

"Were you poisoned?" She handed him a handkerchief.

Ayden wiped his face and mouth, then shook his head. "I believe I was possessed by a demon."

The woman blinked at him, then withdrew a flask from her coat. "It's water, not whiskey."

Ayden took a sip, waited, then sipped again. "Thank you." He handed the flask back and rested his forearms on his raised knees. "I'm Ayden MacKenna."

"I know who you are." She stoppered the flask and slipped it back inside her long tan overcoat.

Ayden looked up at her, and their eyes met. "Lisbeth Coleman, I presume."

She nodded once, lifted her chin, and stared down the road toward Boston. "It's not good for you to be alone and helpless. Any of the others," she glanced down and met his gaze, "and I do mean any of them, would kill you."

Her bearing and self-confidence were not that of a young girl. The small wrinkles around her eyes portrayed a more mature woman than Jason had led Ayden to believe. This woman was too mature to be Isaac Coleman's child. Perhaps his younger sister?

"But not you?"

She smirked at his question. Rather than answer, she reached out a gloved hand to help him stand. "We have at least three miles to walk before we *might* find a cab. If you think you can, we should get moving."

Ayden brushed his palm against his slacks, took her outstretched hand, and staggered to his feet. He gripped her shoulder as his head spun.

"Easy. MacKenna. If you're going to faint, sit back down."

"I'll be fine. Just give me a moment." He inhaled deeply, then coughed. His lungs burned, and bitter bile stung his throat. Finally, he nodded and met her concerned gaze. "Let's go."

As they walked, the pain in his thighs and calves eased, but his lungs continued to catch and burn. He gasped a quick breath and asked, "You're Isaac's daughter? I thought you were much younger."

Lisbeth chuckled. "I'm certainly older than that group of socialites on the hill believes, but Isaac is my father." She lifted one eyebrow and smirked at him. "He's older than he looks as well."

"You don't care for the Brahmin's then?"

"Some of them are decent; others aren't. I don't have as much interaction with others my own age, but the younger set." She shook her head. "Horrible."

"Why pretend to be younger than you are? I would find that uncomfortable, even with your *glamour talent*."

"It is. I'm taking two years away from the trappings of society and hope to make a fresh debut as an older, wiser Lisbeth Coleman."

"Is that what your father would have you do?"

She looked up at Ayden out of the corner of her eye. "Of course."

"You thought well enough of Jason Harris, though."

"I did. Jason was one of the few decent ones. His wife, too. I met her once at a Halloween social before they wed and moved away."

"Did your father have Jason and Amy watched?"

"No. We only kept eyes you and the Prescott house."

Streetlights in the distance hailed the return to the city proper.

Ayden stopped walking and hung his head, his hands on his knees. "A moment, please. I must catch my breath."

"Why did you start running, anyway?"

"I told you; I was possessed."

Lisbeth rolled her eyes. "Possessed by demon rum, perhaps."

Ayden chuckled and shook his head. "I wouldn't believe it either, had it not happened to me."

"You've been walking past the Prescott house almost every night for months. I'm curious as to why."

Ayden tipped his head and slanted his gaze up at Lisbeth's back.

Her thick white-blonde hair hung in one large braid down her back. The man's brown overcoat she wore looked two sizes too large for her frame. Instead of a top hat, a worn brown bowler tipped the top of her eyebrows.

"Someone assaulted one of the Prescott's guests as they arrived on Christmas Eve. Did you not see the assault?"

"Someone may have. I wasn't there that night." Lisbeth paced away, then returned. "Who was harmed?"

"An employee and friend of the Prescotts, Halstead Coffrey. He took a nasty blow to the head with a club, and they split his lip and blackened his eye with their fist."

She shook her head. "I've heard nothing about an attack."

Ayden nodded and straightened as they stared at each other. "If you say so."

Her gaze frosted, and she turned and walked away.

Ayden followed slowly at first, then faster until he caught her and then matched her pace.

"I didn't mean to offend you. I'm still not well, and I am more than grateful for your help tonight."

Lisbeth sighed. "I know."

After another quarter of a mile, Lisbeth hailed a cab. "Back to the Prescott's or home?"

"Home, please."

"Take us along the wharf to Revere's Tavern, North End."

The cabbie nodded, "Yes, sir."

After they were seated and the carriage began to roll, Ayden cleared his throat. "Does your magic project those male features for everyone to see? Including him?"

"Of course."

"But I don't."

"Not now, no."

"How do they work? Your glamours? That's not a skill I'd ever imagined."

Lisbeth shrugged, and a slight smile dimpled her cheek. "Some secrets a girl must keep to herself."

"Are you the only one in your coven with that skill?"

She nodded. "As far as I know."

"Then I'd guess you like carving witches onto the side of pumpkins."

Her eyes widened. "How did you know it was me?"

Ayden smiled and leaned back against the cushions. "Someday, we'll trust each other enough to share our secrets."

"You think so?" Lisbeth raised one eyebrow. "Not while you belong to a rival coven."

"I haven't belonged to a coven since before you were born, and I'm not in one now." He dropped his voice and leaned forward. "Lisbeth, your father worries about things that aren't real."

She turned her head and gazed out the window, her lips pressed as though to still her words.

At Revere's, he exited the cab and closed the door, and they stared at each other for a few moments.

"I forgot to mention that Mrs. Prescott had visitors the earlier today. Amy returned home with two older men. They looked remarkably similar."

Ayden stared at her, then whispered, "Bernard and Bayard James?"

"The James brothers?" Lisbeth's brows rose, and she nodded. "Margaret's brothers, I should have guessed."

"I don't know why they'd be with Amy or why Amy would be in Boston. She went west with her husband, and as far as I know, they remain in Colorado."

"Perhaps it was someone else then. I did want to mention it to you because it is exactly what my father fears will happen—that the James family will return."

"But they didn't remain, correct?"

"No. They went inside for perhaps thirty minutes, then left. I can't even be sure the men were Margaret's brothers."

The Prophecy of the Twins, but Chantal James won't be back.

Ayden forced a smile for the coven leader's daughter. "Good night, Lisbeth, and again—thank you."

Ayden tapped the side of the cab and waved the driver forward, then wrapped one arm around the ache in his side and walked into the tavern.

Chapter 10

Tea and Surprises

Margaret Prescott

Margaret stared solemnly at her image in the dressing table mirror. In vain, she tried and failed to find her daughter's face in her reflection.

Amy, I miss you so much.

How could the *Prophecy* have happened after all our sacrifices to prevent it?

And how can I be here, contemplating a tea and dinner party while my daughter faces almost certain death at the hands of a monster?

"Margaret? Are you ready?" Robert's voice echoed from the entryway downstairs. "Wrigley is waiting, and we have to be back for supper with Hal and Ayden by seven."

She turned her gaze from the mirror and watched raindrops beat against her windowpane for a moment, composing herself. With thoughts as heavy as her heart, she rose with a sigh and left her room.

At least the weather matches my mood.

She would have called off both social engagements if she could. No wonder Robert looked at her oddly these last few days. She hadn't been the same since she'd received the magically imbued presents from her mother. Concern for her family's safety and her own preyed on her mind. No one in her life, except those far from her arms, could understand her fear.

The Prophecy is happening, just as my mother predicted.

Worse, Margaret could not be there to help protect her loved ones. Reaching into her pocket, she gripped the satchel her mother had sent for Robert and pulled the beautiful shawl, woven with defensive magic, close around her shoulders.

She paused at the top of the stairs to watch her husband struggle with his neckerchief in the entry.

"I'm ready. So sorry to run us behind." She held the rail lightly as she descended.

Robert glanced up. "We aren't late. Yet. Can you arrange my ascot?"

"Of course." At the bottom of the stairs, she took hold of Robert's silk. "Do you have a pin?"

"Oh, yes. Here."

Margaret adjusted the neckerchief and secured the pearl studded tie tack. "There." She gave his chest an affectionate pat. "Here. I've a gift for you. Do you like the scent?" She held the small pouch up for Robert to sniff.

"Why, yes." He took the satchel from her hand and inhaled again. "What is it? Lavender and clove?"

"Possibly." Margaret shrugged. "Put it in your inside pocket. You'll smell nice."

Robert tucked the scented bag into his jacket.

Margaret mustered a smile for her husband, retrieved an umbrella and her beaded handbag from the entry table, and then passed over the threshold while Robert held the door.

A brief shower pelted the carriage as they headed to the south end of Beacon Hill. Had it been sunny, they could have walked. However, Jason's parents lived in one of the few Brahmin homes with an expansive lawn and stables. It would be best for the Prescott's to arrive fresh instead of walk-weary and rain-soaked for tea.

A manservant answered the door and led them to the summer room. Instead of the dining tables that filled the same area during the Halloween masque, white wicker chairs cushioned with colorful pillows, a large settee, and a wooden table, all faced the rain-soaked garden window. Ferns and ivy graced the floor from pots and hung from the ceiling to create a green and white tropical paradise.

Rose waited serenely on the settee while Spencer Harris stood gazing out tall glass windows at the rain-soaked garden.

"Mr. and Mrs. Prescott," the manservant announced, then backed from the room.

"Margaret!" Rose's shrill voice rose along with her hand, and she waved across the room. "Do come, have a seat."

"Give me strength," Margaret whispered to Robert.

"You'll be fine, and we won't be here long." Robert stepped forward and shook Spencer's hand. "Good to see you again."

"I'm anxious to hear about the progress of our ship, but first, look at our blooms!" Spencer led Robert back to the windows.

"Sit here." Rose patted the cushion beside her. "I'll ring for refreshments."

Margaret folded her skirts beneath her legs and sat beside Rose. "Thank you for inviting us."

"It was Spencer's idea." She pulled the braided cord beside the couch. "He's been anxious about the ship and wanted to speak to your husband."

"I see."

"But he just couldn't bear the thought of going inside one of those—" Rose stopped abruptly and pulled the cord again. "Where is that maid?"

"Ma'am?" A young woman in a maid's livery hurried Rose's side.

"Tea for four and be quick about it."

"Yes, ma'am." The girl gave a short curtsey and rushed from the room.

"Do you find it difficult to keep help?" Margaret asked, then mentally bit her tongue.

"There is constant turnover." Rose shook her head in disgust and brushed imaginary lint from her skirt. "It is impossible to maintain good workers these days, don't you agree?"

The men returned from the windows and sat in tall white chairs across the table. "No tea yet?" Spencer complained.

Rose rolled her eyes and gave an exaggerated sigh. "It will be here shortly."

Even as Rose spoke, a maid hurried in with a silver tea service and prepared their repast while their conversation continued.

"As I was telling Spencer, our ship, which I intend to name Amylia, will be ready to sail at the end of July," Robert stated. "As you may know, most ironclad merchant vessels are built in Northern England and Scotland. The Amylia will be christened in River Clyde outside of Glasgow."

"Scotland! Good heavens," Rose declared. "I will not travel all the way to Europe to see our ship christened."

"I didn't realize the construction was that far along." Margaret blinked with surprise at her husband.

"I'm just pleased this venture is finally getting underway," Spencer added.

"How long will it take to reach China?" Rose squirmed in her seat, flashing an excited smile at Spencer.

"Well," Robert sat forward and rubbed his hands together. "Not long at all. However, we intend to trade at each port until our last stop in China. My warehouse is filled with tobacco, cotton, mineral oil, and lumber, which we will load onto the Amylia before we disembark from Glasglow. We pick up some cargo in Bombay, of course, then on to China for silk and spices."

"How will you fill our ship in Scotland with the merchandise from your warehouse?" Rose tipped her head.

"One of my other ships, either the *Atlantia* or the *Anatasha*, will ferry a second crew and special cargo earmarked for the Orient run to Glasglow. After she is loaded, the Amylia will continue to China, while the other ship will take on cargo and return to Boston via the West Indies."

"Yes, but how long until *we* reach China?" Rose snapped, pressing her lips.

"It will take approximately fifty additional days to reach China. Once there, we will sell the remaining cargo and purchase exotic Chinese goods to fill our hold. Then we retrace our course home. There will be fewer ports of call on our return as most Chinese and Indian items are intended for sale here in the States. We should arrive in Boston before Thanksgiving." Robert smiled as the maid filled his cup. "Thank you."

"That long? And what do you mean by most?"

"Rose, dear. We must trust Mr. Prescott knows his job and what is best for his business." Spencer nodded as the maid poured tea into his cup and added one sugar.

"Hmph." Rose crossed her arms and sat back with a pout on her lips.

"Have you chosen a captain?" Spencer asked before he bit into a scone.

Robert glanced at Margaret, then shook his head. "I've not made a final decision."

Margaret sipped her tea and remained silent. Robert's excited behavior and peculiar wording regarding the trading voyage made her uneasy.

I must be imagining things. Robert's use of 'we' could have been a slip of the tongue.

"So, we won't have the China goods until the fall," Spencer clarified.

"Merchants will be anxious to procure these items for their Christmas stock. The timing is perfect." Spencer reached for another cookie.

"Have you heard from Jason?" Margaret asked Rose, anxious to speak of something besides the joint venture.

"Why would I?" Rose asked with a raised eyebrow.

Margaret glanced from Rose to Robert, caught Spencer's annoyed stare, then smiled brightly at Rose. "I suppose you wouldn't, now that you mention it."

"Margaret is hoping for news about our daughter." Robert sat his cup on the saucer.

"Does she not write to her mother?" Rose asked with a grin.

"Oh, she does." Margaret paused to take a sip of tea, then put the cup and saucer on the table. "Quite often, in fact." She curled her lips in a forced smile for Rose. "Do forget I asked about your son."

"I do say," Robert interjected, earning both women's glare. "I believe we should be going. Dinner party tonight, you know."

"And again," Spencer lowered his little finger and set his teacup on the table. "We decline your invitation," he stood and arched his lower back, "with the deepest of regrets."

Margaret dabbed her lips with the napkin and placed it beside her plate. "Thank you for your hospitality." She stood and brushed her skirt.

"I'll call for the maid to show you out." Rose pulled the cord.

Outside, the sun had broken through the rain clouds even though rain still sprinkled from the sky.

Margaret opened her umbrella and handed it to Robert, who held it above their heads.

Wrigley brought the carriage around, and they headed for home.

"Please don't ask me to attend another tea with those people." Margaret brushed droplets from her skirt.

"I doubt we shall be invited again." Robert chuckled, then stilled Margaret's hand. "I can conduct business with Spencer Harris at the warehouse. I only thought it would be nice to socialize with them since our children are married."

"I understand your reasons. However, they are insufferable. They're both arrogant and ugly minded. It's a wonder Jason is such a pleasant young man coming from such stock."

"I believe they consider me a tradesman and you a mere tradesman's wife. In their view, Jason married down."

"He what?" Margaret jerked her hand away from Robert. "Your family owns ships, and mine owned property. They have some nerve."

"Your mother sold most of her properties after your father died, correct? You might consider investing your unused dowry." Robert looked out the window as they pulled to the curb in front of their home. "It's grown to a sizeable amount with interest, and since Amy has gone, you need something to occupy your clever mind."

"Perhaps I shall."

Inside, the enticing smells of Mrs. Bengston's cooking filled the house.

"I'm going to change." Margaret took the umbrella from her husband and shook it out. She put it in the holder to dry and tossed her reticule onto the entry table. "Our guests should arrive within the hour."

"Good." Robert opened the closet, removed his top hat, and set it on the shelf. "I need something to wash the taste of their refreshments out of my mouth."

With Peg's help, Margaret dressed in her red dinner gown, which had a satin drape in front and a mid-sized bustle behind. Multiple strokes from a long handle brush made her silver-streaked auburn hair shine. Peg pulled the locks into a simple loose bun at the back of her head held tight with a ruby-bedecked long-pronged comb.

As Peg hurried downstairs to answer the door, Margaret opened the center drawer of her dressing table. Shoved to the back of the drawer, wrapped in a large white handkerchief, was Amy's blood-encrusted comb she'd used to fend off Donetta Dunham's attack several years ago. She touched the cloth hesitantly.

What made me think of this comb?

The unpleasant afternoon with Jason's parents, no doubt. Donetta's injury was the prime reason for Jason's estrangement from them.

Why have I kept this bloody weapon?

Happy voices raised in greeting, made her shove the drawer shut and come to her feet. She looked at her face and gown in the mirror, wishing for less silver hair and fewer lines beside her eyes, then left her room to go down to greet her guests.

She and Robert sat at opposite ends of the shortened table, with Ayden on her left and Hal to her right.

Peg and Wrigley declined to join them this evening, opting instead to share their meal in Wrigley's small apartment.

Once the table held Mrs. Bengston's baked cod, a spring salad, beans, and corn muffins, the cook bowed to Margaret and Robert with a smile. "My nephew is coming by my house tonight, and I promised my husband I'd be there, so I'll be here to clean up the kitchen in the morning."

"Peg and I can clean up, Mrs. Bengston," Margaret assured the cook. "Go, be with your family."

"Thank you, ma'am. Enjoy your dinner." The cook returned to the kitchen and then made her exit through the back door.

Margaret smiled at the gentlemen seated at her table. "We must manage on our own this evening. But since Peg removed the inserts, our dining table is now an appropriate size for four." Margaret placed a portion of salad on her plate and then passed the bowl to Hal. "And we may easily serve ourselves."

At the end of the meal, Robert rose and refreshed water and wine glasses, then remained standing until Margaret looked at him curiously.

"Our newest ship, built in partnership with Spencer Harris, will be christened the *Amylia*, after our daughter. She shall voyage to China, stopping in Spain, Portugal, India, and a dozen other ports. The christening will be at the end of July in Glasgow, and she will set sail immediately thereafter."

"Splendid news!" Hal raised his glass. "To the *Amylia*."

Everyone drank a sip of wine to that announcement, yet Robert remained standing.

"Is there something else, Dear?" Margaret sat her glass down and touched her napkin to her lips.

"There is." Robert nodded, unable to meet her eye. "I intend to captain the *Amylia* on her maiden voyage."

"You?" Margaret gasped. "Do you think that's wise?"

"What about the warehouse? Your other ships?" Hal sat his wine glass down, his face pale.

"I would ask that you, Hal, take care of the warehouse. You know what our stock is, what is due to come in, and how I like things arranged."

"I don't know." Hal blinked quickly and looked away. "I don't know."

"I'll make the arrangement formal and officially hire you as my warehouse manager." Robert raised his glass to Hal, but Hal never looked up.

"Hal might take care of the warehouse, but he's not a businessman." Margaret fought the feeling of abandonment that washed over her. "Who will your clients meet to arrange delivery and make payments?" She reached over and gripped Hal's trembling hand.

"Ayden understands business and has become as much a part of our family as Hal. I intend to offer him a partnership in my shipping business and hope he will agree to manage things for the brief time I'll be gone. I promise, there is nothing difficult." Again, Robert raised his glass to Ayden, but his enthusiasm faltered.

Robert did not receive the response he had hoped.

Hal rose to his feet, his gaze pitched down at his plate. "I don't know how Margaret feels about this, but I am against it." He tossed his napkin to the table, spun on his heel, and left the dining room. Heavy footfalls echoed through the room as he stomped up the stairs.

Robert started after him, then stopped to look at Margaret, supplication apparent on his face.

"Go after him," Margaret scolded. "He's alone, and I..." her gaze darted to Ayden then back to her husband, "...am not."

With a brusque nod to Ayden and Margaret, Robert followed Hal up the stairs.

"Today has easily been *at least* three days long." Margaret heaved a sigh and smiled with resignation at Ayden. "Will you take Robert up on his partnership?"

Ayden shook his head. "I don't know what to think. Did you know about this?"

"No, but I'm not surprised. It's obvious Robert has given this a great deal of thought."

"Why do you say that?" Ayden asked.

Margaret shrugged one shoulder as she turned the wineglass stem between her fingers. "Making Hal the warehouse manager gives him a reason to wait for Robert's return. Hal has a place to live and an income while Robert is off meandering the seas. My greatest surprise is that he isn't taking Hal with him." Her throat tightened, and she took a sip of wine, then returned the glass to the table, turning it a few more times before she continued. "As for the partnership with you, I'm less sure of his motive." She glanced up at

Ayden, and his dark eyes captured her gaze. "Perhaps it's his way of giving us his blessing."

Ayden's brows rose with surprise, and he looked away. He picked up his wine and drained the glass, swallowing the rich red liquid. "Why would he do that?"

"He knew of my feelings for you, although he never had a name or face to measure against my longing."

"Even after you were first married, and your daughter was born?" Ayden lifted his gaze from his wine glass to Margaret.

"He knew." Margaret nodded. "He's always known. Robert and I may not speak of our most intimate emotions, but we know each other well." Gathering courage, Margaret lifted her hand to caress the side of Ayden's face. "I know for certain he wants me to be happy."

Ayden turned his head and kissed the palm of her hand, then took her fingers in his grip. "You're not concerned about the scandal?"

"We've kept Robert's indiscretions secret for over twenty years. He's discreet, and when in public, he and I have honest affection for each other, and it shows." Margaret leaned forward, her gaze dropping to Ayden's lips. "No one is privy to what we hold in our hearts, or what takes place beyond our doors, except us."

Chapter 11

Dinner and Disappointment

Ayden MacKenna

Margaret's slightly parted lips moved to taste his and drove Robert's announcement and proposal for partnership from Ayden's thoughts. He responded to her gentle, questioning caress with a tenderness of his own, cautious at first, then deeper as the wine on her lips and tongue mingled with his own.

No!

Ayden pulled away and shook his head. "A kiss beneath the mistletoe is one thing, but this—this continuous simmering passion between us—is another. You honestly believe Robert would approve of this—of us?"

Her face flushed; Margaret sat tall in her chair, lightly touching the utensils before her. "What do you suppose Robert and Hal are doing at this instant? Should I think less of the man who shared his name and raised my child?" Her narrowed, pain-filled eyes captured his gaze. "He has always known I loved another. *Always*. And I knew his physical desires never included me."

"You knew?" Ayden rose to his feet, unable to sit still a moment longer. "Did you know of his predilections when you agreed to marry him?"

Margaret stood and pushed her chair to the table. Her palms rested on the backrest while her fingers stretched in agitation. "Did I know? What does a child that age know of life and love? I knew Robert responded differently to my presence than other men. He was and shall ever be my dearest friend." Her gaze raked Ayden from the top of his head down, lingering below his belt. "But then, the only experience I had with a man's desire for me was you." Her voice dropped, and she looked away. "And that hardly counts."

"Hardly counts?" Ayden yanked his chair out of the way and stepped toward Margaret. "What we shared hardly counted to you?"

She turned to face him, eyes narrowed. "We were obsessed with each other. Bedazzled. Completely over the moon and insane with love." Tears filled her eyes as she spoke. "We existed in a fantasy that could never have survived our reality." She looked down, as tears etched her face. "We were just too caught up in the moment to realize it. The magic that filled my soul disappeared when you did."

Ayden ran his hand over his face and turned away. He couldn't deny their youthful passion, but what of now? Could he continue to love someone else's wife?

I already do.

But would that be enough?

"Please tell Robert I'll be happy to handle his business affairs while he's at sea. There's no need to make me a partner. I'll meet with him at the warehouse this week or next, and we can go over his books and processes." He walked to the entry closet and retrieved his hat. When he turned to call farewell, he found Margaret standing beside him.

She'd wiped the tears from her cheeks, but the sadness in her eyes remained, a reproach for his harsh words. "Our conversation took an unexpected turn. I apologize if I offended you."

"I'm not offended." Ayden placed his top hat on his head. "Just confused. Still yearning for that unrealistic fantasy, I suppose."

"You don't have to leave." Her glance strayed to the silence up the stairs.

"I do, for now." He followed her gaze upstairs, then looked down and touched his lips softly to hers. "I must understand within myself the difference between what I want and what I can have. Then we will speak of this again."

Chapter 12

Sail away

Ayden MacKenna

The early July heat made Ayden's room unbearably hot. It was time—or past time—to move his meager belongings to the upstairs apartment.

Marion and Dolly did not intend to return to Boston. Instead, Marion wrote him a letter explaining the situation and offered to sell Revere's to him, but Ayden did not have enough cash to make a decent offer.

Ayden gathered the few possessions he'd acquired since moving into Revere's three years ago. All the jewelry he owned had been gifts from the Tulls—tie tacks and cuff links. He kept them in a small box for trinkets. He'd built a simple clothes rack to hang his two nice suits. Again, both gifts from Marion and Dolly. He'd kept his voluminous black robe and worn garments from India, three pairs of work clothes, two kerosene lamps, and one unused candle.

Overall, not much to recommend me.

The furniture in the upstairs apartment would remain since the Tull's new home in Georgia came well fitted. Harry and a friend made the round trip to his parents' new place to deliver clothes and personal items his parents wanted to keep. What remained at Revere's would stay with the upstairs apartment.

Ayden barely remembered the layout from the few times he'd been inside the Tull's home.

He assembled his clothes on the bed, placed the trinket box on top, and then looked around. He'd have to make another trip for the lanterns—or leave them if there were lights upstairs. With a thought, he doused the flame, then gathered the four corners of the bedcover and hoisted his belongings over his shoulder.

He maneuvered through the dark but familiar stockroom and climbed the stairs. Instead of turning left to the office door on the upper landing, he reached to his right, opened the door to Tull's old apartment, and stepped inside.

In the darkened silence he paused to listen to the unfamiliar rooms before him. Expanding his senses, the swell of the rising tide across the harbor road spoke to him of freedom. Closer at hand, a voice raised in laughter reached him from the tavern downstairs, reminding him of friendship.

He'd spent the last few days with Robert, becoming acquainted with his incoming ship schedules, pending deliveries, and procedures. Keeping business books had become second nature to Ayden. Keeping up with Robert's accounts wouldn't be the problem.

With his mind, he put flame to wick throughout the apartment and looked over his new abode from the doorway. The makeshift bindle held over his shoulder.

From the small entry, he blinked solemnly at himself in a full-length mirror across from the door. To his right, the living area extended the full length of the small apartment with a back exit onto a railed landing with stairs which led down to the alley.

A red couch and matching cushioned chair, angled to face the empty fireplace. It flared momentarily with his elemental flame, then faded back to stone. End tables with lanterns gave the room a warm hue.

Past the mirrored entry, a cased opening led to a side of the apartment he had never seen.

Through the opening, and to his immediate left was a washroom. Ahead and to his right, a small kitchen with a coal-burning stove, small table and cupboards. An opening on the far side of the kitchen led to a short hallway and bedrooms.

Ayden peeked in the first bedroom. A narrow bed and short chest of drawers took most of the space in the small room. He flicked his wrist, and the room went dark.

Down the hall, he entered the main bedroom. In front of him stood a tall armoire. Angled in the corner between windows was a matching chest of drawers. The large bed stood against the inside wall with a nightstand on one side and a cushioned chair on the other.

He placed his items on the bed and unpacked his clothes. He set the trinket box atop the chest of drawers, hung his suits in the armoire, and then turned to look at the bed.

Oh, my dear Margaret.

How often had he dreamed of sharing a bed, life, and family with her?

He wandered back through the apartment. The furniture was nice, but it didn't belong to him.

Not unlike Margaret.

He unlocked and opened the outside door, inhaling the night air from the deck. At this height, he could see the city rise to Beacon Hill and feel the movement of the water in the harbor behind him.

Robert would sail for Glasgow later today, and Ayden promised to meet him and Margaret at the pier to wish him bon voyage just after high tide.

With a heavy sigh, Ayden returned inside and locked the outside door. He hurried down the stairs and into the tavern. He'd help Harry close and clean up for the night and then try to get a few hours of rest.

Ayden swept the floor while Harry wiped down the surfaces. As usual, their easy conversation was sprinkled with Harry's funny stories and Ayden's low chuckle.

"Did you finally move upstairs?" Harry asked.

"Just tonight. Somehow it feels... unnatural."

"You'll get used to it."

Ayden paused his sweeping and looked at Harry. "Are you still living in that small house you rent?"

"Yes, but I've been working with a fishing crew three days a week, so I'm barely there."

"Fishing? Really?" Ayden chuckled. "I had no idea. Why fishing?"

Harry stepped to the next table, wiped it clean, and gazed at Ayden. "To be outside on the ocean. To watch the sunrise as they pull the nets in."

"Crab?"

"Crab. Lobster. Shrimp. Whatever we catch in the net. I love it." He stepped to the last tabletop, pushed the small lamp to the side, and wiped the top.

Ayden emptied his dustpan into the trash. "I have a friend who owns ships. In fact, he will set sail today to take possession of his newest vessel in Scotland. After that, he'll continue on its maiden voyage to China."

"Can you imagine?" Harry flipped the hand towel into the air and caught it with a laugh. "Exotic ports, the wind in the sails."

"You would go to sea then, more than on a fishing rig?"

"I might." Harry rounded the bar and tossed the cleaning rag in a pan below the counter. "I'd certainly give it some thought, especially a merchant vessel like your friend's."

Ayden carried the broom to the stockroom entrance. "I'm going to go up and try to get some sleep before I have to be at the pier."

"I'm almost finished." Harry arranged glasses beneath the counter. "I can lock up."

"You know, now that I'm upstairs, you can sleep in the stockroom apartment."

"Thanks." Harry brushed the hair from his eyes. "But you know I like to get away from this place when I'm not working."

"Good night, then," Ayden called and headed upstairs to the unfamiliar rooms.

After Ayden undressed and climbed into the large bed, he stared wide-eyed at the dark ceiling. He could feel the soft swell of waves as they rolled inland bringing the morning tide, but the calming ebb and flow didn't lull him to sleep. Instead, as always, his thoughts returned to Margaret and the sweet kiss she offered at the Yuletide dinner party.

She was all he'd ever wanted in the world, and now, when she offered her affection so sweetly, he turned her away.

Why do I have such difficulty with this?

It's not as though he would interfere with her marriage to Robert. By all accounts, Robert welcomed Ayden and his affection toward his wife. And Margaret had not suffered in loveless or miserable marriage. Clearly, she and Robert cared deeply for one another. Also apparent was Robert's relationship with Halstead. That being outside the boundaries of acceptable association, Margaret's marriage kept Robert safe from scandal.

But what of Margaret? What of her desires and affections?

Ayden rolled to his side, and the nightstand lamp flared with a thought. He stared at the flame and paged through memories—Brown's farm, the small apartment where he and Margaret met, now Wrigley's home, followed by the lost years in India.

He could summon scenes from the past easily, but they didn't help. With a nudge, he moved from remembrance toward precognition. The memories from the past faded until only the flicker of light remained. After several moments, subtle movement caught his attention. As he stared, the outline firmed, and the scene unfolded.

Robert strode up the footway, then paused to look back at the wharf.

Margaret held Hal's arm as they watched his impending departure, tears in their eyes.

The vision faded as his eyes closed, and he drifted into a restless sleep.

Ayden donned his top hat as he exited Revere's. He walked briskly along the wharf to the departure pier, worried he may have risen too late and missed Robert's send-off.

Two men pushed away from the tavern front to follow at a discreet distance, as always.

Ayden continued north, past the passenger liners and the burned-out shell of the Harbor's Delight, to the piers where the merchant vessels docked.

Patriotic banners waved along the waterfront in the soft summer breeze, ready for the upcoming Fourth of July celebration.

Half empty, a large wagon stood near the gangway as deckhands loaded the last merchandise onto Robert's ship, the Atlantia.

On the near side of the gangplank waited the Prescott's carriage. Wrigley held the reins as the bustling port activity flourished all around them. Margaret, Hal, and Peg stood beside the vehicle with Robert, dressed in his captain's uniform.

Margaret glanced over her shoulder in Ayden's direction as Robert and Hal spoke quietly. She raised a gloved-covered arm and waved as she caught sight of him. She spoke in Peg's ear, nodded, and then left the shelter of the buggy to meet him on the pier.

"I'm so glad you were able to make it." She took his arm and slowed his pace. "I'm both excited and terrified for Robert, and he is so happy."

"How's Hal holding up?"

"There haven't been tears yet, thank goodness. I asked Hal to come to dinner tonight, but he said he intends to return to the warehouse as soon as Robert boards. He claims he would be unfit company for the rest of the day."

"He's probably correct." Ayden gave Hal an understanding look as they approached. "Oh, I want to tell you I moved into the upstairs apartment. I'm not sure why it took me so long."

Margaret smiled at him. "That's good. You deserve it for all the work you do."

Robert gave last-minute instructions to the longshoremen loading the cargo. He lifted a hand in greeting to Ayden, dodged two men carrying the last large piece of freight, and then returned to his family. "The tide has changed, and it is time for me to depart."

He hugged Hal, clapping him on the back. "You'll be busy, and I'll be back before you know it."

Hal nodded as Robert released him. "Please take care of yourself."

"Always, for you." Robert held out his hand to Margaret. "Thank you, my dear, for letting me sail this last time."

"As if I could stop you."

Robert wrapped his other arm around her shoulders, drew her close, and kissed her forehead. "Take care of everyone, as I know you will. And please, my dear, enjoy what has returned to you. It is a gift."

Margaret reached up on tiptoes and kissed Robert's cheek. "Hurry home, sweetheart."

Robert released his wife and crossed to Ayden. "I trust you to take care of all I hold dear."

Ayden gripped Robert's hand. "It shall remain as you left it."

Robert shook his head and chuckled. Leaning closer, he whispered, "Lord, I hope not, or Margaret will never let me hear the end of it."

Ayden blinked, surprised Robert would speak of Margaret in such a coarse manner.

Robert laughed at Ayden's expression and shook his hand again. "Well then, at least wish me luck."

"Of course." Ayden smiled. "Fair winds, my friend, and following seas. Your home and hearth are safe with me until you return."

Robert released Ayden, touched Margaret's hand briefly, then turned to Hal, but he had already departed.

Robert hesitated only a moment before climbing the gangway. At the top, he paused to look back and smile at his family.

Once aboard, the sailors lifted the long ramp and stowed it on the ship. Bells rang, and Robert shouted orders to the deckhands. The tide had indeed turned, and crewmen aboard tugs in the harbor signaled departing ships with flags on how to proceed in an orderly manner.

A black cloud belched from the rear stack as Atlantia cast off. Powered by coal, steam turned the propellor and moved the ship into the harbor channel. The crew would hoist Atlantia's sails once they reached the open sea.

Robert, on the master's deck, gave all his attention to the tug signaling his larger vessel.

Margaret held a handkerchief over her nose. "Sweet Goddess, I can hardly breathe."

Peg escaped the thickening air by retreating to the carriage.

A black scarf covered Wrigley's face, allowing only his eyes to shine from beneath his bowler. "Are you coming with us, or am I dropping you at the tavern?"

"He's coming home with us for dinner," Margaret replied to Wrigley, then entered the carriage.

"Unfortunately, I cannot." Ayden shook his head at Wrigley, then leaned in to speak to Margaret. "I'm sorry, but I must return to Revere's. Perhaps another time." He prepared to close the carriage door but paused at a snort from Wrigley.

The old driver shook his head and gave Ayden a narrow stare. "Get in, man. The least I can do is drop you up the way."

"All right. Thank you." Ayden took the empty seat across from Peg and Margaret and shut the door.

As soon as the carriage turned around and headed up the harbor road, the air cleared, and Margaret shook her once white hankie out of the window. "Soot! One reason I avoid the harbor."

"The wind direction was unfortunate." Ayden offered Margaret his pocket linen, but she waved him off.

"I'm fine. I know it's not always like that."

"I won't be able to join you for dinner tonight, either." Peg looked from Ayden to Margaret. "I have a ticket to an orchestra performance at the Music Hall."

Margaret's eyebrows rose in surprise. "Will you attend by yourself?"

Peg blushed. "No, well—not exactly. I'm meeting a friend there."

Ayden and Margaret shared a glance as Peg turned back to the window.

"Does your uncle know?" Margaret asked.

"He knows I'm going and will meet my friend there."

"Which friend? Do I know them?"

"No, I don't believe you do. I met him at the market in town, and we've spoken several times there." She plucked at her gown. "I know this is irregular, but we will be in a public place enjoying the music. The Hall is just past the Commons, off Park and Tremont."

"I know you can take care of yourself. I only wonder if a chaperone would be in order."

"I don't hold the social position that you and Amy do. No one will think anything inappropriate about my attendance."

"I'm sure you're correct—."

"I can take care of myself." Peg bristled. "I'll be home after the performance."

"Let us know how you like the concert. I've always enjoyed listening to music." Ayden smiled at Peg, then glanced out the window. "I believe this is my stop." Ayden opened the door as the carriage pulled to a halt and stepped from the rig.

Margaret continued to stare at Peg, the corner of her bottom lip caught between her teeth.

"Wrigley," Ayden asked as he closed the carriage door. "Are you aware of Peg's plans for this evening?"

"I am." Wrigley gave Ayden a short nod.

Ayden stepped back as Wrigley shook the reigns and mouthed, "He knows," to Margaret.

Margaret nodded and raised her hand in farewell as the carriage pulled away from the tavern.

Chapter 13

Coming Home

Margaret Prescott

Peg escaped from the carriage the moment Wrigley stopped in front of their house.

Margaret waited for Wrigley to place the step, then took his hand as she descended to the street. "Thank you," she said. "Would you like to join me for supper in the dining room?"

"Ah," Wrigley shook his head. "I would, but I already have plans for this evening. I'm sorry."

"No, no. That's fine. Another time."

Inside the house, she encountered Mrs. Bengston as she put on her coat. "Dinner is ready and still warm on the stove. I apologize for leaving before serving, but the mister sent a note saying he's feeling poorly. He asked if I could come home. I didn't think you'd mind."

"Of course, you must go. Let me have Wrigley drive you."

"I don't think so. It would take longer to go around and pick me up than it will to walk across the park and down the way." Mrs. Bengston tied the ribbons of her bonnet beneath her chin and picked her basket up from the entry table. "Just send me a note when you need me again."

"I will, and I hope Mr. Bengston will be alright."

"I'm sure he will. Good evening to you."

Margaret watched Mrs. Bengston disappear down the street and unlaced her bonnet.

Am I hungry? No. I should put Mrs. Bengston's dinner away.

She pulled off her gloves, tossed them on the entry table with her hat, and closed the front door. She found the kitchen tidy, with the stew covered on the unlit stove and the baked bread on the counter beneath a clean cloth.

There is nothing to do here until these cool down.

Surprised to hear footsteps rushing down the front stairs, Margaret hurried into the dining room in time to see the hem of Peg's gown disappear out the front door and hear it shut.

"Oh. Have fun, dear," Margaret called to the empty room.

Robert's ship sailed before noon, and she refused to wait alone in the empty house for Peg or Wrigley to return.

Why is Ayden pushing me away? Perhaps it is time I ask.

Making a sudden decision, Margaret grabbed her bonnet and a light shawl from the closet. She would confront Ayden and make that man talk with her. Once they were alone, she could reason with him.

Margaret locked the front door and walked briskly to the Commons. The warm afternoon mocked her shawl, but it would be chilly this evening.

Since I intend to stay at Revere's until Ayden and I can come to an understanding, one way or the other, it might be late.

The shadows of the trees seemed to whisper to her as she crossed the park. Reaching the other side, she stepped into the short queue and gave her destination to the valet, who directed the cab and helped Margaret into the vehicle.

Inside the tavern, Margaret approached Harry at the bar. "Good evening, Mr. Tull. Is Ayden here?" she asked, her voice tinged with urgency.

Harry smiled at Margaret and nodded. "He's upstairs in his apartment. Would you like me to send Glenda to fetch him?"

"I don't think that's necessary." Margaret smiled but felt her cheeks blush. "It's just up the stairs in back, correct?"

"Yes." Harry grinned. "At the top, it's on the right."

Margaret's heart pounded as she ascended the stairs, her mind racing with thoughts and emotions. She knocked on the door, and when Ayden opened it, their eyes met with longing and frustration.

"Margaret." Ayden inhaled deeply and stepped back as she walked through the doorway. "I'm surprised to see you. Please, come in."

"Thank you, Ayden." She saw her red face in the entry mirror and turned away.

"I wanted to see you. We need to talk."

"You're right." Ayden nodded. "Please make yourself comfortable. Can I get you something to drink? Would you like to see the new apartment before we talk?"

"Yes, to both. Just water for me, please." Margaret draped her shawl over the back of the couch and untied her bonnet. "Have you had dinner?"

"No. Paperwork kept me in the office. Did you have your meal?"

"Actually, no. But let's see your new place first, shall we?"

Ayden gestured to the room. "The sitting room. The far door leads to a landing with stairs down to the alley." He rounded the mirrored divider. "A small writing desk here, and through the archway is the kitchen. To your left is the washroom." He paused to let Margaret look around. "Then through this opening are the bedrooms. A small guest room here." He swung open the door for her to look inside. "And the master bedroom is at the end of the hall."

"This is much larger than the room downstairs," Margaret commented and continued into the main bedroom.

"Yes, it is."

They both stared at the bed for a moment. "Perhaps I could get the water?" She forced brittle smile and looked up at Ayden.

"Oh, yes. Please." He held out his arm.

Margaret preceded him to the kitchen. "I'll have a seat."

Ayden nodded and continued to the cupboard and icebox.

Margaret strolled past the fireplace arrangement and sat at one of the two small sofas across the table from each other at the far end of the room. "Is the furniture new?"

Ayden set the cooled water on the table and sat across from Margaret. "No. The Tull's new home had furniture. They took only their personal items."

"I see." Margaret sipped the water and resisted the urge to hold the cool glass to her cheek.

I might as well get to it.

"Ayden, you know how I feel about you. How I've always felt."

"I know, Maggie," Ayden whispered. "I feel the same about you."

"Then why the hesitation." She sat the glass on the table and held out her hand. "I want to be with you, Ayden," her voice trembled, "in all ways."

Ayden nodded. "I know, as do I." He didn't lift his eyes to meet hers. "But it feels wrong. Even though I know Robert would approve of our affair because he's with Hal, it still does not make it right."

Margaret shook her head, her voice firm. "I disagree. Robert has given his blessing to us. Why should we deny ourselves this happiness?"

"I want you as my wife." His eyes, raised to meet hers, were torn with sincerity. "It is what I've always wanted."

"And we were robbed of that, I know. But to deny ourselves this opportunity to give, love, and share…"

"Margaret, I don't disagree with any of that."

"Then what?"

He took her hand across the table. "What would everyone think?"

"Everyone who? Who would know besides us?"

"Anyone who discovers us or suspects. The Brahmin. Wrigley and Peg."

"Wrigley is far too observant and has always known about Robert, although he never speaks of it. Peg is too young to bother with something like this. We've fooled the Brahmin for over twenty years." She flipped her hand. "Now is our time."

"I don't know…"

"Yes, you do." Margaret stood, drawing Ayden up with her. "Can we at least try?"

"Now?" His eyes widened and he grinned, with more interest than hesitancy.

She tugged his hand and drew him through the kitchen, down the hall, and into the large bedroom. Pins scattered across the floor as she shook her head and ran her fingers through her hair. Then they stilled. "I have scars."

"As do I. Some, you can even see." Ayden's fingers unhooked the small button on her bodice.

"I may know where to look." She whispered as she tipped her head back, offering her lips.

"Yes. You may, indeed." Ayden replied, drawing her close, pressing his hungry mouth to hers in surrender.

Chapter 14

Family Fractured

Lisbeth Coleman

Flames rose high into the night sky, and ash sparkled a fiery red as it floated down around the coven members. Raised arms fed the flame with elemental magic. Their black robes and dark masks hid their identity from all but the God and Goddess.

The full moon hung high above the middle-distance racetrack on her father's equestrian farm, not far from the small Concord community and a comfortable distance north and west of their Boston home.

Lisbeth lowered her arms as her father droned on about the loyalty owed to the Lord and himself by the coven members gathered in the warded circle.

Fewer and fewer members each month.

Her father could not understand how his obsession with Ayden MacKenna, fed by ludicrous tales from his lieutenants, Milton Kohler and Gordon Carmichael, drove normal members away from their coven fellowship.

As it stood, since MacKenna's arrival in Boston, they'd lost five—no six—members and their families.

Three stopped attending gatherings and avoided her father after the big fire in Boston. Three more last year after a mob burned down a brothel on the dock. No one bothered to explain what connected those events to Lisbeth, but she had her suspicions.

After her father elevated Milton and Gordon to his lieutenants, and because Ayden knew them, surveillance on the rival coven fell to the few remaining men in the Coleman coven.

And they have had enough of father's nonsense.

Lisbeth didn't mind loitering outside the Prescott house. It was the perfect excuse to leave her family home and be away from her parents. At two and thirty years, she was well past the marriage market, and there were no single male witches her age in the coven.

A bitter truth my mother must come to terms with.

There were unmarried men within their Brahmin social circle, but they thought Lisbeth a young pimpled-faced debutante, too crippled by shyness to speak more than two words.

I'm done with the lies, the half-truths, and the deceptions.

As soon as the corners released their *elemental-wards*, Lisbeth spun on her heel and stalked toward the house.

She pulled off her robe and mask in the mudroom, stuffed them into her saddlebag, and headed for the stables. Dressed in her usual male garments, she slung the saddlebag over her shoulder and selected a familiar pair of leather gloves from the shelf at the stable door. She pulled them on as she decided on a horse. Lisbeth owned three of the fifteen thoroughbreds housed in her father's stable. Unfortunately, she could only take one.

Father will sell the other two in his fury at me for abandoning him. So be it.

She opened the stall of the black Arabian stallion. Nero danced as she stroked his ears and hugged his throat. "I love you, my beauty." Lisbeth gifted him an apple from the barrel, and as he chomped it down, she closed the stall door.

Next, she visited the dun gelding at the end of the row. Shephard nuzzled her hair when she hugged him farewell, gave him an apple, and moved on.

Lisbeth stopped at the tack room, picked up her saddle, then lugged the leather seat to the rack in the center of the aisle and opened Bravo's stall. Her quarter-horse gelding, a palomino color, pawed the straw in anticipation.

"Yes, I know. You've been waiting." As she saddled her chosen mount, she spoke the words to the glamour spell, altering her appearance as she worked.

By the time she tightened the girth strap, she was no longer the blonde-haired woman who'd entered the stable.

A slender young man with dark hair and a drooping mustache swung into the saddle. "Let's go, Bravo before Father thinks to look for us here."

She left the stable door open as she rode into the darkness, following the familiar roads back to Boston.

Why should I limit myself to Boston?

She had the means and the magic to go anywhere, to start over as anyone she chose.

It is time to make a fresh start.

Chapter 15

Traveling Companions

Melvyn MacKenna

Minster Stevens finished the Lord's Prayer and whispered, "Amen," as he closed his Bible. "May your father find eternal rest with the Lord." He laid a comforting hand on Melvyn's forearm as he passed.

"Thank you, Reverend," Melvyn whispered.

The short Protestant service for his father came with the cost of the simple coffin and burial plot. He knew his father wouldn't mind being laid to rest in a church's small graveyard, and Mel wanted his father's grave tended, not forgotten at the edge of a pauper's field.

I know the Lord and Lady understand.

For his entire life, Mel and his father were the only ones he knew who held faith in the Ancient Male and Female Divinities and were able to wield *Elemental magic*. However, from things his father uttered in his last few weeks, he knew they were not the only ones who did.

His father wanted him to seek them out. "For fellowship, son. You need others like yourself."

"Are you saying other people can call *Fire* and commune with the spirit in animals?"

"And more. I've been selfish and over-cautious. Since your mother passed, I've sheltered you too much. When I'm gone, promise me you'll go north to Boston. There's a coven there, or there used to be, run by Garrett Brown. And if you can't find him, look for Margaret James, although she may have married. My point is, there are others like us, but be cautious."

Mel waited beside the open grave with the plain pine box until the gravediggers returned to cover Lyam MacKenna with the earth he loved.

Goodbye, Da.

At least his father would be with his brother, Ayden, and their mother again.

Melvyn hung his head as wave after wave of loneliness washed over him. Each step away from his father's grave gave him physical pain, low in his gut.

Promise me you'll go to Boston and find others like us.

His father's last words repeated in his head.

But be cautious.

Mel paused at his dappled gelding and brushed a tear from his chin. He'd given away or sold everything in the small house he and his father shared. There was nothing left in the home but an old broom.

In his saddlebags, he carried a change of traveling clothes and a good suit. Using his father's roan as a pack horse, he stowed his camp roll, a tin pot and pan, and small items he wanted to carry into his new life.

He'd considered taking the train or catching a ferry to Boston, but he wanted to keep both horses. Besides, it would save precious money to follow the well-travel road north to Hartford and on to Springfield, then east to Boston. Once in Boston, he would need to pay for a boarding house and look for work.

It would take the better part of a week to make it to Boston, but Mel was in no hurry.

He checked the girth strap and the lead for the pack horse, mounted Dapper, and rode away from the churchyard.

It clouded up several times as he traveled through Connecticut to Springfield, but it never rained. Each night, different traveling companions gathered around a communal campfire and spoke of where they were from and where they were heading.

Some planned to travel further south than he had come north, all in search of a better life and future for their families. Each night, when the others finished with their tales, Mel asked if anyone knew a Garrett Brown or a Margaret James, but none had.

As the sun set on his last night before arriving in Boston, Mel tied his horses to the line strung between two tall trees, saw to their comfort, and then pulled his bedroll from Whistler, his father's roan. He found a level patch of ground between the horses and the fire, rolled out his gear, selected a few items, and then sauntered to the large communal fire.

He had passed smaller campfires along the road, but this large firepit had the most people. More travelers meant more chances for someone to know of work in Boston and to ask about Brown and the James woman.

Mel squatted near the fire and unwrapped three thick pork sausages he'd purchased from a farmer along the road late that morning. He skewered the spiced meat rolls with a long metal rod and laid them across the cooking forks he placed on either side of the fire. "These are to share," he stated, then poured water from his canteen into his father's old tin coffee pot, threw a handful of coffee grounds in, and shoved it beside the coals. "I don't have enough cups, but the coffee is also for everyone."

A family of three huddled together, the young son holding tight to his mother's skirt. The boy stared wide-eyed at Melvyn, then yanked on the skirt. "Does he mean us too, mama?"

Mel chuckled. "I do, young man."

"We don't have anything to share," the mother's voice held shame and a bit of fear.

"Maybe not this time, but someday you will. When you can share, do so—and remember me."

Beside them, two men joked, obviously friends or travel companions. "We have some greens, onions, and carrots we picked."

"Eddie raided a garden." One of the men laughed and playfully slapped his companion's arm.

Eddie shrugged and shook his head. "A weed filled and abandoned garden. We rescued these vittles from being overrun."

As the two men emptied their pockets, the mother sat her son on his father's lap. "I can clean those and use our pot to cook them in." She gathered the offerings in her apron and carried them to the family wagon.

A lone rider, seated far away from the two men and the fire, rested against his saddle.

"You're welcome to share as well, if you're not hungry, we'll have coffee soon." Mel nodded to the loner. When he'd first approached the fire, he thought the loner was a dark-haired man with a drooping mustache, but now he sensed something else.

It's as though my eyes see a gray wolf, but my magic insists it's a bear.

The dark-haired stranger pushed back his hat and gave Mel a friendly smile. "Thank you, sir. Your spirit of generosity shall brighten our evening."

Mel turned away with a nod and attended the fire. He pulled on one of his thick leather gloves and turned the meat to sear the other side. "You're welcome." Discomfort crawled along his spine. His high level of *Earth-magic* made him secure in his surroundings, but it warned him there was something wrong with the new stranger.

As the meat sizzled, dripping fat into the fire, and the vegetables boiled, Eddie pulled a small guitar from his saddle kit and brought the instrument to the fire. He quietly strummed a tune while the food cooked.

When the sausage had browned, Mel removed the rod from the fire and held the hot metal in his gloved hand as the woman pushed the sausages onto a large plate.

She quickly sliced them into thick medallions, then set the wooden serving dish on one of the rocks that circled the large firepit.

After the woman strained the vegetables and placed them on a dish next to the meat, the group approached the fire with their plates or cups and served themselves. There was ample food to accommodate the six adults and one child.

While they ate, Mel talked about his trip north from New Haven and his hope of finding the people his father spoke about in Boston.

"My mother died in the Boston cholera outbreak of '49. After she passed, my father fled the city and took me to New Haven. Before Da died, he asked me to return to Boston and seek out a couple of people he remembered."

"We're down from Boston." Eddie nodded to his friend, then set his empty plate on the stones. "Who're you looking for?"

"Two people. I don't know what connection, if any, they have to each other. One is a man named Garrett Brown, the other, a woman named Margaret James."

"Yeah," Eddie's friend grunted, then leaned back. "I know Garrett Brown. I'm not sure if it is the same man your father knew. He's an old cuss and a judge for the City of Boston. He'd have to be about to retire."

Eddie nodded. "I've been in his court."

"Imagine that." Eddie's friend poked his side.

"I might have information about the James women." The dark-haired man had moved forward to eat and sat beside Melvyn.

When Mel turned to him, the man's face wavered as though viewed through melting candle wax. Mel quickly looked back at the fire. "Is that so?"

"Would this Margaret be a member of the Brahmin James family? The same ones who had a fall out with the MacKenna clan years ago?"

Mel rose to his feet and stared hard at the man beside him. "MacKenna?"

The stranger dropped his plate by the fire and stood to face Mel. "Yes. Does the name MacKenna mean something to you?"

With a sudden movement, Mel reached out and gripped the man's arm. A strange tingling covered his palm as the face before him cleared. No longer a dark-haired man, he stared into the blue eyes of a pale-haired woman.

Don't betray me. I have information you seek, information you need to know.

Her thought came to him the same way his horse warned him of a sore hoof or a rattler.

Whoever she is, she wields strong Earth-magic.

"Who are you?" Mel whispered.

"I lived in Boston." She glanced at Mel and smiled. "I was heading out of town, but now—." She shook her head. "Never mind." Her voice softened, "I know, *knew,* the daughter of the woman you search for." Her voice remained deep, as though she still portrayed a man.

And perhaps she does, to everyone else.

"Margaret's daughter?"

The woman nodded. "I didn't know Amy well, but we'd spoken."

"Who are you?"

"Call me Lis for now," she said softly in her low tone. "I'll ride back with you to town tomorrow. We can discuss *your Earth-magic,* among other things."

She knows of my magic!

Mel had never met someone else with *elemental magic,* much less one so powerful they could hide their face behind another. Then again, he only knew of himself and his father, who had any magical skill at all.

"I accept your offer, but first, tell me how you know the name MacKenna." Mel stepped toward the horse line, then waited for Lis to follow.

"The James and MacKenna families were rivals—years ago, or so I've been told. This rivalry took place long before my family moved to Boston." Lis passed Mel and reached for the palomino.

The horse bumped his nose to her hand in greeting.

"This is Bravo."

"Bravo is well cared for and happy to be with you," Mel asserted. "What happened to the MacKennas?"

"How do you know he's happy?" Lis turned to him with a smile. "And I don't know what happened to the MacKennas. They left Boston a long time ago." She rubbed Bravo between the ears and fed him a treat from her pocket. "What's your interest in them anyway? I thought you were looking for Margaret James?"

"I am. I only wonder why you mentioned the name MacKenna."

Lis stroked Bravo's neck, then walked past Mel toward the fire. "It's a long ride to Boston. We'll have time to talk. As for now, I'm turning in."

Heavy clouds obscured the sunrise, and raindrops scattered across the dry ground as they broke camp.

"We need the rain." Lis pulled on an oiled hooded jacket. "But it would have been nice to reach Boston without getting drenched.

Mel nodded as water dripped from his hat. "I've had fine weather this entire journey until today. Luckily, we're only a few hours out from town."

Lis shrugged. "We'll still be soaked—and muddy." She looked up at the threatening sky and wrinkled her nose.

"I'd like to find a room close to a bathhouse." Mel checked the lead to the packhorse. "Everything will be damp and will need to be laid out."

"Or you could find one with the new plumbing. Some hotels and boarding houses have a bath inside now."

"I'm not sure I can afford one of those," Mel laughed.

Lis glanced over her shoulder and said, "With your *Earth-skill*, you could magic the dirt away."

"As could you, I imagine, but a warm tub of water in front of a fire would suit me just fine right now."

"Who taught you about your magic?" Lis smiled at him with a question in her eyes.

"My father. He's the only other person I know who had the skill. His best magic was *Earth-magic*. He had a way with animals." Mel glanced at the woman riding beside him, dressed as a man. The way she rode told him she'd grown up riding astride. "You were going to tell me how you knew the name MacKenna."

"That's right." Lis raised her eyebrows. "However, I'll let Margaret James tell you that."

"So you are taking me to her?"

"Not directly. I'm taking you to someone who knows Margaret James far better than I do. I've only met her in passing at a party years ago." Lis cast a curious glance at Mel. "And why are you so curious about the name MacKenna?"

"It's my name." Mel tipped his dripping hat at Lis. "Melvyn MacKenna. I should have introduced myself sooner, but my father warned me to be cautious."

"Your father gave you good advice." Her smile widened. "I'm pleased you make your acquaintance, Mr. MacKenna. My name is Lisbeth Coleman," she lowered her voice, "and you are safe with me."

Mel fell behind while traffic traveling in the other direction increased. As the storm abated, the road filled with travelers.

Lis called back to him, "I'm going to take the harbor road around. I know a place we can eat, and you might find a room."

Mel shook the last raindrops from his hat and nodded to his companion. "And a bath."

Lis laughed. "And a bath."

Before long, the tall ships in the harbor filled the eastern horizon, reflecting the late afternoon sun bright against the storm moving out to sea.

Lis dismounted at a dock-side tavern and wrapped her reins around the hitching rail. "We can ask about a room here. If they have one, I'll help you unload your packhorse."

Mel nodded. "I can do that, but it is kind of you to offer." He tied Dapper's reins to the rail, unknotted the lead rope to Whistler, and tied it to the rail. Too tired to notice much else, he followed Lis through the doors.

Chapter 16

Family Found

Ayden MacKenna

The early diners were leaving the tavern, making room for the later guests and card players.

Ayden helped Glenda clear and wipe the tables. He glanced up as a couple of men entered the front doors. One of the trail-weary men seemed familiar, but his companion's face fell from Ayden's mind as soon as he looked away.

One of them is wearing a glamour. Lisbeth?

Ayden finished with the last table while Glenda directed the men to a table near the bar. The mustached man crossed the room, but the other remained in the doorway, pale as ash, his stare clutching Ayden.

Ayden straightened from wiping the table, concerned for the young man's health. He tossed down the cleaning rag and stepped forward. "Are you ill, son?"

"Da?" the man uttered, then his eyes rolled back in his head, and his knees buckled.

Close enough to catch him before his head struck the floorboards, Ayden lowered the man to the ground and looked for his companion.

The dark-haired traveler hurried over and crouched across from Ayden. "You must look like your father. I had no idea seeing you would be more than a happy surprise for him."

Ayden narrowed his eyes at the speaker as the glamour mask fell aside. "Lisbeth!"

Her blue eyes begged for understanding. "I met this man on the road last night and brought him straight to you."

Ayden shook his head. "I don't understand."

"I believe he's your brother."

Melvyn?

The tall man Ayden held in his arms couldn't be his brother, could he? That little boy stopped aging in Ayden's mind when he'd sold into bondage aboard Magi Rakesh's ship.

"I barely recognize him," Ayden murmured. His hand still clutched the man's nape.

Melvyn's eyes fluttered and opened. He stared at Ayden and then shook his head. "Blessed Goddess, what's happening to me?" He pressed his eyelids closed and rolled his head away. When they reopened, he turned his head to find Lisbeth. "You're still here."

"I am." She took his hand. "Mel, I'm sorry this was such a terrible shock. I thought it would be a welcome surprise."

"How?" Mel glanced at Ayden, then back to Lisbeth as he sat up. "I don't understand."

"He's your older brother."

"My brother...." Mel struggled to his feet, stepped back, and ran a hand through his hair. "My brother died."

Ayden shook his head. "No, I didn't die."

"Then where were you? Da grieved for you," Mel's face crumbled. He took a deep, steadying breath and whispered, "We needed you."

Lisbeth looked over her shoulder at the men from her father's coven, who watched with interest. "This is too public. Is there somewhere we can go?"

"Yes. You're right, of course." Ayden held out his arm toward the back of the tavern. "My apartment is upstairs." He stepped aside to make room for Melvyn to pass.

"I have things on my horses I need." The color returned to his face, as he retrieved his hat from the floor and then looked at Ayden. "I can't leave them outside."

"I can take the horses to the stable," Lisbeth offered.

Melvyn began to shake his head.

"They will hold your things, take care of your animals, and have them for you when you leave," Ayden assured his brother. "After we talk, you can walk down the street and get your things."

"I want Lis to stay with me—us," Mel said.

Lisbeth made a shushing sound. "Softly. There are too many ears and eyes here."

"That's fine, Mel. Your friend should stay." Ayden studied the tavern patrons and found Harry's eyes upon them. Ayden crossed the tavern and spoke soft and low to Harry. "That's my brother. I need his horses outside taken to the livery and his belongings stored until he comes for them. Can Kit handle that?"

Harry glanced through the kitchen window.

The young dishwasher's hands held an oval serving plate, which he carefully dried and placed on the shelf.

"He can. Two horses?"

"Make it three. My brother's friend is coming with us."

"Kit!" Harry called. "Come out here. I have an errand for you."

A tall, gangly youth hurried from the stockroom to the bar and stood beside Ayden. "Yes, sir?"

Harry smiled. "Remove your apron and hang it on the hook inside the stockroom door." When the lad returned, Harry continued. "There are three horses outside. Walk them to the livery. Have the stable workers unsaddle and store the packs and goods for us. The horses are to be brushed and fed."

"Give them my name for all three," Ayden interjected. "And have them send the bill to me."

"I'll show him the horses," Lisbeth spoke up, then waved the young man toward the door. "Come with me." The pair walked outside.

Ayden glanced at Melvyn and found the younger man staring hard at him. *He thought I was our father and acted if he'd seen a ghost.*

Realization washed over Ayden, and he caught his breath. He covered his mouth with his hand and turned away from Melvyn, struggling to control his emotions.

Father had been alive all this time.

Harry leaned close and whispered, "Are you unwell, Ayden? What's going on?"

"Nothing. I'm fine." Ayden sniffed and shook his head. "I just received some bad news." He turned back to Melvyn as Lisbeth entered the tavern.

She hitched up her trousers and headed for Melvyn. "Ready, kid?"

Melvyn nodded, and both lifted their gaze to Ayden.

"Follow me." He led them into the stockroom and up the inside stairs. On the landing, he unlocked the door and led the group inside. "Take off your coats and make yourselves at home. I have water in the icebox, but the harder beverages are downstairs. I rarely have guests." He poured water into the three glass jars and carried them into the living area.

Both Lisbeth and Melvyn stood awkwardly near the door.

"Please, sit. We have some catching up to do." He placed the water on the center table, then sat on the couch facing his two guests.

Lisbeth tugged Melvyn's sleeve. "Come on. You both know things the other needs to learn." She sat on one side of the empty couch, leaving the other side, across from Ayden, for Melvyn.

Ayden took a sip of water. "The last clear memory I have of you is sitting outside our house, digging in the dirt with a spoon Mother gave you."

"You have memories of our mother. That's more than I have." Melvyn raised his glass but hesitated, his gaze on Ayden. "Both you and ma have always been dead to me." Without drinking, he sat the glass back on the table. "Da *said* you were dead. How is it you're here? Where have you been?" The pain in his eyes came across as clearly as the accusation in his voice.

Ayden rubbed his hand across his face. "I was in India, for the most part. Several years after I escaped, I spent working to earn my way back here. When I returned to Boston, I tried to find you, but you had gone."

"Escaped?"

Ayden nodded. "*Magical bondage.* The twenty-year contract ended, and I ran."

"Magical contract," Melvyn scoffed. "You could have just left and come home. Father needed you. Do you know how hard it was for him to raise me alone?"

"It was an *Earth-magic* contract, signed in my stolen blood while I lay unconscious." Ayden shook his head. "I could not break it. I wanted nothing more than to come home."

Lisbeth opened her mouth as though to speak, but a knock on the outside door halted her comment.

"Ayden?" Margaret called in hushed tones from the landing. "Are you in there?"

With a brief glance at his guests, Ayden rose and moved to the outside entrance. With his mind he released the protective wards and opened the door. "Margaret. I didn't expect you. Please, come in."

Chapter 17

Circle of Trust

Margaret Prescott

"Thank you." Margaret smiled as she stepped across the threshold. "I wouldn't have bothered you, but I can't find Hal..." She halted when she caught sight of the guests in Ayden's apartment. "I'm sorry. I've interrupted."

"Think nothing of it. Please, come in." Ayden held out his arm, and the two men came to their feet. "Here are friends and family. One you know, and one I'd like you to meet."

Margaret shook her head. "I know neither of these gentlemen, surely."

A dark-haired, mustached man stepped forward and held his hand to Margaret. As their palms touched, he murmured, "Lisbeth Coleman."

Margaret gasped as the handgrip firmed, and the face began to change. She blinked furiously, thinking a bit of lint must have flown in her eye.

The dark hair whitened and lengthened; the man's shoulders narrowed. Even the bones in the hand she held undulated in her grasp.

"Use your *Earth-sense*. The stronger your skill, the easier it is to reveal the *glamour*," Lisbeth instructed.

Margaret nodded, and Lisbeth's face became clear when she blinked again. The blonde woman, dressed in men's dusty and worn attire, resolved before her eyes.

Margaret gazed at Lisbeth's actual face for the first time. "I might have recognized you on the street, but perhaps not." She released Lisbeth's hand and took a step back. "I always thought you were younger than Amy."

"No. Young Lisbeth was simply another glamour." Lisbeth's cheeks flushed as she resumed her seat. "A ruse I employed for father to ferret out information from the Brahmin children."

Margaret shook her head in wonder. "Ayden mentioned your miraculous abilities, but honestly, had I not watched the change with my own eyes, I would never have believed it. *Earth-magic?*"

Lisbeth nodded. "*Earth* and *Air*, a bit of *Water* too, I think. The more *Earth-magic* someone has, the harder it is to maintain the illusion. Physical contact impairs the *glamour* as well."

"You use three magics?" The other man in the room stepped forward, his words tinged with awe.

"I do." Lisbeth smiled up at the younger man. "I'm best with *Earth* and *Air*, but I practice *Water* and *Fire* as much as possible to strengthen them."

"Do you recognize him?" Ayden spoke in a low tone to the woman by his side, glancing at the younger man.

Margaret shook her head. "There is a vague sense of familiarity, but no. we've never met."

Ayden grinned. "Perhaps you did when he was little more than a babe."

Margaret gripped Ayden's forearms and laughed as her eyes widened with joy. "You found him?"

"Lisbeth did and brought him to Revere's."

Margaret smiled with delight at the new, mature Lisbeth. "Thank you."

"You are welcome, Mrs. Prescott." Lisbeth reached for her water. "He came to Boston to find you, not him." She lifted her glass toward Ayden.

"Me?" Margaret stared at the youthful version of Ayden. Now that she knew who he was, the resemblance to the Ayden she remembered from her youth was striking.

"Then, by all means, let me introduce you." Ayden gestured toward Melvyn. "Margaret, may I present my brother, Melvyn MacKenna. Melvyn, this is Margaret Prescott."

"Margaret *James* Prescott," Lisbeth added, placing her glass on the table.

Melvyn's brows rose, and his eyes widened. "I... ah. I'm pleased to meet you." He held out his hand, and Margaret stepped forward, hesitating only slightly. The last hand she touched had given her quite a surprise.

Melvyn's callused hand gripped hers gently, a warm touch he shared with his brother.

"A pleasure to meet you too. I saw you once when you were too young to walk. Your mother held you in her arms."

"You knew my mother?"

"Yes." Margaret nodded as she released his hand. "Our parents belonged to the same coven and met monthly at the Brown farm." She glanced up at Ayden. "I knew your brother best as we were of an age, but I also knew both your parents."

"Would that have been Garrett Brown?" Melvyn's glance shifted from Margaret to Ayden.

"Yes, that's right. Garrett was our coven leader," Ayden replied.

"Father asked me to find him as well."

"Did he say why?" Margaret released his hand and stepped back.

"Not precisely. Da didn't want me to be alone with *elemental skills* that no one I knew shared." Melvyn glanced at his brother. "I know he would have returned to Boston if he knew you were here."

"I know," Ayden murmured.

An awkward silence followed until Margaret smiled at Lisbeth and Melvyn, then turned to Ayden. "Again, I'm sorry to intrude, but I must locate Hal. He has missed two meetings this week, and the tailor on Summer Street and the owner of the dry goods on Broad Street have been by the house asking for Robert."

"When did you last see Hal?"

"It's been at least a week." Margaret shook her head. "Actually, I don't believe I've spoken to him since Robert sailed." She walked to the door. "If you hear from him, tell him I must speak with him immediately."

"I'll go to the warehouse tomorrow, contact the buyers and arrange to deliver their goods."

"Thank you." She took his hand and squeezed it. "I don't know what I'd do without you. But for now, I must go. Wrigley waits for me downstairs." She tipped her head to Ayden's two guests. "I'm more than pleased to remake both of your acquaintances. I hope we can visit again soon."

Ayden followed her out of the door, and she turned to look at him. "You have your brother back."

"So it would seem."

"And Lisbeth Coleman? She's so different. Can you trust her?"

"I think so. Lisbeth helped me before when she had no reason to, and I get the impression she has left her father's home for good."

"Really?" Margaret blinked in surprise. "Where is she staying?"

"I don't know—nowhere yet, as far as I know." Ayden lowered his voice. "I think she was leaving Boston when she ran into Melvyn and decided to bring him here."

Margaret nodded. "I'd offer to take her home with me, but I live too close to her father's house for her comfort, I'm sure."

"I'll suggest she use the cot in the stockroom until she finds a place or decides to leave town."

Margaret nodded, then reached up and gave Ayden a quick kiss on his lips. "I'm happy for you."

Ayden bent his head for a more substantial kiss, then released her. "I'll come to your house tomorrow." He looked down at the alley and then narrowed his eyes at Margaret. "Wrigley's not down there, is he?"

"No, but I asked the cabbie to wait just around the corner. I'll be fine." She raised her chin to admire his long, dark lashes as his eyes closed, and they kissed goodbye. "Go get to know your brother. Bring him to dinner tomorrow night. And find Hal."

"I will."

When Ayden released her hand, Margaret hurried down the steps. At the bottom, she glanced back to find him watching. She lifted her hand in farewell, then hurried around the corner to the cab that waited.

Chapter 18

Rumors and Stories

Melvyn MacKenna

Melvyn tried not to eavesdrop on Ayden's conversation in the doorway and turned his attention to Lisbeth. "We should go. I still need to find a bed for tonight."

Lisbeth heaved a small sigh and rolled her eyes. "You came a long way to find these people, and now that you've met your brother, you're too tired to get to know him."

"Oh, you mean the brother I thought dead my entire life." Melvyn glanced toward the doorway.

Ayden had stepped outside and pulled the door close behind him.

"That wasn't his fault," Lisbeth reminded him.

"No?" Melvyn leaned forward, his voice lowered and filled with irritation. "Are you saying it was my fault?"

"Of course not." Lisbeth pressed her lips and narrowed her eyes. "There's no need to assign fault in unfortunate circumstances."

Melvyn took a deep breath and sat back. "You're right. I'm being foolish. It's been a hell of a week."

Ayden closed the door and returned to his guests. "I'd wager you're hungry and would like to have dinner, maybe get cleaned up and settle in for the night. Do you have a place to stay lined up?"

"No, not yet." Melvyn rose and faced his brother across the table. "Speaking of that, I should start looking."

"I have a suggestion, if I may." Ayden pointed across the room. "There's a guest room right down the hall. Mel, you're welcome to stay here until you find accommodations more to your liking."

"I don't want to impose—" Melvyn began, but Ayden waved off his concern.

"Nonsense. I would love to get to know my brother. We're all the family we have left." Ayden smiled as Lisbeth came to her feet. "I also have an offer for you. There's a room at the back of the stockroom. It's small but comes with a bed and dresser. I lived there before I moved up here. You're welcome to stay as long as you like."

"How generous," Lisbeth replied with a smile.

"Also, feel free to use the water closet through there. The previous owner had one installed for his wife before they moved, and it's quite nice."

"Do you own the tavern now?" Melvyn asked.

"No." Ayden led the way to the door. "I only manage it. I know Revere's recently sold, but I've yet to meet the new owner."

At the base of the steps, Ayden led Melvyn and Lisbeth through the stockroom to the small room in back. He opened the door and gestured for Lisbeth to enter. "It's not big, but it is available, and the price is right. That door leads to the alley." He pointed at the exit across the room.

"Those are some impressive wards." Lisbeth lifted an open palm to the alley door and her eyebrows rose. "Are you overly cautious or afraid of something?"

Ayden chuckled. "Your father didn't tell you he paid me an uninvited visit?"

"No. When was this?"

"Last fall. I was recovering from a gunshot wound. He came through that door to try to hasten my departure. Luckily for me, he miscalculated how incapacitated I really was."

"That sounds like my father." Lisbeth glanced around the tiny room and then nodded with a smile. "I'll take it until I decide what I want to do next, but I must maintain my disguise. Men from the coven still watch you."

"I am well aware of that." Ayden pulled the room door closed.

Lisbeth paced away and then turned. "You'll need to address me as something other than Lisbeth while I wear this disguise."

"Agreed." Ayden lifted a small key hung from a nail beside the door and handed it to Lisbeth. "Your room key, Madam. Should we call you Lester? If I slip and call you Lis, it will sound like I'm saying Les."

"Very clever." Lisbeth chuckled. "Lester, it is."

Melvyn walked beside Ayden as they entered the tavern. "You were shot?"

Ayden nodded and selected the table near the bar. "Indeed, I was." He sat, leaned back, and pointed to his right side. "One bullet. Right about here."

"Who did it?"

"Fanatics who were outraged about a bawdy house down the dock. I was in the area at the wrong time. There was a spattering of gunfire, and I was hit. Margaret's husband and the warehouse manager, the one she can't find, brought me here." He raised his hand and signaled the waitress. "The Prescott warehouse is a block from where the riot occurred."

Glenda worked her way over to their table and spread her bright smile to each man. "What can I get for you?"

"Glenda, this is my brother, Melvyn, and his friend Lester. They'll be staying with me for a few days."

"Nice to meet you." Glenda winked at Lisbeth.

"Would you bring us three daily specials for dinner and a round of cider?" Ayden grinned widely at Melvyn and Lisbeth. "Li Qiang is the best cook on this side of town. You're in for a treat."

"How long have you worked here?" Melvyn asked.

"Three years. I got a sweeper and cleaner job the day I returned to Boston."

"You've only been in Boston three years?" Melvyn shook his head. "You have done well for yourself very quickly."

"That's true. However, I worked in a mercantile growing up, where I learned to maintain a ledger and understand the importance of building relationships with customers and vendors." Ayden took a sip from the cider Glenda delivered to the table. "That, and I got on well with the owner and his family. They're good people. They trusted me, and I never betrayed that trust."

"But Lis...I mean, Lester's family doesn't trust you." Melvyn tasted the cider, then took a larger sip. The apple flavor was fresh and crisp, with only a noticeable twinge of alcohol.

Lisbeth laughed, then spoke softly, low enough for only their table to hear. "A few of my father's members, who knew your brother when he was younger, believe him to be the devil incarnate. They convinced my father his presence in town would draw the powerful James family back and create a coven war."

"James? As in, Margaret James?" Melvyn looked from Lisbeth to Ayden.

"Yes, and no. Coleman is concerned about Margaret's brothers and mother, not her." Ayden shrugged and spun his glass on the table. "And I admit, were they to return, it could pose a problem."

"What?" Lisbeth leaned forward. "Are you saying it's true? The MacKenna's and the James' families were what—at war?"

"Oh no—that's far too dramatic." Ayden shook his head; his gaze fixed on the table. "Margaret and I were close as children and very much in love as we grew older. Unfortunately, her mother blamed my family for the death of her husband. Which was, of course, absurd, but grief does strange things to one's ability to reason." He downed his cider and raised the empty glass to catch Glenda's eye.

The group sat in silence as Glenda refilled their glasses and then hurried away to the next table.

Ayden poured a small amount of table salt into his hand and held it in his fist for a moment, his lips working in silent prayer, and then he tossed the salt over the table.

"A silence ward." Lisbeth nodded in appreciation.

"I doubt your watchers can overhear us from across the room, but I'll take no chances." Ayden took a deep gulp from his glass, then looked at his table mates. "Margaret's mother was obsessed with a prophecy she'd heard as a young woman. It dealt with demons and magically skilled twins. Even though she had already given birth to twin sons, she believed the prophecy spoke of her grandchildren. Powerful twins who would somehow summon a demon."

"She sounds hysterical," Melvyn commented.

"I thought so, too." Ayden nodded to his brother. "And to make matters worse, since I am a pyromancer, she felt that if Margaret and I were to marry and have children, they would be the ones to release the demon."

"A pyromancer?" Melvyn sipped his cider. He glanced at Lisbeth. "What's that?"

She shrugged her shoulders and returned her attention to Ayden's tale.

"A pyromancer can see images within a flame. Sometimes, the pictures are of future events. Sometimes of the past. I've learned over the years that crucial details are often missing, and directing my visions has proven difficult." He gazed solemnly into Melvyn's eyes. "I looked for you and Father in the flames so many times. I swear, I never saw anything that could have led me to you.

I discovered our mother died when I returned. I always assumed you were alive—but I could never see where you were."

"All is well, Ayden. I believe you." Melvyn reached across the table and gripped his brother's arm.

"So, Margaret's mother disapproved of your relationship with her daughter." Lisbeth looked up from her glass, her eyes narrowed. "That couldn't have been easy to live with. Where are Margaret's brothers and mother now?"

Ayden gazed intently at Lisbeth —so long that Melvyn thought he wouldn't answer. Finally, Ayden gave a nod of his head as though he'd come to a decision.

"I believe her mother is dead, killed by the demon she predicted for so long."

Lisbeth chuffed and sat back, shaking her head. "That's absurd."

"As for her brothers, I think they've gone west to Amy and Jason, where they prepare for the arrival of said demon."

"Where did you obtain this dubious information?" Lisbeth sat up as Glenda approached with their plates.

The special was a chicken dish with homemade dumplings. The gravy was highly seasoned, dark brown, and delicious.

"I've never tasted anything like this." Melvyn savored another mouthful.

After the group had feasted, Ayden took a sip of cider and cleared his throat.

"Lester, do you remember when you followed me from Margaret's house to the river road and past where the city ends?"

"I do."

"I was sick nearly to death. I told you then I'd been possessed by a demon, and you laughed and said—"

"Demon rum." Lisbeth nodded. "I remember. Are you telling me you were serious?"

Ayden nodded, never looking away from Lisbeth's stare. "The demon took me as I passed Margaret's house." He glanced at Melvyn. "It paid no attention to my panic, nor to the woman when she spoke to me."

"Woman?" Melvyn gripped his glass, enthralled by his brother's tale.

"Yes. A voice I would always recognize." Ayden sipped his cider. "Chantal James. Margaret's mother."

"What's this?" Lisbeth countered and rolled her eyes. "Your tale grows taller by the moment."

"Chantal told me the demon had killed her and imprisoned her spirit to usurp her *elemental-skills*." Ayden set his glass on the table and then pushed it away. "She was formidable with fire, as are her sons and daughter. It's their primary power."

"What else did she say?" Lisbeth glanced over her shoulder, then pushed her glass away as well.

"That the demon hunted the twins. It makes sense if they were who you saw at Margaret's earlier that day."

"I suppose." Lisbeth looked across at Ayden through narrow eyes. "Then why didn't the demon simply kill you and take your pyromancy skill? Why leave you at the edge of town?"

"I don't know." Ayden shook his head and shrugged. "The beast might have realized my body was done. After I fell, before you reached me, I saw a crow. It stretched its wings, shuddered, then called loudly and leaped into the air. That was when the demon left me." Ayden looked from Lisbeth to Melvyn. "And possessed the crow instead."

Lisbeth visibly shivered. "I heard the crow call in the dark. As I ran toward you, I saw it take flight."

"I wonder if the demon ever found the twins." Melvyn emptied his cider and sat it in the center with the other two.

"Have you told Margaret you spoke with her mother?"

"Her *dead* mother?" Ayden's gave Lisbeth an incredulous look and shook his head. "Of course not, and you won't either. How could I tell her such a thing? Besides, Margaret corresponds regularly with her daughter. If this prophecy has indeed happened, Amy will tell her."

"If they win," Lisbeth muttered.

Ayden nodded but continued to stare hard at Lisbeth.

Melvyn heaved a sigh and ran his hand down his face.

Enough of this, I need to sleep, and I'll have nightmares as it is.

He stood and stretched. "I accept your offer of the room, brother mine. However, I'll need to get things from my pack."

"Same." Lisbeth stood and nodded at Melvyn. "I'll go with you to the livery."

"Your horses are stabled under my name. Kit can run over to let the stable-master know you're coming." Ayden pushed his chair back and rose in one smooth motion, then stepped to the bar. "Kit?" he called through the kitchen opening.

The young man's narrow face appeared; eyebrows raised to his hairline. "Yes, sir?"

"Run over to St. John's livery. Let the stablemaster know the owners of the horses stabled under my name will need access to their gear."

"I will, sir." Kit worked the strings behind his back, then pulled the neck bib strap over his head then disappeared from the window.

Through the window, an elderly man with his long hair wrapped in a topknot took his place. He spoke harshly to Ayden and shook a spoon at him to punctuate his foreign words."

"I know," Ayden replied. "If I wanted an assistant, I should have hired one, not a dishwasher, but this is urgent, and Kit will be right back."

The cook disappeared to the sound of pots and pans crashing.

Ayden turned, his hand covering a grin, then shook his head, his eyes alight with amusement. "Li Qiang is unhappy with me for taking Kit away again."

Kit hurried through the stockroom door, shoved a bowler hat on his head, and scurried across the tavern to the exit.

"If you don't know where the livery is, you should follow Kit." Ayden pointed to the closing tavern door.

"I know where St. John's is." Lisbeth pushed the stray hair from her face and looked at Melvyn.

"Bring your things to alley door," Ayden instructed. "Knock and I'll release the wards."

"As you wish." Lisbeth turned from Ayden to Mel. "Shall we?"

Melvyn smiled at his brother then followed Lisbeth across the tavern and out the door. He caught up to her as she turned inland.

A block ahead, Kit stopped at the livery stable and hurried through the gate.

"What do you think about the demon nonsense?" Lis asked and chuckled.

"I don't know." Mel shrugged. "Most everyone I've met so far are elemental folk, in one way or another. Who's to say there aren't demonic ones as well."

He turned and found Lis contemplating him. "What? Do you disagree?"

"Not at all," Lis said, thoughtful. "Not at all."

Chapter 19

Word from Glasgow.

Ayden MacKenna

Ayden settled into the wooden chair in his former room downstairs and stared at the door while waiting for Mel and Lisbeth to return.

After he'd filled Harry in on his brother's surprise appearance, Ayden informed the bartender that he would be away from the Tavern most of the day tomorrow.

Accepting a partnership with Robert hadn't seemed fair to Robert, as Hal handled the deliveries and warehouse, leaving Ayden to keep only the monthly financial ledgers.

Now, with Hal missing, he would need to manage the receiving and delivery duties at the warehouse and perhaps more—all things that were difficult to think about with Melvyn newly returned to his life.

He stared at the oil lamps lit in the small chamber as he waited.

Did I try hard enough to find them?

He rubbed his eyes and swallowed the lump forming in his throat.

Three hard raps on the outside door brought his head up, and he rose from the chair. A wave of his hand cleared the wards, and he opened the door. "Quick indeed."

Melvyn entered first, his saddlebag slung over his shoulder and a heavy leather pack in each hand. "We cleared out the storage. No sense leaving things there." He stepped into the room. "We asked Kit to take the horse back. I hope that's all right."

"Of course."

Lisbeth followed Melvyn with a single saddlebag. She let it slide from her shoulder to the floor and closed the door. "If you give me a moment, I'll use your upstairs tub first."

"You know your way. After we stow these in his room, Mel and I can enjoy a cider." He took one of the leather bags from his brother. "Oh—" Ayden paused in the doorway. "Do you want me to put the wards back up?"

"Thank you, but I can ward the door." She crouched down and unbuckled the bag. Lacy women's undergarments filled her hand, and she shoved them back in. "Must be the in other one." She chuckled to herself.

Ayden smiled at her girlish laugh, closed the door, and followed Mel up the stairs. After depositing the saddlebag in Mel's room, he waited by the cold fireplace for Mel to finish unpacking. A short light tap warned him that Lisbeth was ready for her bath, and Ayden opened the door.

"I can heat the water before we go downstairs if you like," Ayden offered.

"Not necessary. I have enough *Fire* to heat water." Holding a set of clean men's clothes, Lisbeth closed the washroom door.

"You're all so skilled compared to me," Melvyn complained as they returned to the tavern.

"You have at least two skills, correct?" Ayden pointed at an empty table near the far wall, and the two men crossed the room.

"All I know is *Earth*." Mel smiled at Glenda as she followed them to their table.

"Cider, please, Glenda." Ayden settled into his chair, his back to the wall, with a clear view of his watchers.

"Me too." Mel dropped into the chair beside Ayden.

When Glenda moved away, Ayden threw salt in the air to shield their conversation. "You do have a secondary skill. Did father not work with you to develop your magic?"

Melvyn's eyes narrowed, and his lips thinned. "Da was busy being both my mother and father. We didn't have a lot of time for magical elemental nonsense."

"I don't mean to offend or cast our father in any unfavorable light. But he would have never considered it nonsense—it's part of who we are."

The conversation paused as Glenda brought their drinks. "Where's your other friend?"

Ayden shook his head. "He may be along shortly, but Glenda, I don't think he's your type."

"You never know." She winked at Ayden, grinned at Melvyn, then moved on.

"If you like, we can try simple tests to gauge your skill with other elements."

"Tomorrow?" Melvyn asked, then took a long drink of the cider.

"No. Tomorrow, I must find Hal and settle a couple of deliveries for the warehouse. Then, we'll have supper at James' home in the evening."

"Margaret's house?"

"Yes."

"I'm invited?"

"Both you and Lisbeth are. You'll meet more magic users there."

"Garrett Brown?"

"I don't know, but it's possible." Ayden finished his drink. "He's been to dinner at Margaret's before."

Lisbeth walked to the table but didn't pull out a chair. "I'm done upstairs and I'm going to bed."

"Would you like to have dinner at Margaret's with us tomorrow night?" Ayden asked.

"Oh... into the lion's den with both feet." She wrinkled her nose and chuckled. "It will be nice to see the inside of the house after staring at the outside for years." She tipped her head toward the back room. "Goodnight."

"Goodnight." Both men replied in unison as they watched her weave through the tables in her Lester *glamour* and pass through the stockroom door.

"She is very nice." Mel finished his cider.

"Yes, she is. Nothing like her father."

"He won't be at dinner tomorrow night, will he?"

"Not unless he turns up uninvited. He tends to do that."

Melvyn stood and looked around the tavern, then down at his brother with a grin. "I will take advantage of your washtub and then go to bed. It has been a terrible week—except for finding you."

Ayden rose to his feet and held out his hand to Melvyn. "Brother."

"Brother." Melvyn took his grip.

Ayden blinked to clear the moisture from his eyes as Melvyn turned, gave a cordial nod to Harry behind the bar, then left the room.

I have a brother.

Of course, he'd always had one, but Mel had been little more than a babe in a memory that never aged. Hopefully, the man who slept in his guest room would become a brother *and* a friend. Ayden held up his empty glass and waited for Glenda to round the tavern to his table.

"Another?"

"Last one tonight, then I'll find my bed. I'll be out tomorrow day and night, so you know."

"Harry, Li Qiang, and I can manage things here." She flounced off in her good-natured way, waving to a few regulars as she returned to the bar to fill her tray.

Ayden nursed his last drink for an hour, looking into the lantern flame in the center of the table. As he finished his drink, a voice whispered from the flame.

"For what do you search tonight, Ayden MacKenna?" Miera's voice, soft and distant, queried.

"Nothing. A past lost to me, I suppose." His lips moved, but his reply came from his mind.

"Look ahead, dear friend, not behind."

"You're right. Good night, Miera."

Only silence answered from the flame.

He glanced at the watchers' table near the door, but both men appeared asleep. Without disturbing their slumber, he went upstairs to bed.

An argument in the other room woke him. Sunlight streamed across the dresser where Caz slept peacefully on his candlestick.

The voices are familiar, and yet...

He sat up and ran his fingers through his hair.

Melvyn, Lisbeth, and—Wrigley?

He pulled on his trousers, picked up his shirt, and rushed through the apartment.

In the center of his living area, Lisbeth and Mel faced off against Wrigley.

"I'm saying I don't know who you are. I came here to speak with Ayden MacKenna, and I'll do that before I take my leave, thank you very much."

"And as *I* said before, he's still asleep."

"Asleep or dead, don't you mean!" Wrigley looked from Mel to Lisbeth. "Don't think I can't see who you are behind that masculine face, little Miss Lisbeth Coleman. I know who your father is too, and what he's like."

"What?" Her voice broke as she gaped at the older man.

"You just said you didn't know who we are." Melvyn stepped forward.

"I don't know who *you* are, young Mr. Needs-a-haircut. I guessed who she is from Margaret's description of her *glamour-skill*—and don't think I can't see right through them on my own, young miss."

"Enough!" Ayden pushed his arms into his shirtsleeves and marched into the living area. "Wrigley, this young man is my brother Melvyn. You may have met him the night he was born."

Wrigley's lined and leathery face underwent several changes, ranging from delight to skepticism. He looked Melvyn up and down with a single raised eyebrow and thin pressed lips. "How do you know that's true?"

"Lisbeth brought him to me yesterday, and I am positive he is my brother. *That* is not up for discussion." Ayden finished buttoning his shirt, then began to tuck it into his trousers. "What are you doing here, anyway?"

"Margaret sent me to find you. She's had disturbing news and wants to speak with you immediately."

"News from Amy?"

"What?" Wrigley shook his head. "No, no. Not from Amy. Whatever made you think that?" He waved his hand in dismissal. "She'll tell you in person. I'll wait for you downstairs." He paused, then dipped his head to both Melvyn and Lisbeth. "Nice to meet you both." With a quickness that belied his age, he stepped outside. His boots echoed his passage down the wooden stairs.

"What a strange man," Lisbeth commented as she closed the door. "How did he get past your wards?"

"Wrigley?" Ayden ran a hand across his brow. "Maybe I forgot to reset them last night."

"No, I felt them when I opened the door." Melvyn shook his head. "Did opening the door from the inside disarm them?"

"No." Ayden shrugged. "Maybe," he called over his shoulder as he stepped into the water closet. He pumped a handful of water, splashed his face, then ran the moisture through his hair before drying his face with a towel. Absolutions accomplished, Ayden hurried to the outside door. "Wrigley's waiting."

He picked up his jacket, slipped it on, and took his brown bowler from the hook. "Mel, why don't you come with me?"

"If you like." Mel pulled on his dusty outer frock and found his half-crushed wide-brimmed felt. "What about you?" He looked at Lisbeth as he set his hat.

"I can't go with you. I've some errands to run. If I'm to present myself at the Prescott home tonight for dinner, I have a few purchases to make." She opened the inside door. "I'll see you both at dinner."

"Margaret likes to dine at seven," Ayden called.

"Noted." Lisbeth shut the door.

When both men stood on the outside platform, Ayden lifted his hand and sealed the outside door, then hurried down the steps with Melvyn close behind him.

Wrigley waited in the driver's seat of the Prescott carriage, holding the reins. "I'm glad you took your time."

Ayden chuckled at Wrigley's rough demeanor and opened the door for his brother. Once seated, he appraised his brother as Melvyn watched the city pass by the carriage window. "What do you think of Boston?"

"I haven't seen much of it yet. Are all the roads made of stone?"

"Most of them. The further you travel north, the fewer cobblestones you find."

Melvyn nodded as though this made perfect sense, and Ayden stifled a chuckle.

Wrigley called to the brothers as they exited walked to the Prescott's front door, "Go on in. Margaret knows you're coming, and Peg might be out with her fella."

Ayden knocked on the door, then turned the knob to enter.

"Who's Peg?" Melvyn asked as they stepped into the home

"Wrigley's niece. You'll likely meet her tonight."

Margaret waited in the sitting room; a letter crumpled in her hand. She rose to her feet as Ayden paused at the door. "The *Atlantia* never made it to port."

"What?" Ayden held out his hand for the letter.

"The letter is from the harbormaster at River Clyde. The *Amylia* still rides in the harbor." Margaret rubbed her hands together as she paced to the window. "He wants to know what we intend to do."

Ayden looked up from the official's letter to Margaret. "He's declared the *Atlantia* missing and has requested ships sailing that route to keep a lookout for her." He glanced up from the missive. "Where are your other ships?"

"The *Anatasha* and *Arcadia*?" She turned from the window and faced Ayden. "*Arcadia* runs what Robert calls the sugar route. Jamaica, Belize, Florida, and the eastern seaboard up to Canada and back down."

"And the other?"

"*The Anatasha* has no set route. Robert and the captain—Captain Singer—plan each trip's route based on crop yields or expected shortages." She shrugged. "Gut instinct sometimes, I'm not sure."

"Where is the *Anatasha* now?"

"I've no idea. You'll have to check Robert's paperwork at the warehouse. Does it matter?"

"Probably not, but I'll check." Ayden closed the distance between them and touched her arm. "How are you?"

Margaret turned, slipped inside his jacket, and wrapped her arms around his waist, laying her forehead against his chest. "I was afraid when Robert told me he would sail to China, but I never thought I would actually lose him."

He gathered her in his arms and kissed the top of her head. "We haven't lost him yet. It's too soon to say why he is late."

She tipped her head back and gazed into his eyes. "This will devastate Hal."

Ayden nodded and pushed an errant lock of hair behind her ear. "I know."

"Excuse me." Peg's voice from the entrance reached Ayden. "May I help you?"

"I'm waiting for my brother." Melvyn must have eased from the sitting room when Ayden and Margaret embraced and waited near the entryway.

"Really?" Peg drew out the word to indicate utter disbelief.

Margaret moved out of Ayden's arms and touched her handkerchief to the corner of each eye. "You'd best save Melvyn before Peg throws him out."

Ayden straightened his jacket and strode from the room.

"Are you saying another of you is wondering about the house?" Peg stood on the stairs, dressed in a light green day dress, clutching a small bag in one hand, with both fists braced on her hips.

"Good morning, Peg." Ayden moved to stand beside his brother and gave Peg a short nod in greeting. "You certainly look lovely today."

"Mr. MacKenna. I had no idea you were here." Peg's glance darted from Ayden to Melvyn and back. "I was just on my way out when I discovered—," her voice faltered.

"My brother. His name is Melvyn, and he arrived in town last night." Ayden turned to Melvyn. "Mel, this is Wrigley's niece, Peg Johnson."

"I never would have guessed they're related," Melvyn muttered, his face shuttered and tight. "Miss Johnson." He spoke louder and dipped his head slightly.

Peg sniffed at his curt greeting. "How do you do, Mr. MacKenna? It is MacKenna, is it not?"

"It is," Melvyn responded shortly.

"Oh, Peg." Margaret beckoned from the sitting room. "I've had some distressing news. Do you have a moment?"

"Yes, of course." She hurried down the stairs, past the men, and paused in the doorway to the sitting room. "It was nice to meet you, Mr. MacKenna."

"Dinner at seven?" Ayden called over Peg's head to Margaret.

"Yes. Mrs. Bengston will be here shortly to begin preparations."

"We'll be back by six-thirty, and we'll bring Lisbeth with us if that's agreeable."

"That will be perfect." Margaret drew Peg into the sitting room. "Please, sit with me."

Ayden opened the front door, stepped out, and waited on the stoop for Melvyn to follow and close the door.

"What was the urgent matter, if you don't mind me asking?" Melvyn followed Ayden down the walk and across the cobbled street.

"Robert, her husband, left a little over a week ago on one of their ships bound for Glasgow. They're adding a new ship to their small fleet and were expected to arrive with extra crew to pilot the vessel home." He followed the walk to the park entrance and then turned in. "He never arrived. Margaret received a letter from the harbormaster asking what Robert wants to do." He shook his head and slowed his pace. "The harbormaster didn't realize the ship's owner was on the missing ship."

Melvyn stopped walking and stared agog at Ayden. "You're friends with Margaret's husband? Does he know about you and, um...his wife?"

"Hmm, yes. Robert and I are more than friends, to be honest. Robert made me his partner in the shipping business before he set sail. I thought it was to secure Margaret's livelihood should something unforeseen happen. But now, I'm not so sure." A new sense of urgency filled Ayden, and he continued quickly through the park.

Melvyn followed. "Where are we going now?"

"To look for Robert's close friend, Halstead. He oversees their warehouse, which is a good place to start. Since Robert sailed, Hal has missed two delivery dates. I need to find Robert's shipping and receiving log and distribution schedule, reschedule the deliveries, and discover what happened to Hal."

"Where did you learn how to do all this?"

"Honestly—" Ayden paused his quick step and looked back at Melvyn, then slowly shook his head. "I learned all this, and much more, while in India. In many ways, I grew up there." Ayden turned, hurried out of the park, and raised his hand to call a nearby cabbie. He gave the driver the warehouse address and took a seat beside Melvyn. "The warehouse isn't far."

Inside the Prescott warehouse, Ayden headed to the office at the back of the large building.

"You always carry the keys to their warehouse?" Melvyn asked as he looked at the model ships on the shelves.

"When Robert gave me the key, I just put it on my keychain." Ayden sat in Robert's chair and opened a large leatherbound book in the center of the desk. "This could tell us something." He read for a few moments, then scribbled a few notes with the pencil and a scrap of paper he found in the desk drawer.

"Find something?" Melvyn looked over Ayden's shoulder.

"The two appointments Hal missed and what he was to deliver. I'll need to reschedule those deliveries." He tucked the note in his breast pocket. "What's more interesting is the cargo manifest for the *Atlantia*." He looked up at his brother. "That's the ship that disappeared."

"What's interesting?"

"I don't know—I can't pinpoint any discrepancy." He ran his nail down the cargo manifest. "Robert told me he typically ships lumber, tobacco, fish, and crops like potatoes and tomatoes to Europe. However, for this run, he intended to carry more cotton and mineral oil for trade in the Orient. Once he arrived in Glasgow and took possession of *Amylia*, the cargo and extra crew would transfer from *Atlantia*. After that, *Amylia* would sail toward China, and *Atlantia* would take on finished goods in Europe and return to sell here."

"Why is that interesting?"

"I don't know." Ayden rubbed his eyes. "He's listed the trip's cargo, food, water, and coal requirements. There's something here I'm not seeing, or maybe I'm imagining things." He shrugged and closed the binder. "Hal's room is upstairs. Let's see what we find."

Hal's sleeping area was in disarray, with clothes strewn across the bed and floor. The wardrobe doors were open, drawers out, half emptied.

"Is this normal?" Mel asked, looking over the contents of the bureau. "What a mess."

"Someone either took him, and they searched the room, leaving this disarray, or he packed and left abruptly." Ayden tossed a torn shirt into a drawer.

"Who would do this?"

"There are a few possibilities." Ayden straightened the mattress on the bed frame and looked out the dirty window. "A group of religious fanatics roam the docks. We had a run-in with them at a bawdy house the night I was shot. Hal and Robert brought me here first, then to Revere's." He turned and looked at Melvyn. "Hal was attacked on Christmas Eve just outside of Margaret's house. I don't know if the same fanatics have followed Hal or if it could be Lisbeth's father and his coven trying to scare us off, and they mistook Hal for me."

"Are you saying both groups wish you harm?"

"Possibly." Ayden nodded. "But I see nothing here that sways me in either direction. He could have ravaged his room while rushing to pack."

"Pack?"

"No one has seen Hal since Robert departed. Perhaps he boarded the *Atlantia* before it set sail to remain with Robert."

"You say that as though they have a—relationship."

"They do. An intimate partnership they've shared for quite some time."

"But...what about Margaret?"

"Robert is her husband, and she loves him."

"And you?" Melvyn raised one eyebrow and squinted at Ayden.

"Margaret knows about Robert and Hal, just as Robert, and I assume Hal knows about Margaret and I."

Melvyn shook his head. "This is hard to understand."

"I agree, it's an unusual situation."

"Could Robert and Hal's relationship anger the fanatics?"

"That's a possibility, but it's too soon to know for sure." Ayden kicked several articles of clothing toward the wardrobe and walked past Melvyn and out the door. "First, I must apologize to two buyers and reschedule their deliveries."

"And then what?"

"Get dressed for dinner with Margaret. Tomorrow, I think I should speak with the leader of the religious zealots terrorizing the whore houses along the wharf and find out if they've harmed Hal."

"I should go with you." Melvyn nodded and followed Ayden out of the warehouse.

Chapter 20

Measured and Fitted

Melvyn MacKenna

Melvyn found the early afternoon spent watching his brother cajole an angry, dry-good owner both interesting and instructive.

Ayden took command of the merchant, angry with the delay, and put the man's annoyance to rest. His brother smiled and apologized as he smoothed the shop owner's ruffled feathers with a wave of his hand, or so it seemed.

Where did he learn this?

When they left Clinton's Dry Goods, the owner laughed and patted Ayden on the back. He was happy to do business with Prescott Imports and looked forward to his delivery later that week.

"Where to now?" Melvyn matched his brother's long stride as they paced up the street.

"Thatcher's Tailoring. Archie is an old acquaintance of mine. This shouldn't take much time, then we can head back to Revere's and dress for dinner."

Melvyn had never attended a dinner party and never considered what he might say to a woman as grand as Margaret Prescott or as lovely and spirited as Peg Johnson. He brushed at his coat and hoped he would find time to repair the sleeve on his best shirt for tonight and brush his jacket clean.

The bell above the door rang as they entered, and a number of shoppers turned at the chime.

Mel nodded and smiled, but most had already moved away.

Ayden headed for the back of the store and called hello to a balding man with a measuring ribbon hung around his neck. The two shook hands and spoke while Melvyn looked around.

Bolts of fine material were displayed to allow shoppers to feel the different fabrics. Melvyn touched the last six, marveling at the colors and feel of the various threads beneath his fingertips.

"He's your height. The shoulders appear about the same. It wouldn't take long to make a few alterations."

Mel glanced up and found the proprietor and Ayden staring at him.

"Measure him up and make a second suit as well. Mel can pick the fabric." Ayden shook the tailor's hand. "And we'll get your fabric shipment delivered by the end of the week."

The tailor shook his brother's hand, then turned to Mel. "Archie Thatcher. Nice to meet you, young man. I made suits for your brother when he first came to town."

Melvyn took the older man's hand. "Nice to meet you, sir."

"I saw you admiring the tweed. If you like, I'd recommend the darker herringbone pattern for menswear just over here."

"Yes, I like that." Mel touched the soft woolen fabric and smiled at the tailor.

"Good then." He pulled a bolt of fabric from beneath the counter display and pointed toward a curtained area. "We'll just take a few measurements and adjust your brother's suit, and you'll be set for your dinner party tonight."

Mel pulled back. "I'm taking Ayden's order?"

"One of the suits in my order," Ayden said from behind. "The other will be ready when we negotiate our new deliveries."

"We'll finish your second suit with his lovely herringbone tweed in two weeks."

Archie proclaimed, and ushered Melvyn behind the curtain. "We'll be right back," he said to Ayden.

"Take your time."

Behind the curtain, Archie's assistant waited.

"Please remove your jacket," the tailor instructed. "Luca will take your measurements."

As Luca measured Mel, he called out numbers to Archie, who made notations on a small card.

"Very similar to your brother, Mr. MacKenna. You're just an inch shorter, and your arm length is shorter by a half inch. These alterations will take no time at all."

Mel nodded, but the tailor appeared to require verbal affirmation. "Um, thank you."

"Not at all, not at all." He noted Melvyn's neck size. "While you wait for the adjustment, might I suggest the haberdasher across the street? They have an assortment of hats, gloves, handkerchiefs, and undergarments that should fit the bill."

"Yes." Mel peeked out a gap in the curtain and saw Ayden standing near the exit. "Are you finished measuring?"

Luca nodded, and Archie handed Mel his jacket. "We'll have your suit tailored by this afternoon."

Melvyn took his jacket, nodded to Luca and Archie, then slipped out from behind the curtain and followed Ayden out the door.

Ayden pointed across the street, and Melvyn groaned. "What now?"

"Gloves, a new hat, handkerchiefs, and underclothes." He looked down at Melvyn's boots. "Boots?"

"Is everything I wear that bad?"

Ayden chuckled. "Not at all. But if you are to assist me, and I hope you will because I need help, you must appear a man of business."

"And less like a farrier for hire."

"Helping me pays better." Ayden smiled and held open the haberdashery door.

Melvyn selected a tall charcoal derby while Ayden ordered the other incidentals. "Archie has my brother's measurements if you need them. We'll take the hat, gloves, undergarments, and handkerchiefs today."

They walked down to the shoemaker and ordered ankle-height lace-up boots, another pair of black slip-on gaiters, and a pair of spats. After selecting a premade black belt in the correct size, they returned to Archies for a final fitting.

Back at Revere's, the men had time to wash, dress, and catch a Hansom to Beacon Hill for dinner.

"We're early," Melvyn noted as they stepped from the cab.

"I always try to arrive early when Margaret is expecting me."

"Why is that?" Mel sat his new derby on his head and straightened his new jacket.

"I left her waiting for over twenty years." He raised one eyebrow at his brother. "I promised never to make her wait for me again." Ayden paid the driver, then strode down the walk to the door.

Melvyn hurried to catch up. "I don't mean to argue the point, but it doesn't appear she waited. She married while you were gone and had a child."

"I do have eyes." Ayden knocked on the door.

Wrigley, wearing his wrinkled and dusty driver's suit, opened the door. "Good afternoon, brothers MacKenna. Please come in."

"Wrigley." Ayden removed his hat and handed it to Wrigley. "Are the ladies in the sitting room?"

"Margaret is in there, Peg is still upstairs, and Mrs. Bengston is in the kitchen." Wrigley pointed to the sitting room, then took Ayden's and Melvyn's hats and set them on the shelf in the understairs closet. "Please, make yourselves at home."

Ayden entered the sitting room. "How are you feeling? We could have called the dinner off, you know."

"I know." Margaret rose and wrapped her arms around Ayden's waist. "But I hate to cancel plans at the last minute."

Melvyn followed Wrigley past the sitting room into the dining area. The large table, set for six, held three place settings on each side. Da had attempted to teach Melvyn manners and the niceties of social dining, but Mel had hardly listened.

I'm going to make a fool of myself.

"I don't eat with the family." Wrigley stood in the doorway, grinning at Melvyn as though he could read his mind. "Watch your brother and Margaret. Use the utensils they do. You'll do fine." A wicked grin split his face, as if to contradict everything he'd just said. He uttered a high-pitched chuckle, shook his head, turned, and walked through the next room and out the back door.

Delicious aromas emanated from the next room, along with a lightly hummed tune that felt somehow familiar. Stuck between intruding on Ayden or following the grumpy driver, Mel paced along the table to study the drawings hung on the wall.

The framed sketches were in pencil and contained details that astounded Mel. A sparrow, its wing extended as though injured, stared up at the artist. Each feather appeared so genuine Mel ached to touch it and feel its silky vane.

The fear and pain sketched in the small bird's eyes pierced him as though the injured animal lay before him, and he touched it with his *earth-sense*.

How can I possibly feel this?

Was it the artwork itself or something more?

He moved on to the next drawing—this one of a horse. Head hung over the stall door; the animal knew love beyond measure by his mistress. The dark equine eyes waited patiently but also held anticipation for the promised apple placed out of sight of the artist's pencil.

How can I know these things? What type of magic is this?

He rounded the end of the table, eager to look at the sketches hung on the opposite wall.

"I see you've found Amy's drawings." Peg hovered at the entrance in a dark blue dinner gown. "She enjoyed sketching animals." Peg's hair, arranged in artful curls atop her head, with a few dark tendrils allowed to escape along her neck and temple, made her appear a Grecian Goddess. "She captures the subjects wonderfully, but the injured bird puts me off."

Suddenly thankful for Ayden's new suit, Mel struggled to find something intelligent to say. "I understand that. The artist has certainly captured the poor bird's fear and pain." Sketches forgotten, he stepped forward and smiled at Peg. "Amy is the artist, you say?"

"Yes." Peg nodded and moved around the table to examine the bird. "Margaret's daughter. Amy could draw almost anything—animals and people—living things mostly. The sketch at the end there is of her husband, Jason."

Mel turned from Peg and studied the black and white sketch of a young man's face, his hair, a riot of curls, perhaps a bit too long. From the detailed pencil illustration, Mel knew the man's eyes were a vivid blue, and his teeth straight and white above an impressive strong jaw. "He loves Amy very much," Mel blurted.

"Why on earth would you say that?" Peg laughed. "I'm not saying he doesn't love her, but that certainly wasn't what I thought you'd say."

Mel smiled at Peg's musical laughter. "What would you have me say?"

"Most people comment on how handsome Jason is."

"They do?" Mel looked at the drawing again.

But that isn't what Amy sees.

Instead, Melvyn knew how deeply Jason's feelings ran and how desperate he was to stand on his own and take care of his wife without help from his father.

"Yes, you're right." Mel turned from the drawings. "Amy's husband is quite handsome."

"Quite?"

Melvyn shrugged. "He finds people's reaction to his looks amusing."

Peg's eyes widened, and her head shifted to one side as she studied Mel. "You know him then?"

"No."

She can't see the hidden depths layered into each drawing.

"It's just a guess." He indicated the hint of a smile on the drawing's lips. "He seems amused by all the fuss."

Peg narrowed her eyes as she studied Melvyn. She opened her mouth to speak, but a knock at the door interrupted her. "Excuse me." She brushed past Mel and crossed to the entry to open the door. "Oh! May I help you?"

"Good afternoon. I'm Lisbeth Coleman. Mrs. Prescott invited me to dine with her this evening at seven."

Melvyn followed Peg to the door and gazed at Lisbeth in wonder. He'd half expected her to arrive wearing her wrangler glamour, but not as the Boston princess she was.

Lisbeth's white-blonde hair had been curled and gathered at the back of her head. Loose radiant curls framed her face, and a thick braid hung over her bare shoulder. Her off-the-shoulder gown in a rich dark burgundy clung tightly to her generous curves, with an overskirt drape of black lace gracing the front above her black shoes.

Behind her, an older gentleman with a black top hat and cane paid the cabbie and proceeded up the walkway.

"This might be Lisbeth," Ayden said as he approached the corner of the sitting room. He stopped at the sight of Lisbeth in her finery. "It is most certainly, Lisbeth. Come in!" He gestured to the older gentleman behind her. "You too, Garrett. I'm glad you could make it."

Peg scooted behind Melvyn and headed down the short hall to the dining room and into the kitchen.

Margaret beamed at her guests and opened her arms. "Welcome. Welcome! I'm so glad you were both able to come tonight. Today's news had me down, but your wonderful faces have lifted my heart."

Garrett kissed Margaret on both cheeks and looked at her sternly. "You received unwelcome news?"

"I did, and I'll tell you more later, but first there are introductions in order. Garrett, this beautiful woman in the magnificent dress is Lisbeth Coleman. Her family are Boston Brahmin royalty if such a thing exists."

Garrett swept the top hat off his head and bowed. "Miss Coleman, it is genuinely nice to meet you."

"Lisbeth, this distinguished gentleman is Judge Garrett Brown of the Boston Circuit Court."

"I'm pleased to make your acquaintance, your honor."

"Please, no honorifics. Call me Garrett."

Margaret stepped forward and indicated Mel. "And this young man is Ayden's brother, Melvyn. He arrived in town just recently."

"Mr. Brown." Melvyn shook Garrett's hand. "My father always spoke well of you and asked me to find you and remember him to you."

"Your father is a fine man." Garrett gave Ayden a confused look. "Am I to understand Lyam has recently passed?"

"Yes, sir. It's only been a few weeks."

"I am sorry for your loss." Garrett reached out and gripped Ayden's arm. "And for yours as well."

"Thank you," Ayden murmured and closed the door behind Lisbeth. "Now, there is more room to get acquainted in the dining room, and it smells like Mrs. Bengston may have dinner on the table."

Garrett set his hat in the closet, then wrapped Lisbeth's hand around his arm. "If I may escort you, my dear."

Lisbeth's grin widened. "I'd be delighted."

"Margaret?" Ayden held out his arm.

Margaret hugged his arm and followed Garrett and Lisbeth into the dining room.

Melvyn stood alone and marveled at the company he kept tonight.

Da would be both proud and amazed.

"And all of them are like me, able to manipulate natural elements." Mel spoke softy to himself.

Ayden turned and looked at him. "Are you coming?"

"I am, indeed."

Chapter 21

Arrivals

Margaret Prescott

"Where would you like us to sit?" Garrett inquired as Margaret and Ayden entered the dining area.

"If you and Lisbeth would take the seats at the far end, across from each other, then Peg and Mel in the center seats."

Peg gave Margaret a nod of understanding, then smiled as Garrett held her seat.

Ayden seated Lisbeth, pointed at his brother's chair, then rounded the table and held Margaret's chair.

"Mrs. Bengston cooks delicious dinners for us. As you know, I'm no hand in the kitchen. Since Amy married and left home, Peg has graciously agreed to join me at meal-time, so I don't have to eat alone. Our cook is the only staff I employ, and we serve ourselves by passing the platters around the table."

"You mean to say Peg sups with you and Robert now?" Garrett asked.

"No. Just me. Robert is often away at dinner time, entertaining clients."

"Is that where he is this evening?" Garrett shook out his napkin, placed it on his lap, and gave Margaret his full attention. "I don't mean to pry."

Deep breath.

"Actually, no." She looked down at the table, then back to Garrett. "I believe everyone here is aware of the letter I received today from the harbormaster, except you, Garrett and Lisbeth." She placed the napkin in her lap. "Robert sailed for Europe a month ago. That crossing normally takes between seven and nine days. Based on the harbormaster's estimate, Rob should have arrived weeks ago."

"Dear Goddess!" Garrett exclaimed. "What's being done?"

"All ships leaving Glasgow are asked to keep a lookout for the *Atlantia*." She shrugged and looked away. "Other than that, we can only wait."

"Two of Robert's ships are on this side of the Atlantic. As soon as they reach Boston, I intend to send at least one of them to Glasgow on the same passage Robert described in his office log." Ayden spoke down the table to Garrett and Lisbeth. "If nothing else, the *Amylia* should be brought home unless we can find a captain willing to make the China run."

"Spencer Harris will have a say in that—he owns half the ship." Margaret's eyes widened. "And he doesn't know Robert is missing."

"Does he know about me?" Ayden asked, placing a dollop of mashed potatoes on his plate and then passing the dish to Peg.

"No. Robert and I aren't particularly fond of Jason's parents."

"I'm not surprised," Lisbeth interjected. "Spencer and Rose are horrible snobs, even for the Brahmin elite. They're quite disliked by everyone I know."

"I performed the wedding ceremony between Amy and their son if I remember correctly." Garrett passed a bowl of steamed greens and then took the potatoes from Peg.

"You are correct; however, Jason is estranged from his family, which surprises no one."

"How are the Harris's involved with Robert's ships?" Garrett asked.

"Robert needed capital for the new steamer and agreed to allow Spencer to invest half on the *Amylia*." Her plate full; Margaret folded her hands on her napkin and waited for the rest of the table to finish filling theirs.

"Pardon me for asking, but how does this involve Ayden?" Garrett passed the potatoes and folded his hands in his lap as well.

"Robert made Ayden a full partner in his shipping business before he sailed. Which means..."

"That Ayden has to deal with Spencer." Lisbeth laughed with delight. "I hope you are up to the task."

"I'm sure he is," Melvyn put in. "He's quite the diplomat. He had the merchants who missed their shipment happy as larks before we left their offices."

"Shipments missed because Robert is away?" Garrett raised an eyebrow.

"You are quite the busybody, Your Honor." Lisbeth smiled and winked at the older man.

"There is a story there as well, but first, let us thank the Lord and Lady for their gifts and ask our Lady to watch over those away from us tonight."

Margaret reached across the table and took Ayden's hand, then offered her open palm to Melvyn.

When all hands clasped, forming a circle, Margaret closed her eyes.

"Lord and Lady, be welcome at our table.

We thank you for your abundance tonight

as we share your bounty with friends and family.

God and Goddess, extend your sheltering light to our two loved ones

who are away from us this night and guide them safely home."

Margaret opened her eyes and looked around the table.

Ayden's dark eyes displayed warmth and support. He gave a nod and released her hand.

"Nicely done, young Margaret." Garrett arranged his napkin and picked up his fork. "I couldn't have done better myself." He paused and touched his bottom lip with his forefinger, brows drawn together. "Two who are away, you say?"

"Robert and the warehouse manager, Hal," Ayden replied.

"Ah! I see. And there is the reason the deliveries were overdue." He pushed a piece of chicken across his plate and then looked at Ayden. "Any idea where your manager could have gone?"

"A few ideas I intend to explore this week. You've heard about the fanatics plaguing the docks and bawdy houses."

"I have. They style themselves *The Pure Fire of Boston*." He pierced the chicken with the tines of his fork. "I've had two of them in my courtroom on assault charges just this month."

"We had a couple of run-ins with them last fall. Once along the wharf, and another when they came into Revere's looking for trouble."

"And Christmas," Margaret put in.

"We don't know for sure." Ayden looked from Margaret to Garrett. "But we suspect they may have assaulted Hal on Christmas Eve as he arrived for dinner."

Garrett swallowed his bite of chicken and touched his napkin to his lips. "Then their group would be a good place to start looking for your missing manager. Any other leads?"

"You must always suspect my father." Lisbeth folded her napkin and placed it on the table near her plate. "He is plagued with fear Ayden and Margaret have begun a rival coven to supplant him in Boston, or, worse yet, draw the terrifying James brothers back to town." She pressed her lips as she gazed at Ayden. "My father would use any ploy to frighten you away."

"And your father is...?" Garrett folded his napkin and looked across the table at Lisbeth.

"Isaac Coleman."

Garrett blinked, and his smile faltered. "You're Isaac's daughter. I'm not sure how I missed that connection."

"You know my father?"

"Not personally, no. But I keep in touch with a few of my old members, and they've spoken to me about this new coven and its leader." Garrett chuckled. "If he worries about a rival coven, it's a good thing he doesn't know about our dinner tonight."

Ayden, Margaret, and Lisbeth replied at the same time.

"He does."

"He already knows."

"He's heard."

"How could he?" Mel exclaimed. He looked from Garrett to Ayden. "We've been here less than an hour."

"Six witches having dinner at Margaret James's house, one being his daughter, would be worth sending one of the sentinels to warn my father. Our townhouse is not that far from here."

"Isaac's coven not only watches Revere's." Ayden set aside his napkin as he spoke to his brother. "They watch this house as well."

"Then they saw you come in," Mel gaped at Lisbeth, "and you knew they would."

"I knew." Lisbeth nodded, lifted one shoulder, and looked at Margaret and Ayden. "I don't mean to cause trouble, but I wanted to get to know you—" she hesitated, then added, "—as the real me."

"I doubt there will be any trouble," Ayden assured her.

A sharp rap on the door followed his words.

"When you speak of the devil..." Garrett chuckled.

"Hush now, Garrett," Margaret scolded. "You're like to give the younger ones a fright."

"What younger ones?" Melvyn asked.

Peg stood when the knock sounded, then looked from Garrett to Margaret as they spoke. "Wrigley's out back if we need him." She passed behind Ayden and rounded the end of the table. "I'll get the door."

"I can get it." Ayden pushed his chair back to stand.

Peg held up her hand to stop him. "It's routine for me to greet callers near dinnertime." She grinned over her shoulder at Melvyn, wrinkled her nose, and said in a stage whisper, "I'm not scared."

Lisbeth and Garrett chuckled as Margaret turned to watch Peg answer door.

It can't be Isaac. Perhaps it's Hal.

Peg brushed her skirt and then opened the door. Her brows went up, her mouth dropped open, and she threw her arms wide and shrieked. "It's you!"

Adrenaline shot down Margaret's spine at Peg's cry, and she came to her feet.

Ayden moved quicker and rushed past Margaret to Peg.

Margaret stepped forward and saw who Peg was holding in her arms.

"Mama!" Amy released Peg, untied her bonnet, and flung herself down the hallway, past Ayden, and into her mother's arms. She pulled her head back and looked into Margaret's eyes. "You're astonished to see me. You didn't get our letter?"

"No, but you're a welcome surprise, my dear." She wrapped her arms around Amy and looked past her shoulder.

Jason stepped through the door and hugged Peg quickly, then offered Ayden his hand and an engaging grin. "It's so good to see you again."

Margaret pushed Amy to arm's length and beamed at her daughter, caressing her face. "I'm honestly glad you're here."

Amy's brows drew together. "Is something wrong?" She looked in the dining room and shook her head in confusion, lowering her voice. "I see we've interrupted."

"Nonsense. Besides, you know almost everyone here."

"I only recognize Judge Brown."

Margaret grinned. "The young man is Melvyn, Ayden's younger brother. He's just arrived in town, and the woman you already know."

Amy leaned to one side and observed the white-haired woman. "She's familiar…"

"Lisbeth Coleman." Margaret raised her brows and smiled. "But not as one would expect."

"No." Amy narrowed her eyes at her mother. "Are you sure?"

"I am. Lisbeth is a witch and adept at *glamour magic*. She never was the shy young debutant who caught fire."

Amy blinked with surprise at her mother. "But why?

"Ah, a tale for another time. I'll re-introduce you. You'll like her."

"All right, but first, where's father?" Amy lowered her already quiet voice to a whisper. "Alyse waits in the cab. The man she intends to wed is with her. He wants to ask father for her hand. We know her existence will shock Father, but it's time he knew the truth, don't you agree?"

Margaret opened her mouth, closed it, and looked over at Ayden as a peculiar mix of panic and anticipation filled her gut.

My daughters found each other, and now the rest of the world will learn the secret of their birth. Goddess, give me strength.

"Alyse is outside?" Margaret muttered more to herself than to Amy.

"She is. Should I have her come in?"

Margaret pressed her lips. "Yes, but let's move to the sitting room and leave my guests to enjoy their dessert." She touched Peg's arm as she passed to return to the dining room. "Please make our guests at home while I have a brief meeting with my daughter. This shouldn't take long."

"Of course," Peg said to Margaret and then continued into the dining area. "There is pudding to enjoy while Mrs. Prescott speaks with Amy. Who would like to try a cup?"

Chapter 22

Truth Revealed

Ayden MacKenna

"It's wonderful to see you. Have you eaten? There's plenty left from dinner to share." Ayden offered, drawing Jason forward.

Jason hesitated and cast a glance out the open door. "We didn't arrive alone."

"You have others with you? Bring them in. I'm sure Margaret won't mind."

"I, um." Jason hesitated, took a deep breath, and lowered his voice as he leaned forward and whispered, "Amy wants permission from her mother first."

"Indeed?" Ayden raised an eyebrow and turned his gaze to Margaret and Amy.

Margaret's worried eyes captured his glance.

"Margaret?" Ayden stepped towards her; concern and confusion clouded his thoughts.

Margaret drew Amy forward and proceeded past Ayden with a shake of her head and into the sitting room. "We shall receive the new guests in here." She glanced over her shoulder at the men in the entryway. "Jason, bring them inside—directly in here. Ayden, I'd like you here." She sat slowly on one side of the settee and arranged the fold of her skirt.

Ayden blinked. The questions Margaret's odd behavior provoked circled his mind so rapidly that they left it blank. "As you wish, my dear." He followed mother and daughter into the sitting room, then crossed to the far side to stand behind the settee. He folded his arms and gave his full attention to the door.

Amy's head turned as he strode past. Once he took his stand behind Margaret, Amy transferred her bewildered gaze to her mother.

Margaret ignored Amy's odd look and shifted in her seat, her focus on the door.

"This way, yes—right through here." Jason appeared for a moment; his arm extended toward Margaret.

A cloaked woman strode past him. Head down, she walked directly to the center of the room, then turned toward Margaret. Her face was shadowed and hidden beneath her hood.

Behind her, a big man, both tall and broad-shouldered, ducked his head to pass beneath the doorway.

Ayden stared at the woman's tall escort. He could easily have been the tallest man Ayden had ever seen.

The man pulled a tan Stetson from his head and smiled as he calmly met Ayden's gaze.

"Jason, come in and close the door, please," Margaret requested, her voice tight.

As the door snicked shut, the woman in the center of the room lifted her hood and looked around.

"Lord and Lady, be good," Ayden muttered.

The woman's dark travel dress was more serviceable than the gay fabric and design Amy wore, but her face and eyes drew him in and captivated his wonder. "What trick is this? A *glamour?*"

Fast asleep in the stone amulet around Ayden's neck, Caz stirred sharply, then jumped with excitement or warning.

Identical twins run in the James family.

The duplicate vision of Amy stared into his eyes.

This is Amy's twin.

"Margaret?" The cold-heartedness necessary to separate these two babes, and this one from her mother, astounded him.

And I thought what Chantal did to me was inhumane. What Margaret did to these children, to her daughters, was beyond redemption.

Mustering as much composure as he could manage, Ayden smiled at the couple. "Please have a seat and be welcome." He extended an arm toward the settee where Margaret sat straight-backed and stiff across from the two matching chairs.

The woman ignored him and instead, held out her hand. "You must be my—" she sniffed off the end of her sentence, then looked up to him and took a deep breath. "You must be Robert. I'm Alyse—James." Her eyes burned questions into his as she pressed her lips to still some barely held emotion.

Ayden took her cold hand in his and then shook his head. "I'm sorry, I'm not Robert. My name is Ayden MacKenna. I'm a friend of your family." He glanced over Alyse's head at Jason.

"I apologize." Jason straightened and pushed away from the closed door. He had an inscrutable smile as he stepped toward the couple who stood before Margaret. "I should have made proper introductions. Mr. Leigh, may I present my mother-in-law, the esteemed Mrs. Margaret Prescott. Standing beside her is our good friend, Mr. Ayden MacKenna. Margaret, Ayden, allow me to introduce Mr. Jimmy Leigh. Jim is the Harris Highlands Ranch foreman, and I believe this may be his first visit to Boston. He accompanied us to speak with Robert on a very welcome matter. Ayden, you've already met Amy's twin sister, Alyse James."

"Mr. Leigh." Ayden extended his hand to the foreman.

"Jim or Jimmy Leigh suit me best." Jim gripped Ayden's hand in a firm handshake.

"Jim then. A pleasure to meet you."

"Ma'am." Jimmy Leigh reached over the table and took Margaret's hand for a moment, then returned to his place behind Alyse.

"A twin sister," Ayden said into the awkward silence as he glanced from Margaret to Amy, then settled his gaze on Alyse. "I'm surprised, and then again, I'm not. Twins do run in your family. Tell me, how did the three of you ever keep such a secret?"

"They didn't know, Ayden." Margaret's dull, soft tone held more than a modicum of guilt. "No one in Boston knew."

Ayden's gaze returned to Margaret. After a moment, he shook his head. "That can't be true. You knew. Robert must have known."

"No." Margaret shrugged one shoulder, her eyes cast down on her hands as she worried the material of her skirt. "Robert never knew both twins survived. He wasn't allowed in the room when the girls were born."

"But after—"

"There was never an after." Her tear-filled gaze rose to meet his. "They took Alyse away immediately, before I even gave birth to Amylia. They wrapped my darling child in a blanket, and she was gone."

"Who is they? Your mother?"

Margaret nodded. Her glance touched both girls; the tears on her face matched theirs, and then she looked back at her hands. "And brothers. They had a wet nurse waiting in a wagon behind the carriage house. The girls never knew they had a twin until recently."

"Why would Chantal do that? How could you allow it?"

"I didn't have much choice at the time, did I?" Margaret replied, her accusation sharp, and lamps flickered around the room as her bruised gaze tore into Ayden's. She took a deep, calming breath. "Mother believed separating my daughters to be the only way to avert their death—all of our deaths."

"And she was right," Alyse softly replied, her eyes downcast. "Our first *twyning* fulfilled the prophecy and caused the demon to stir. He escaped hell to find us." Her attention rose to her mother. "*Grandmère* paid for her knowledge and our escape to find Amy with her life."

Margaret nodded solemnly. "After your spring visit, I thought that might be the case."

Ayden swallowed. *Now is not the time to speak about my encounter with the demon and what I know of Chantal's death.*

"But the demon and his curse are behind us now." Alyse pressed her lips with determination. "And I'm here to meet—and speak with my father."

"Your father is not in town at the moment." Margaret brushed at her dress, then glanced up at Ayden. "Robert sailed a month ago to Scotland to take possession of his newest ship."

Alyse shuddered and paled visibly. She straightened as she stepped back toward her twin. Her gaze remained fixed on her mother. "Say that again," she whispered.

Margaret blinked and smiled at Alyse. "I'm sorry, my dear, but your father is not here."

Relaxing against the wall beside Amy, Jim's head came up and straightened.

Caz pounded hard against his stone enclosure, forcing Ayden to rest his hand on the necklace beneath his shirt. "Shh, Caz," he murmured.

Alyse reached out to Amy with her arm, and they clasped hands.

"No!" Amy shook her head. "That can't be."

"I'm never wrong," Alyse replied. Her eyes remained on her mother.

"What's the matter?" Margaret asked.

"Mother, you know how I sometimes have waking visions and can scry for omens in water?" Amy glanced at Ayden, then returned her focus to her mother.

Margaret nodded.

A tingling began low in Ayden's stomach.

How had I never noticed?

He stared at the twins holding hands, and the image of his brother came to mind. Mel would be only a few years older than these young women.

The resemblance is unmistakable. How did I never guess?

"Alyse has a *spirit-gift* as well." Amy paused and glanced around the dining room.

Jason touched his wife's shoulder and nodded, lending her his support.

"What gift is that sweetheart?" Margaret's pale skin seemed even paler in the gaslight.

"I'm a *truth-reader*," Alyse said in a hushed tone. "In most cases, I must seek to read a person's honesty. At other times, the turbulence of their dishonesty bubbles out with their words, and I know, without trying."

Brace yourself. Miera's voice flickered with concern from the wall sconce flame.

Are you aware of what happens here?

Three spirit-gifted so near each other have caught my attention, yes.

Margaret heaved a sigh. "Robert sailed for Glasgow several weeks ago. The harbormaster wrote to me when his ship did not make port when expected. As far as I know, neither he nor his ship have been located."

"True." Alyse murmured.

Margaret met her daughter's gaze. Neither flinched.

Amy looked from her mother to her sister. "Then where is the lie?"

"Mama, where is our father?" Alyse spoke into the silence of the room.

No one moved, held in the tension on Margaret's face. "I just told you."

"No. You told us about your husband."

Margaret's brow rose, and her mouth fell slightly open as she gasped.

"Alyse, stop it." Amy pulled her hand away from her sister's grip.

Alyse shook her head. "I can't stop. Anger sparkled with tears in her eyes. "I will not accept one more lie from this family. I've lived with their falsehoods my entire life. I came here to make myself known and speak with my father." Her attention turned back to her mother. "Where is my father?"

"I don't know."

"A lie. You do know."

Margaret gulped back a sob; her eyes brimmed with tears as she shook her head.

Ayden lowered himself onto the settee beside Margaret and drew her into his arms as she sobbed. "Your accusations, even if correct, are dangerous to your mother—to your entire family." He stared hard at the twins and then at Jason and Jim. His heartbeat was like thunder, keeping time with Caz's attempts to free himself from the amulet.

"Ayden, don't," Margaret begged.

"Tell me!" Alyse's words were sharp, and the flames flared in their glass lanterns.

Startled gasps could be heard outside the room, and a pounding began at the front door.

"Compose yourself!" Ayden stood and faced Alyse. "Regardless of who your father is, you are in your mother's house, and you will control your magic."

Alyse narrowed her eyes and raised both fire-filled hands in a rage, but Ayden clenched his fist by his side.

All the lanterns in the house went dark.

"What?" Alyse opened her empty hand in confusion. "How is this possible?" Her angry gaze jumped to Ayden. "Give it back!"

The two stared at each other angrily.

Jimmy Leigh rounded the low table and rested his arm around Alyse's shoulders. "I know you're upset, but there is no danger here, except maybe you."

"If you promise to control your outrage, I'll return the fire—daughter."

Alyse blinked, her eyes opened wide, then a tiny smile of satisfaction lifted her lips. "I knew it."

Margaret pulled the handkerchief from her dress sleeve and covered her face as she sobbed.

Amy muttered, "No." Then moved closer and shouted at Ayden, "No! You are not my father."

"He is," Alyse decreed softly. "Mother knows the truth, even though Mr. MacKenna still has doubts."

"I don't doubt." Ayden shook his head. "I should have figured this out before now."

"My father is Robert Prescott." Amy declared sharply, her chin quivering. "Don't do this, Mama. Where is my father?"

"Amy," Jason soothed and gripped her shoulders, but Amy shook him off.

"No!" She pointed her finger at Margaret. "You *know* Robert Prescott is my father."

"Robert raised you and loved you your entire life. Robert is your father in all the ways that matter to a child."

"And you lied to him? About me, about us?" Amy clenched and unclenched her fists, fighting to control her emotions.

"Of course not. Robert and I were the only ones, until now, who knew you were not—that he was not—" her voice faltered and faded.

"Your mother didn't know?" Ayden handed Margaret his dry handkerchief.

"I don't think so." Margaret shook her head and dried her cheeks. "She may have guessed, but she never asked."

"Ayden is right about one thing; this may not be spoken of outside this room." Jason stepped past Amy, then turned and addressed the twins and Jimmy Leigh, casting glances at Margaret and Ayden. "For the rest of the world, Robert Prescott must always remain Amy and Alyse's father." He swallowed. "That your children were separated at birth can be attributed to a child stolen by an unstable mother, but the scandal of a pregnancy out of wedlock—the family's reputation would never recover."

Ayden nodded. "I agree, but I want to tell Mel. He's part of this family now."

"Who is Mel?" Alyse asked.

"My younger brother." Ayden looked from Amy to Alyse. "Knowing what I now know, you and he share a remarkable resemblance."

In the relative quiet of the room, a voice from outside the door said, "They won't mind. We're family and know what this is about."

The door swung open, and Bayard James grinned at his sister as he tossed his hat back to a dumbfounded Peg. "Hello Mags. I see the girls found you..." his voice trailed off as he came to a halt, and his gaze settled on Ayden.

Ayden turned to Bayard James. Every nerve down his arms and along his spine surged with suppressed rage.

Bayard's grin widened into a beacon of joy. "Ayden! You're alive and home. I can't say how glad I am to see you." He stumbled aside as Bernard pushed past.

"What is he doing here?" Bernard's arm rose, palm forward as a swirling fireball formed between his fingers.

A cacophony of voices erupted around Ayden.

Margaret jumped to her feet. "Bernard, what are you doing?"

"Uncle Bern, stop!" Alyse's arms came up as she stepped in front of Ayden.

Jimmy Leigh moved quickly, inserting himself between Bernard and the rest of the room. "You need to calm down, Bern." He glanced shortly at Bayard and then returned his hard stare to Bernard. "Now."

Bernard's bowler hat flew in the air as he fell forward into Jimmy Leigh's arms.

Past the doorway behind Bernard, Melvyn hefted a large cast-iron skillet over his shoulder, prepared to strike again. "Lisbeth told us who they were and that there'd be trouble."

"And I told you they were family!" Garrett yelled in exasperation. "Now look what you've done."

Chapter 23

Aftermath

Jason Harris

"Will he be all right?" Lisbeth whispered to Jason as they waited inside Margaret's guestroom.

"He will. My wife and her sister are healers—well, together, they heal." Jason shrugged one shoulder. "They would explain it better than I."

Amy and Alyse hovered over their uncle Bernard, communicating with nods and silence that Jason had become used to when it came to his wife and good sister. Each twin held one hand to opposite sides of their uncle's skull. Two distinct aura hues surrounded the women's hands beside the man's head. Amy's soft gold, while Alyse's aura had a warmer, orange tone.

Lisbeth lifted her shoulders. "It's just...I feel responsible. I didn't mean for Mel to physically assault their uncle. You see, I've been told for years how dangerous the James brothers are and how much devastation would ensue should they return to Boston."

Jason turned his attention from the bed to the companion beside him. "Shy, young Lisbeth Coleman. Not so childlike and not shy at all. What did Margaret call it, a *glamour?*"

"If anyone knew about my *glamours*, it would be you." She smiled at Jason, then returned her gaze to the twins. "It's just as surprising to find a fully human man married into a witch family—and aware of it. I always wondered how your marriage would turn out."

"I became extremely open-minded when presented with undeniable evidence." He grinned and winked. "That is to say, I came around."

"Father claimed Margaret had given up her magic, and her daughter, with her human husband, had no skill. I proved him wrong the night of the masquerade."

"The fire was your idea then?"

Lisbeth raised one shoulder. "Actually, no—but it was my *fire*. I recognized another witch's magic when Amy's mother snuffed it out."

"And I would have sworn you were no more than fourteen that night." He edged forward to catch her gaze. "I know it's rude to ask, but you must tell me, what is your age in truth, young Lisbeth?"

Her grin broadened into a smile. "Only *you* could ask a woman her age and get away with it, Mr. Harris. I'll be five-and-thirty this fall."

"I'd say you don't look a day over twenty-five, but how would I really know? Your *thug-in-the-night glamour* was ever so convincing. You nearly scared me to death."

Lisbeth chuckled and rocked back on her heels with delight. "That was fun for a while, but honestly, my father's obsession ruined the coven and all it could have been. I'll never go back to him."

Amy and Alyse rose in tandem then turned to face Jason and Lisbeth.

"Uncle Bernard will sleep for quite some time. The damage appeared minimal for such a hard hit on the head." Amy tidied up the nightstand, taking the bowl of warm water and cloth with her.

Alyse paused before Lisbeth. "Amy told me she knew you before she met Jason and that you are able to disguise your physical appearance quite successfully."

Lisbeth nodded. "She's correct."

"And how you appear—now—is your undisguised form?"

"It is."

"Do you intend any harm to my family or my uncle?"

Lisbeth straightened; her brows furrowed. "What a thing to ask."

"A simple yes or no will tell me the truth."

"No. I intend no harm to you, your family, or your uncle."

"Good." Alyse turned to Amy. "Let's go down and ask Mother if there is anything we can do to help find Robert, um—father."

"I agree. And we need to go back to the hotel for the night. There aren't enough beds here for all of us."

"Bernard won't be going anywhere." Jason shook his head. "Do one of you intend to stay here with your uncle?"

"I'll stay with him." Lisbeth offered. "If I leave now, my father's watchers will follow me back to where I'm staying, and I prefer they don't know my whereabouts. I'll sneak out in disguise with the morning deliveries, and they won't know to follow me."

"Hmm." Alyse looked from Amy to Lisbeth. "All right and thank you. It's been a long day and an odd evening. That said, I'm happy we met, Lisbeth."

"I am glad to have met you, as well," Lisbeth said as Alyse left the room.

Amy handed Jason the bowl of water and took Lisbeth's hands. "I wish you hadn't had to hide yourself when we met before. I think you and I could have been great friends."

"No doubt, although I may have been too old for your friends."

"Ha! As you well know, they were never my friends." Amy released Lisbeth's hands and followed her sister down the hall to the stairs.

Jason paused to watch the tall blonde woman seat herself in the chair beside Bernard's bed. He backed away from the door but hesitated as she spoke softly to her charge.

"So, you're the man who frightens my father so." She rested her palm on his forehead and then along the side of his face before she relaxed back in the chair and folded both hands across her lap. "It may have been the brash bravado I witnessed tonight which impressed your contemporaries in Father's Coven. They've convinced him you are a monster and to be avoided at all costs." She closed her eyes and grinned. "I do so love that in a man."

Jason smiled at Lisbeth's sentiment and followed his wife down the stairs.

Chapter 24

Unfinished Reckonings

Ayden MacKenna

Except for those attending Bernard, and Garrett—who made his goodbyes with haste when Jimmy Leigh carried Margaret's brother upstairs—the family and guests gathered around the dining room table.

Ayden chose the chair at the close end of the table where he could watch down the hall toward the front door and through the kitchen to the back.

If my daughter were in a house filled with people who I thought were my enemies, nothing would stop me from getting to her.

As though thinking of Margaret's twins caused one to appear, Alyse hurried down the stairs and crossed to the dining room.

"Will he live?" Ayden asked with a smile.

"Of course. It was never in doubt—without any thanks to your brother." She raised one eyebrow at Melvyn.

"I've said I'm sorry. I don't know what else I can do." Mel pressed his lips and kept his head down, tracing a pattern on the tablecloth. "I thought you were all in danger. I felt his magic ignite just as Lisbeth gasped that they were the notorious James brothers, it seemed like what I should do." His gaze flickered to Bayard, who sat across and down the table from him.

"Bernard is... rash." Bayard offered Mel a smile. "He mistakenly assumed Ayden must be here to seek retribution for an assault he suffered twenty-odd years ago."

"The assault hurt less than the years of bondage. That cost me more than you will ever know." Ayden's gaze moved from Bayard to Margaret and finally rested on Alyse.

"We all thought—well, I thought—you'd be back in a week, as powerful as your skills were even then." Bayard lifted his gaze filled with sincerity to Ayden. "I'm sorry for what we did to you."

Margaret remained unusually quiet. Her attention moved from her brother to Ayden, then Mel as she followed the conversation. She took a breath, then halted whatever she'd been about to say and pressed her lips.

"Mags?" Bayard questioned. "Speak your mind."

"I'm not sure I should. What right do I have to be angry at secrets kept from me when all of you were denied the truth I knew."

Amy and Jason came downstairs and stood in the dining room doorway, listening.

Margaret acknowledged them with a glance and then continued. "Even now, there are truths we hold from one another—for safety, for shame..." her words ran out, and she hung her head. "Regardless, I can't believe it was my own family who stole the life I desired from me." Her eyes lifted to Bayard, filled with suppressed tears. "How could you? What gave you the right? Spare me repeating all my mother's demonic terrors. What you did, and what you kept from me about what you did—"

Margaret's gaze shifted to Ayden. "And you. You saw who assaulted you. Yet you never told me who took you away from me, *and you knew.*"

"What purpose would it have served? They were gone." He gestured toward Bayard and hesitated before adding, "Along with your child, as it turns out, which you never mentioned to me or Amy."

"Bitterness will envelope you and tear you apart if you let it," Jimmy Leigh uttered. His voice, low and deep, sucked the conversation from the room. He raised his head and looked at the family gathered in the dining room. "The people you love are here with you—now. And *now* is all that you truly have. Don't waste these precious moments with meaningless recriminations about who knew what and when. It will only lead to more regret, more loss."

"What do you know of loss?" Margaret's heated retort rasped from her trembling lips.

"More than you can imagine, ma'am," Jim murmured, then rose from the chair, careful to miss the dangling candelabra over the table as he stood to his full height. "It's late, and we should return to the hotel."

"We're going to leave Bernard here. He's deep in a healing sleep and shouldn't be disturbed." Alyse held her hand to Jim and drew him away from the table. "We'll be back after breakfast tomorrow if that's acceptable, mother."

"Yes, of course." Margaret wiped her tears with her handkerchief. "I apologize for my outburst, Mr. Leigh. I hope you will forgive me."

"Nothing to forgive, ma'am. And please, call me Jim."

"If you stop the ma'am nonsense. You make me feel old."

Jimmy-Leigh tipped his head with a half-smile and followed Alyse to the foyer to retrieve his hat and her light wrap.

"Good night, Mama." Amy kissed Margaret's cheek, then took Jason's hand as they turned to go.

"Good night, Mags. Ayden." Bayard stood and rounded the table, pausing beside Ayden. "I am sorrier than I can say for the part I played in your abduction."

"The last thing I recall before I woke in the hold of Rakesh's ship was the look of profound horror on your face." Ayden rose and took Bayard's hand. "I always knew you were not the instigator of my fate."

Bayard nodded, his face too downhearted to smile, but his lips curled slightly as he followed Amy and Jason to the door.

Ayden turned his gaze to Mel. "You should go with them. It isn't safe for any of us to be alone, especially this evening."

"You're not coming?" Mel stood and stretched.

"As long as Lisbeth is here, there's a possibility her father will show up. I need to stay here."

"I'll keep a lookout for trouble at Revere's." Mel picked up a raw sliced carrot from a serving platter on the table. "And bring a change of clothes back with me for you and Lis in the morning."

"I appreciate it."

Mel nodded his understanding, then hurried to the front door. "Hold up. I'm coming with you."

Peg passed Margaret and Ayden as she returned from the kitchen, an apron tied around her dress. She picked up the platter that held the fresh vegetables.

"Leave those, Peg. Mrs. Bengston will clean up in the morning."

"I won't wash the dishes; just put away food to keep and scrape what will spoil into the compost bucket outside." She picked up the chicken platter, then rounded the table to return to the kitchen. "Excuse me," she said with a grin to Wrigley.

Wrigley's mouth teased a smile. "Oh no, pardon me." He plucked the plate of chicken from Peg's hand and continued to the table, taking Bayard's recently vacated seat. "What I don't eat, I'll bring to the kitchen on my way out." He looked around the table as Peg handed him a clean plate and utensils. "Thank ye, niece."

Peg continued to move plates of food into the kitchen as soon as Wrigley spooned a serving onto his plate.

"I'm surprised you're eating in here," Margaret commented. "You rarely do."

"That's true, but I overheard a few things, and I thought it best to let you know I knew."

"What did you learn?" Ayden chuckled.

"No." He dropped the chicken bone on his plate and rolled the linen napkin around in his hands. "I *already* knew. No need to walk on eggshells around me."

Ayden and Margaret exchanged amused looks.

"Then what *did* you already know?" Ayden leaned back in his chair. "Be specific."

"Ha! Easier to tell you what I didn't know before tonight." He raised one eyebrow as he returned Ayden's stare. "I didn't know it was her brothers who hit you on the head and shipped you off."

"Bernard hit me. They both dropped me in the hold of a ship, where Chantal signed away my life with my own blood." He'd meant to sound amused, to match Wrigley's casual manner, but even now, his anger bubbled to the surface.

Margaret took his hand. "I didn't realize my mother was there."

"Rakesh told me later what happened while I was unconscious."

"I *did* know you carried twins." Wrigley took back the conversation as he picked up another chicken leg. "Any fool could have seen that. I figured your family took one of them away, although Chantal never mentioned it to me, nor did you, for that matter." He pointed the meaty leg at Margaret, then took a bite.

"So, is that all you knew?" Ayden narrowed his eyes at the older man.

Wrigley chewed, swallowed, then waved the bitten leg at Ayden, his voice low. "I suspected the twins she carried were yours." He tipped his head and the chicken leg toward Margaret. "You remember, I worked for your mother as a handyman after your father passed. I was in the house on and off for years, and your brother," he pointed the leg toward the ceiling, "the one upstairs with the Coleman girl, talks very loudly. He aired his suspicions about you two on a regular basis. And I knew the two of you were close even back at Brown's farm." He took another bite, chewed, swallowed, and grinned at Ayden and Margaret. "And I can count."

"Is that true?" Peg gasped from the doorway. "Amy is *your* daughter?" She looked from her uncle to Ayden."

"Margaret Johnson, that is a family secret, and I'll thank you for keeping your voice down." Margaret hissed at Peg. "Not everyone in this house right now knows about that."

"I'm sorry," Peg whispered. "I was just surprised, is all. Does Amy know?"

"She does. The family knows, and now you and your uncle. Your parents named you after me, and I consider you family, but Lisbeth Coleman and Garrett Brown do not know, nor do I want them to. There are already too many who *do* know to keep this scandal much of a secret. The Brahmin will be utterly horrified, especially Jason's parents."

"No one will know," Ayden comforted. "And no one would believe the rumor anyway. No one remembers I was even around back then."

Wrigley tossed the last piece of chicken onto his plate and wiped his mouth. "Several in Coleman's coven knew you when we followed Garrett. Isaac Coleman is a Brahmin and their leader to boot. If the suggestion hasn't been raised already, you can make a wager it will be speculation soon enough."

"But that's a thin thread. I doubt Spencer Harris would put any stock in a rumor like that, especially if it cast aspersion on his son." Ayden passed Wrigley's plate to Peg.

"He might," Margaret muttered. "Spencer and Jason don't get along." She waved her hands in the air. "It doesn't matter. I'm not going to worry about it now. Once Robert is home, the gossip mongers will hide their heads."

"One last thing," Wrigley stood and tossed his napkin on the table. "It doesn't matter who saw your brother home. There are enough strong witches here to defend this house, should the need arise, but Mel will spend the night alone."

"Sweet Goddess, you're right." Ayden jumped to his feet. "What was I thinking?" Anxiety and urgency gripped his gut. "I'll bring Mel with me when I return tomorrow." He bent to kiss Margaret's cheek.

"Be sure you do." Margaret gripped his head with both hands and kissed him soundly on the lips. "No more disappearances." She released him and looked at Wrigley. "You could drive him."

The men shook their heads.

"Wrigley is needed here. I'll see you in the morning. And Coleman knows better than to assault me." Ayden hurried from the dining room, pulled his summer jacket and hat from the front closet, then shut the front door soundly as he left the house.

Outside, cicadas sang to the quarter moon. He paused on the front stoop and let the still night settle around him. Then he threw his senses wide.

It was early enough in the evening for a summer stroll, and he sensed the numerous strangers who wandered sedately along the stone paths through The Common.

Ayden opened his eyes. The cobblestones, dampened by humidity, reflected the soft light from the streetlamp. The avenue before him was empty of pedestrians,

And watchers.

Concern quickened his step as he hurried from Margaret's porch and strode north along the residential block. The lack of the ever-present watchers heightened his unease.

If the watchers aren't here, then where? Revere's?

On the park's far side, a row of Hansom Cabs would wait for new fares.

A cab would have me to Revere's in no time.

He hurried across the street, turned onto Walnut, then sprinted toward the park. He impatiently waited for carriages to pass on Beacon Street before he raced across the cobblestones to one of the park's entrances. He followed the path past the pond and beneath the branches of the great elm to the turn-in at Tremont Street, where the coaches picked up their passengers.

Perspiration beaded his brow, and he brushed his forehead with his handkerchief, then shoved it unceremoniously back into his pocket. The line for a cab was long, and he slowed his pace to look over the crowd. He didn't see Mel, the twins, Jason, or Alyse's tall friend Jim, who would have been easy to spot.

They must have already caught cabs.

Unease hung in the air along with the evening's humidity. The jovial crowd waiting in line cast curious glances at Ayden as he swore under his breath and stepped from the queue. He crossed Tremont, dodging through traffic and earning shouts of anger from coachmen.

Past Tremont, the traffic cleared. The newly rebuilt downtown was quiet, with few carriages and fewer pedestrians. Music from a small corner cafe caught his attention but faded as he hurried down the hill toward the pier.

From a crossroad near the end of the long road, a carriage took the corner at a high-speed rate and continued up the hill toward Ayden.

As they drew nearer, Ayden could sense the panic of the horses and slowed his pace to a stop to watch.

Anger radiated from the coach as it raced past, only to have the driver yell and yank the leads so hard the horses cried out. The carriage rocked and swerved onto the curb, barely missing a streetlamp.

The door of the ornate coach swung open, and Isaac Coleman stepped out and advanced on Ayden. "Release my daughter!" He swung his white cane in anger before him. A glimmer of fire traced the staff's arc, then dissipated in the night air.

"I don't have her, Isaac." Ayden took a step toward the angry father. "You know better than most that Lisbeth goes where she will and does what she pleases."

Sparks skidded across the street as his cane slammed down on the cobblestones. "Where is she?"

"No." Ayden shook his head and took another step. "I like Lisbeth much more than I like you. I intend to hold her confidences dear." He unbuttoned his jacket. The sudden warmth from the amulet caused sweat to bead across his brow.

"I know you've seen her."

"I won't stand in the middle of the street and discuss your missing daughter. Perhaps she wouldn't have run away if you weren't such a conniving bastard."

"She didn't run away!" Coleman slammed his walking stick down again in rage. "I ought to cut you to pieces for the mess you've made of my life."

"You can try." Ayden rolled the fingers of both hands into fists, then spread them wide. Electricity sparked between his knuckles, and he gave Coleman a hard smile. "Oh yes, I very much want you to try."

Isaac Coleman shook with fury as he gripped his cane. "There will come a day when you'll know just how I feel." He retreated to the safety of his coach. A shout of "Go!" accompanied by a sharp rap sent the carriage on its way.

Ayden watched until the coach turned onto Tremont Street, then he gripped his amulet. "What is wrong with you?" The pulsating warmth stilled within his hand. He spun on his heel and resumed the quick pace down the hill. Once he reached the harbor, pedestrians were once again in abundance. He threaded between small groups of people on his way up the dock to Revere's, then stepped inside.

The tavern had two full tables. At one, a group of five played a card game called Euchre. At the other, two couples shared a meal.

Behind the bar, Harry polished a glass with a white towel while he spoke with a customer seated at the bar.

Again, no watchers.

Unease grew as he crossed the tavern with a smile and nodded to Glenda. When he reached the bar, he tapped lightly with his knuckles, then turned his back to Harry and the patron he chatted with. It was an old signal they used to convey urgency and the need for confidentiality.

Several moments passed. The deal changed at the table before him.

"What will you have tonight?" Harry said in a soft yet casual voice.

"I'm checking on my brother, and he won't appreciate it." Ayden chuckled as he turned his back to the card game. "Did he come in?"

"Haven't seen him." Harry poured an ale from the tap and set it before Ayden. "I did see Molly. She returned her room key and said she was leaving town. Too many sin-obsessed Prohibitionists coming around for her to feel safe."

"I'm surprised they haven't tried to shut us down." Ayden sipped his brew and cast his senses upward. Mel was not upstairs.

"Even though the prohibition on distilled liquor was lifted, I keep the whiskey and rum under the counter, just to be safe." Harry shrugged. "But the fermented brews don't seem to bother these folks."

"That's good." Ayden nodded. "Whoever controls the state legislature decides what we can sell, and that seems to change daily."

Where could Mel be?

Chapter 25

Borrowed Shelter

Melvyn MacKenna

Bayard spoke over his shoulder as he unlocked the door to his hotel. "You should stay here for the night. It's safer than being alone."

"Are you sure this is necessary?" Melvyn hesitated as he looked up and down the empty hallway. "Besides, how do I know you won't hit me over the head and ship me off to some foreign land?"

"My brother might, but I'm not going to hurt you." Bayard chuckled as he tossed his jacket over the back of a chair, then walked to the chest of drawers while he worked one cuff link loose. "Come in and close the door. I promise I won't bite."

Melvyn entered and closed the door behind him. "It's just—Ayden thinks I'm at his place."

"We can go by there in the morning." Bayard pointed to the far bed. "Bernard won't use his bed tonight. There's even a trundle in the closet should Jim decide to bunk with us." Bay chuckled and dropped the other cufflink on the dresser top. "Not that *that* is likely to happen."

Mel barely heard Bayard's chatter. "If Amy and Alyse are my nieces," his voice rose in hesitant disbelief. "And you're their uncle; doesn't that make us related?" Mel shrugged out of his jacket, his mind awash with the revelations presented that night.

Bayard sat on his bed, pulled off his low boots one at a time, and dropped them on the floor. His brow furrowed. "It should, I think." He shrugged and sighed as he rubbed his high-arched foot. "Brothers-in-law, once removed, perhaps? At least it would if Margaret and Ayden had married."

Mel shrugged as he undressed and got in bed, pulling the covers over his chest. "I'm worried about Ayden."

"Your brother can take care of himself."

Chapter 26

Missing Shadows

Ayden MacKenna

Ayden leaned against the bar and surveyed the tavern while sipping his drink. "My usual shadows are absent tonight, I see."

"A man I didn't recognize came in around suppertime, spoke to them, and they all left." Harry took two empty glasses from Glenda's tray, refilled them, and replaced them. "I worried for you," he said to Ayden.

Glenda smiled at both men, picked up the tray, and moved across the tavern to the card players.

"Not enough to check on me."

"It's been a busy night. I forgot about it until you asked."

"I need to find Mel." Ayden returned his half-empty glass to the bar. "He's probably with Margaret's brother. I'm not sure that makes me feel any better, to be honest."

"Margaret has a brother?"

"Two. Twins." Ayden stepped away, then turned back. "I may or may not be back tonight, but I'll be here tomorrow if you want to get out from behind the bar."

"Much appreciated, but let's play that by ear. Oh, and check upstairs before you begin your search. Mel may have left a note."

"Good suggestion." Ayden changed direction toward the stockroom.

Lisbeth's apartment remained secure with her magical ward. Once up the stairs, he sensed his own ward, untouched since he and Mel left for Margaret's earlier that evening.

He hasn't been back.

No reason to break the ward to look for a note.

Back down the stairs and through the tavern.

Another group seated themselves as Glenda made her way to their table.

"Goodnight, Ayden," Glenda called as she prepared to take the orders from the newcomers.

On the street, Ayden looked up and down the pier but gained no insight.

Mel may have stayed with the girls and Bayard, but which hotel?

There were dozens of hotels in the city. He rubbed his face with his hand as he pondered Mel's whereabouts.

Bayard seemed sincere in his apologies. Surely, he would have ensured Mel reached Revere's safely or kept him close.

He walked to the edge of the wharf and took a deep breath, sending out his senses in case Mel was nearby.

The tiny hair on the nape of his neck rose as he exhaled and opened his eyes.

Someone watches me.

Many men and a few women enjoyed the dock this summer's eve.

Ayden observed the groups passing the tavern as casually as possible when two men loitering near the buildings beside Revere's caught his attention. One stood in front of the shop beside Revere's, and the other lurked near the alleyway that led to Revere's back entrance. They wore similar dark clothing and stovepipe hats and avoided meeting his gaze.

Well hell. Maybe they've seen Mel.

Ayden crossed the street and approached the man in front of the shop.

Upon seeing Ayden's direction, the man clutched the thick tome beneath his arm to his chest. Appearing as if he might run, then thinking better of it, he straightened his spine and met Ayden's eye.

"Excuse me," Ayden began, "I'm looking for my brother. He's a bit shorter than I am and thinner and younger, but other than that, we look much alike." Ayden chuckled, then continued. "He may have been by here earlier this evening."

The man blinked and glanced over Ayden's shoulder, then back to Ayden. He licked his lips and shook his head. "I've seen no one of that description." He cleared his throat. "You're the owner of that whiskey den, aren't you?"

Ayden raised an eyebrow. "It's a tavern, and I only manage the place. The owner recently sold to an investor who has not made the purchase public."

"Liquor is a sin."

"A legal one now that the temperance law has changed again. Besides, Revere's serves excellent meals, coffee, tea, and other non-alcoholic beverages."

"You allow gambling."

"Card games, like Whist, Bridge, and Euchre, are encouraged at Revere's. No money changes hands over the table. Those games are for entertainment only."

"They are the devil's playground. I'm sure Mother McKay would agree with me."

"You think she would?" Ayden shrugged. "Perhaps you and your mother are part of the Pure Fire Temperance movement?"

The man clutched the black leather-bound tome and pressed his lips. "You, sir, are a sinner."

Ayden narrowed his eyes. "To some. But let me ask—do you carry a firearm? Do you fire it into the night where innocent people might be?"

The man's eyes widened, and he took a step back. "How did you...?"

"How did I know?" Ayden moved forward. "Do you also burn buildings to the ground with people inside?"

Finding his passion, the man threw his arms wide, "Sinners! All of them," he shouted, and his chin jutted forward in defiance.

"Guiltless people you judged to be sinners." Ayden clenched his fists, and his voice dropped to a threatening growl. "Reach for that weapon beneath your coat, and you will burn where you stand, I promise."

He turned from the fanatic in disgust and noticed the other man had slipped away.

Probably up the alley.

When he turned back, the Pure Fire Temperance zealot he'd spoken with ran up the pier, dodging pedestrians, still clutching his good book.

"Hypocrite," Ayden muttered, then looked toward the city. "Mel, I hope you're with Bayard because I don't think I will find you tonight. At least you're not with Coleman or these Pure Fire fanatics."

Without an indication of where to look for Mel, the best thing he could do would be to return to Margaret's.

A Hansom cab pulled to a stop beside the harbor, and passengers departed from both sides of the vehicle.

Ayden waved at the driver, crossed the cobblestone street, and helped the last woman from the conveyance. "West side of Boston Commons, please."

"Yup." The driver shook the reins as the door to the conveyance closed.

Ayden sat back and gazed out the window. He'd decided to walk from the Commons to see if the watchers had returned.

He paid the driver at his destination and crossed the street to the residential neighborhood.

As he approached Margaret's, he spotted the two watchers from Coleman's coven loitering across the street. Just before he knocked on the front door, Isaac's coach stopped in front of Margaret's house.

"I knew you had her!" Isaac sprang from the carriage and approached Ayden on the front step. "You've been lying all along."

"Your daughter attended a dinner party here this evening, as I did. However, I left before she did. When we spoke, I had no idea where she was at that moment."

"Semantics!" Isaac yelled as he halted before Ayden.

"Perhaps." Ayden leaned close and whispered, "I'll allow you to ask if she is here. No matter what you learn, you will not be allowed to storm inside and demand Lisbeth submit to you." Ayden smiled at Isaac's ashen face, then knocked on the door. "Behave yourself."

Wrigley opened the door and smiled at the men on the front stoop. "And here's a mismatched set, if I've ever seen one."

"I've come for my daughter," Isaac demanded.

"Your *adult* daughter was invited to dinner. She is no longer here." Wrigley held a small envelope out to Coleman. "She said to give you this when you arrived."

Isaac snatched the missive from Wrigley's hand and tore it open. His face darkened to an unhealthy color as he read her note. Finally, he crumpled the paper and muttered, "That's not Lisbeth," then turned and marched down the walk to the street and his carriage. He disappeared inside without pause, closed the door, and the driver shook the reins.

"Any idea what she said?" Ayden asked Wrigley as the older man closed the door.

"She's upstairs with the brother if you want to ask her."

Ayden raised one eyebrow at Wrigley. "I see. How's Bernard doing?" He removed his coat and placed it, along with his hat, in the closet.

"He woke long enough to tell Lisbeth that Melvyn is with Bayard at their hotel. Overall, I think the rascal will be fine."

"Ayden," Margaret called from the railing above. "I'm glad you're back. We need to talk."

Chapter 27

Everything Else

Margaret Prescott

Margaret closed her bedroom door behind them, shutting out the low murmur of Peg and Wrigley downstairs and Lisbeth's quiet voice down the hall as she spoke to Bernard. The familiar stillness enveloped them, leaving only the soft tick of the mantel clock.

Ayden stood near the empty hearth; his features shadowed in the warm flicker of lamplight. His tension showed in the rigid set of his shoulders and the slight clench of his jaw.

Margaret knew that anguished look; had known it years ago.

Before our world shattered into pieces.

She took a slow, steady breath. "Ayden, I scarcely know where to begin."

He turned to face her. His gaze was intense at first but softened when it found hers. "Start with Robert," he prompted gently. "The message said his ship never made port?"

Margaret nodded and swallowed around the sudden lump in her throat. "Gone without a trace, along with the crew. And Hal—I cannot help but fear the worst. Either taken by those fanatics, or aboard Robert's ship without anyone knowing."

Ayden stepped closer; his voice gentle and reassuring, "We'll find them. Whatever the cost, Margaret. I promise you that."

She hesitated; her heart ached under the weight of everything she had yet to say. "Ayden, it's all too much. With both Robert and Hal gone, the business, the merchants, the ships, and everything else now rest upon your shoulders. You never asked for all of this."

Ayden offered a weary smile, something both sad and gentle. "Neither did you, Margaret. And yet here we stand."

He reached out and took her hands. His touch warm and reassuring, familiar in a way she'd longed for but never allowed herself to acknowledge openly before. Margaret exhaled and let herself feel the comfort of his touch.

"We must keep our secret," she said softly, her voice tight with emotion. "If society learns the truth—that Amy and Alyse are yours, born out of wedlock—the consequences would destroy our family. That secret must remain ours, and ours alone."

"I know." Ayden nodded. "I'll guard that truth as fiercely as I'll guard our daughters. You have my vow."

Margaret squeezed his hands; her fingers brushed the worn scars he bore from his long years away. It felt strange and comforting at once. "Alyse accepts you joyfully. But Amy—Amy struggles with this sudden reality."

A shadow of pain flickered across Ayden's face, breaking his careful composure. "I saw it in her eyes," he whispered. "To Amy, Robert is her true father. I'm merely an intruder."

Margaret's heart twisted. "Be patient with her, Ayden. She grieves a father she adores, and resents a truth forced upon her."

He nodded. His thumb moved gently across the back of Margaret's hand. "I'll wait for Amy for as long as it takes. If she needs patience from me, she will have it."

Margaret sighed; her relief mingled with sorrow. "I should have told you sooner, Ayden. But I lived so long within that prison of secrets—I feared losing everything."

He raised one hand and touched her cheek; his fingertips lingered on her skin. "Margaret, forgive me for my earlier anger. I let my pain blind me and blamed you unjustly."

She leaned slightly into his palm, savoring this brief contact that felt both too much and not enough. "There's nothing to forgive," she murmured. "You had every right to your anger. But the secrets are done now—and perhaps, we can finally mend this broken family." Even as she said it, she knew forgiveness was easier than admitting how deeply his anger had shaken her.

Ayden let go. His expression steadied; determination replaced the shadows in his eyes. "I'll manage Robert's affairs publicly as his partner. Privately, I'll keep searching until we have answers. And together, we'll hold this family steady."

Margaret nodded, heartened by his strength and calm resolve. "We'll do it together."

He turned to go, then paused, one hand resting on the doorknob.

She saw hesitation in the line of his shoulders, the tight set of his jaw—not anger, but something quieter. Sadness. Doubt.

"Ayden?" she asked softly.

He didn't look back at first. "It's strange," he murmured. "How a man can be given everything he's longed for... and still feel like an interloper in his own life."

She crossed to him and gripped his arm. "Is that what you think you are?"

"I wasn't the husband. I wasn't the father. Not when it mattered." His voice was steady, but she heard the pain beneath it. "I feel like... I walked into someone else's home, someone else's story, and all I did was rearrange the furniture."

The truth of his words struck deeper than she expected. For a moment, she saw herself, and her world, through his eyes. Not as an anchor set in a sea of possibilities, but as a history already written.

Margaret turned him toward her and lowered his chin, so his gaze met hers. "Then let me be very clear," she said, her voice low and fierce. "I loved you before I ever knew what a husband was. Before there were rings or names or expectations. What I gave Robert was loyalty. What I give you is *everything else.*"

Ayden searched her eyes, as though searching for truth in what she confessed.

A small nod passed between them, no longer a request for permission, but a vow of understanding.

When he finally left the room, Margaret remained still, her fingers brushed her lips, as she remembered the man who had always been hers—even when the world said otherwise.

Chapter 28

After The Storm

Jason Harris

Jason stood near the floor-to-ceiling window, watching the city rouse beneath the gray, damp morning light. His hands rested in the pockets of the hotel robe. Behind him, coffee cooled on the writing desk, untouched. The clatter of a carriage below echoed up the brick walls, sharp and jarring.

Amy hadn't spoken to him after the revelations last night. Her silence stretched like wire—thin, tight, ready to snap. Not a word since the confrontation, not after the storm of shouting and tears, not even after he'd held her—awkward and desperate—while she shook in his arms.

She sat at the vanity, brushing her dark curls with unnecessary force. Her jaw clenched. The scent of bergamot clung to her dressing gown. It was citrusy and familiar but distant, like everything else this morning.

She looks like a war goddess before battle. He almost said so but thought better of it. Instead, he returned his attention to the window and focused on the scattered drops racing down the glass. "You're still angry," he said, voice low.

Amy set the brush down. "Perceptive, aren't you?"

Jason turned, walked slowly to his wife, and leaned his hip against the vanity. "He didn't know, Amy."

She stared at the mirror, not him. "He might have. All this time, he might have known. He was there. He looked at me like—*like I belonged to him.*"

"He found out last night," Jason corrected. "Same time you did. Alyse saw the truth or lie in your mother's words. *Spirit magic*, remember? She called her out, and your mother—"

"Confessed," Amy finished bitterly. "And just like that, my father's dead and buried and replaced by a man I barely know."

"That's untrue. Your father is missing, and you *do* know Ayden." Jason knelt beside her chair. "And he hasn't taken your father's place, darling. He *is* your father. That's the truth—awful and unfair as it is. But he didn't *steal* that role from Robert. Robert raised you. That doesn't change because of blood. You love him and he loves you. That's real."

Her eyes welled, but she didn't blink. "Ayden doesn't belong in his place. He didn't live this life."

Jason kept his voice low. "Maybe not, but remember, Ayden didn't ask for this either."

Amy finally turned to him and met his eyes. "Do you trust him?"

Memories tumbled through Jason's mind in the time it took to blink at his wife's question.

Ayden rescuing them from the Boston Fire when all hope was lost. Ayden helping find the horse the Fire Marshal commandeered from Jason and Amy, and so much more.

Jason nodded. "We've trusted him before." He took her hand. "And I trust you. I trust that if you take a breath and step back, you'll see this isn't betrayal. It's a wound that needs time."

A moment passed. Then Amy stood, her hand in his.

The Hansom clattered through Boston's cobbled streets. Its lacquered black frame and polished brass fixtures caught the morning light through the breaks in the clouds.

Jason sat across from Amy, who kept her face turned toward the window, arms crossed, lips pressed into silence. Her dark curls framed a profile that refused to flinch, even under pressure.

He watched his wife for a long moment before he glanced away.

Better not to press her now. She'd heard his words at the hotel. What she did with them would take time.

Jason hopped out and offered his hand when the carriage reached the Prescott house. Amy ignored it and stepped onto the walkway alone.

Before he could knock, the door cracked open.

Peg filled the frame, dressed head to toe in a plum-colored day dress, one gloved hand on her hip and the other holding her market basket.

"Well," she said, eyes flicking between them, "you're both still upright. That's a start."

Jason managed to smile. "You look ready for a duel."

Peg smiled as her eyes narrowed playfully. "The Boston Public Market is no gentler than the frontier, Mister Harris. One must be swift, stylish, and armed with sharp elbows."

"My Mother?" Amy asked, ignoring Peg's banter.

"In the kitchen, I think. I know she came down earlier."

Amy moved past Peg without a word and headed for the kitchen.

Peg's sharp gaze followed her, then shifted back to Jason.

"She's not ready," Jason said quietly.

Peg raised a brow. "No one is, really."

Jason stepped inside, pausing to glance upstairs. "Bernard?"

"Still out cold," Peg said. "Their healing knocked him flat. Who knew they could heal like that? Let's not mention Amy has a twin!" She widened and rolled her eyes. "I suppose that is old news after yesterday. Anyway, Lisbeth says Bernard might wake before supper if the house stays quiet." She adjusted her gloves. "Not that it will."

Jason nodded. "So, you're escaping on a Market run?"

"It's the best place to hear news or to forget news. And you could chance to meet an old friend."

He didn't ask who she intended to meet, though her tone curled at the edge with mischief. Peg had always been too sharp to cage and too loyal to distrust. He let it go.

"Do you need anything, Jason?" she asked, her tone serious.

Jason shook his head. "No. We just need time."

"Then I recommend you collect your wife and come with me." Peg's tone softened. "Give Amy time to feel at home in Boston again. Give her time to feel normal. Her world has tilted, and nothing lifts spirits like fresh oysters and unwise purchases."

"Are you sure she is downstairs?" Amy demanded as she returned to the entry.

"Yes. Fairly certain. I was just upstairs. There's only Lisbeth and Bernard up there."

"Hmm." Amy looked from the staircase to Jason. "Perhaps it's just as well Waynoka returned to the Cheyenne. She'd have plenty to say about Lisbeth sitting at Bernard's bedside this long."

Jason exchanged a quick glance with Peg. "Uh."

Peg winked at Jason and linked her arm with Amy's. "Come to the market with me. Both of you. Fresh air, moving targets, and fancy bonnets. What else could you need?"

Amy narrowed her eyes. "I'm not in the mood."

"Then it's the perfect time." Peg turned and called over her shoulder. "Uncle Wrigley! Could you pull the carriage around to the front, please? We are ready to go."

Jason caught Amy's hesitation and gently touched her arm. "Let's just go. A walk won't kill us, and you haven't seen Peg in a long time."

Amy said nothing but didn't resist when Peg steered her out the door and led her down the steps.

Jason helped Amy from the carriage when they reached Market Square. He nodded to Wrigley—stoic and steady on the box—and paused to take in the rush of color and clamor as he released Amy's hand.

Crowds bustled beneath the high, arched canopy. Hawkers shouted prices over bins of oranges, barrels of oysters, and the rustle of fabric stalls. The air smelled of fish, spice, and rain-soaked brick.

Peg let herself out of the other side of the carriage and then darted ahead, weaving through the crowd like she'd been born for it.

Jason stayed close to Amy at first, but she wandered toward a stall of polished stones, entranced by the glossy rocks the vendor displayed.

He lingered a moment before he spotted a shop tucked off the main row. Its sign read *Bartleby's Walking Sticks & Staves*. The bell over the door jingled as he stepped inside. The air smelled of cedar and beeswax.

A white-bearded man behind the counter looked up. "Morning, sir. Something practical or something with flair?"

Jason scanned the rows of canes and tapped one with an iron tip. "Anything... special?"

The shopkeeper's eyes twinkled. "Looking for steel in your stride?"

Jason nodded once. "Something with a blade."

The man nodded slowly. "I might have just the thing. It just came in this morning, although it is rather unusual." He vanished into the back and returned with a long velvet box. He set it on the counter and opened it carefully.

Inside lay a black cane, sleek and unassuming. A silver hawk's head crowned the grip. The shopkeeper pressed a hidden latch near the top. With a soft click, a slender triangular blade slid free of the hollow shaft—an *épée* blade, perfectly balanced, the hawk's head as its hilt.

Jason's breath caught. It reminded him of the swordstick his father had destroyed—the blade he'd once used to protect Amy.

"How much?"

The price stung, but he paid it.

As the shopkeeper wrapped the cane sword, Jason stepped to the front window.

Peg stood across the street at a flower stall, laughing—*laughing*—with Otis Pierce.

Jason's pulse spiked.

Otis leaned far too close to Peg. His smile filled with easy charm. Beside Otis stood Donetta Dunham, the girl his parents had wanted Jason to marry. Dressed in pale green day dress, with a visible bulge beneath her light jacket. A narrow scar sliced across her cheek.

How do they even know each other?

Donetta's gaze suddenly lifted and locked with Jason's. She stilled as her brows rose, then she leaned close to Otis and whispered in his ear.

Something moved behind Otis's eyes. Jason didn't know what, but he didn't like it.

Otis turned toward the window just as Jason stepped back from the glass.

Jason fought the urge to rush out and drag Peg away. But she didn't look afraid. She looked *interested*. The scene tightened his chest.

He thanked the owner, left the shop, and hurried down the side street that led to the Market Square, where Wrigley waited atop the carriage.

"Is my wife back yet?" Jason asked.

Wrigley shook his head once. "The new one, Alyse, showed up. Not Amy."

Jason scanned the market. Too many faces. Too many shadows. And somewhere out there, Amy.

Chapter 29

The Fracture Between

Alyse James

Alyse studied the inside of the Prescott carriage, the weight of silence pressing against the windows as thick as the summer fog off the water. Had her *Grand'Mere'* Chantal not interfered immediately after her birth, she would have grown up as a Prescott from Boston, instead of the orphan James girl from Toronto.

Or, maybe raised as a MacKenna, with parents and a sister, from who cares where?

She touched the tips of her fingers to her head and gripped reality.

No. The Demon would have found and killed us all soon after Amy and I first twyned. No warning. No preparation. No protection.

Their uncles first twyned as toddlers, after all.

Outside, voices drifted in—Jason's sharp question, edged with worry, followed by Wrigley's deep and even tone.

"Is my wife back yet?"

"The new one, Alyse, showed up. Not Amy," Wrigley replied.

A pause.

"That tall fella of hers, Jimmy Leigh, was here too," Wrigley reported. "But he took off chasing something past the stone stall."

Alyse leaned forward, pushed the curtain aside, and caught Jason mid-scan—his pale hair catching the weak light, his expression dark with tension.

"She's not with you?" she asked, voice low.

Jason stepped forward. "I thought she might have doubled back. Can you ask her to come back to the carriage?"

"No. She's pushing me out," Alyse said, frustration rising in her throat. "I've tried to *twyne*, several times, but she won't let me in. She's too angry at my betrayal of Robert."

Jason's eyes swept the crowd again. "I left her looking at polished stones, just down that way." He pointed, then opened his empty hand, as though his wife might magically appear when summoned.

Footsteps pounded the cobbles as Jimmy Leigh ran up. His long coat flapped in the breeze behind him, his boots slick with mud.

"I felt her go," he said, when he came to a halt, his breath ragged. "The pain burned her direction across my forehead like fire. And then—nothing."

Alyse opened the door and stepped down from the carriage. She met Jim at the wheel hub. "What do you mean nothing?"

Jim's jaw clenched. "The thread snapped. She is either no longer in mortal danger," he hesitated, then continued softly, head down, "Or she is beyond our help."

"No... Jim, I *know* she's alive," Alyse comforted the big man with a touch on his arm, and Jason with a meaningful glance. "I feel her. She's just..." Alyse shrugged. "She's blocking me—hard—but she's not dead."

Jason cursed under his breath. "She's taking this too far. Angry at all of us, and then I see Otis Pierce, of all people, chatting and flirting with Peg, and standing with *a pregnant Donetta Dunham!* It gives me an ugly feeling." He tore the brown paper off the cane box in a fury, pulled the polished black walking stick from inside, and gripped it like a saber.

"I'm going to find Amy. Or Otis and Donetta. Someone who can give me some answers."

"Jason, wait—" Alyse began, but he was already walking.

Jim started to follow.

"No." Alyse gripped the arm of Jim's coat. "Let him go."

Jimmy Leigh stayed beside her, his hands twitching at his sides. "That feeling—I've only lost your soul's tether like that a few, horrible times."

"That's Amy's soul out there, not *mine*," Alyse reminded him. "She has her own. You only feel her because of our *Twyne*."

Before Jim could respond, a voice rang above the crowd's noise. "Jason Harris!"

Alyse turned.

A short and very pregnant blonde woman with sharp mousy features stood halfway down the open market street, one hand clutching the swell of her belly, the other jabbing through the air.

This must be Donetta Dunham.

Donetta's pale green jacket hung open. A scar on her cheek shown white and vivid in the morning light.

A dark-haired man flanked her, fists curled at his sides, eyes locked on Jason's retreating form.

"That fella with the pregnant gal is her brother," Wrigley leaned over from his perch on the carriage seat to inform Jim and Alyse. "I believe his name is Nathan."

"You think you can ruin a woman's life and walk away?" Donetta shouted at Jason's back.

Shoppers stopped.

Heads turned.

A ripple of curiosity passed through the market.

Alyse attempted to step forward, but Jimmy Leigh blocked her with one arm.

Jason turned. "What—"

"You scarred me!" Donetta yelled. "You left me with *this!*" She touched her stomach like it was a mark of shame.

Nathan surged forward. "You're a coward, Harris! You hide behind women and blades!"

A sharp police whistle cut through the crowded chaos around them.

Donetta blanched.

"Now!" Nathan grabbed Donetta's arm. "Run!"

They turned and shoved into the crowd, slipping away in the churn of startled bodies.

Jason's face went white. He stood frozen for a breath, *épée* blade exposed, the polished cane, now a hollow scabbard, in his other hand, the box and wrapper discarded on the ground. He glanced at Alyse and Jim, and without a word, he disappeared into the crowd, moving fast, heading in the direction Donetta and Nathan had fled.

Jim moved to go after him again, but Alyse caught his wrist.

"No," she said. "Let's focus on Amy, not whatever Jason does with those people."

Jim hesitated, breathing hard. "He shouldn't be alone."

"He'll be fine," Wrigley chimed in and chuckled.

"He's not helpless," Alyse agreed, but the words tasted bitter. "If Amy is still in the market and no longer in danger, she could return at any moment. We should wait."

They stood in the chaos of the market, the crowd still hummed from the outburst, the space around the carriage stretched empty, like a wound.

Thirty minutes later, Peg returned. Her gloved hand looped through the crook of Amy's arm, the two laughed, their cheeks flushed from the warming air and victory at the market stalls.

Amy carried two small, wrapped parcels under one arm and a paper cone of warm roasted almonds in the other.

Amy stiffened and slowed her pace as soon as she saw Alyse waiting by the carriage.

Peg stopped short. "You're here? What's happened?"

Jimmy Leigh stepped forward and addressed Amy. "You were gone quite some time. I—we tried to find you."

"We were only two streets over," Peg said, confused. "Amy was with me most of the time."

"We couldn't find her," Alyse said tightly. "I couldn't twyne. I thought—"

"That something awful happened?" Amy interrupted. "At least, nothing new since yesterday."

Jim crossed his arms. "You blocked Alyse out. I could feel you in front of me—then the pain vanished."

Amy laughed, bitter and short. "Not this nonsense again."

"It's not a nonsense," Alyse snapped. "You were in danger."

"From what, stale apples? Loud vendors?" Amy shook her head. "You all overreacted."

"No, we didn't," Jim said, his voice colder than he had ever addressed Amy. "A very pregnant Donetta Dunham just accused Jason of ruining her and ran off before the police arrived."

Amy blinked, her posture stiffening. "What?"

"In front of half the market," Alyse added. "Wrigley said her brother was with her. Jason went after them."

Amy paled. "Where is he now?"

Jim scanned the area then leaned in, and replied softly, "We don't know. He didn't come back."

Amy stepped closer to the carriage; her mocking laughter, gone. She looked at the crowd along the street where Jason had vanished. "He went alone?"

"Yes," Alyse said. "He was furious."

"Then why are you still standing here?" Amy's voice cracked. "Why didn't someone stop him?"

"Maybe because you pushed me away, and we needed to be here if you came back." Alyse snapped.

"Your Jason can take care of himself," Wrigley offered.

The air between the sisters crackled like sparked kindling as they waited in silence.

Finally, Peg cleared her throat. "We've waited an hour. The crowd's thinning. Some vendors are packing up.

"Yep." Wrigley unwrapped the reins from the brake lever. "It's time to head back. When Jason returns and the carriage is gone, he'll catch a cab to Margaret's or the hotel."

Jimmy Leigh helped Peg and Amy into the cab. Alyse climbed in after them, her stomach still tight with unease.

The carriage pulled away from the Boston Public Market, one passenger missing, and too many questions left behind.

Chapter 30

Held on Suspicion

Margaret Prescott

The sound of carriage wheels rattled against the cobblestoned street outside. Margaret set her teacup down with a soft clink and rose from the sitting room settee. She moved to the window with a rustle of skirts.

Peg and her twins, followed by Jimmy Leigh, were already heading up the path.

The front door flew open, and Peg charged across the entry and up the stairs.

Amy and Alyse entered together, but their anger at each other hung in their stony silence.

"How was the market?" Margaret asked cautiously.

"Eventful." Amy offered without meeting Margaret's gaze. She walked past her mother and placed her purchases on the edge of the dining room table.

"Disastrous." Alyse countered, unpinning her hat from her hair. "And we couldn't find Jason before we left."

"Stop it!" Amy spun to face Alyse. "You keep making unwanted comments in my head. If it doesn't stop immediately, I will block you out for good."

Alyse rolled her eyes and placed her straw bonnet on the entry table.

Margaret bit the edge of her lip. The girls were still at it. She opened her mouth to change the subject when Lisbeth and Bernard descended the stairs.

"You're up," Margaret announced unnecessarily.

"And feeling much rested," Bernard reassured the small gathering.

"That's good. Let's all have a seat. I understand the market was quite a spectacle, and I want to hear all about it.

Margaret led the way into the dining room. She seated herself at the head of the table, then looked behind the group toward the entry. "I thought Peg was with you."

The sound of rushed footsteps pattered from the floor above and continued to the staircase.

"Here she comes," Lisbeth said as Bernard held her chair. "Thank you." She smiled at her patient as he settled into the seat beside her.

Just then, a solid knock shook the front door.

Peg, who had changed into a dark grey work gown, paused as she reached the bottom of the stairs to tie an apron over her bodice and skirt. She glanced at Margaret for a moment before she opened the door.

A uniformed police officer stepped across the threshold and looked around as he introduced himself. "Good afternoon, miss. I am General Superintendent of Police, Jacob Rehm." He held out folded papers. "Please inform your mistress that I have a warrant to search these premises and for the arrest of Jason Harris on the charge of suspicion of the murder of Donetta Dunham."

"What is this?" Margaret demanded, rising to her feet. "On what grounds?"

The Superintendent turned toward Margaret. "Nathan and Calvary Dunham, Donetta's brother and father, respectively, have filed the accusation, Ma'am. Donetta is missing, with foul play suspected, and a confrontation between the two witnessed, Jason is to be arrested and held for questioning."

He moved to Margaret, still holding the warrant. He stopped before her, offered the search and arrest warrant, then motioned to the chairs. "If you would all remain seated in this room while we search the house, we would appreciate it." He signaled to a young officer behind him. "Officer Daniels will wait with you." Rehm turned abruptly and led the other officers up the stairs past Peg.

Heavy footsteps pounded above them as officers searched the bedrooms, then faded as the authorities made their way to the small third floor.

Peg entered the dining room, leaned against the wall, and glanced with annoyance at Officer Daniels. "I shouldn't have opened the door." She wrinkled her nose at the young officer.

Bernard shook his head. "You couldn't have known, and you wouldn't have been able to keep them out if you did."

"Do you think they'll search the carriage house? Uncle Wrigley won't like it."

Amy and Margaret chuckled.

After the police cleared the third floor, they marched to the carriage house. As they returned through the kitchen, Superintendent Rehm paused before Margaret. "I'm sorry to have disturbed your family, but our search is now complete. I remind you that we still hold a warrant for the arrest of Jason Harris. If he returns to your home, you must report it, or you will be guilty of harboring a person wanted for questioning."

Margaret rose to speak, but the front door swung wide and rebounded against the wall as Jason staggered inside.

His fine morning jacket was creased and dusty. He clutched his once-shiny cane in his hand as he pushed his tangled curls out of his face with the other. His gaze immediately found Amy, and a broad grin split his face. "You're safe. When I saw the police wagon outside, I thought the worst."

Amy came to her feet. "Jason!" Then she covered her mouth with her hands.

The police officers surged through the dining room and into the entry, surrounding Jason.

One of the officers handcuffed the confused Jason, read him the warrant, and marched him out the door before words could be exchanged.

Superintendent Rehm was the last one out. He turned and tipped his cap to Margaret. "Thank you, Ma'am. Sorry for the disturbance in your home. Inquire after Mr. Harris at the station later today or tomorrow." He closed the door.

The silence in the room lasted until they heard the wagon pull away.

Margaret sank back to her chair and placed the still folded warrants beside Amy's packages on the table. "Dear Goddess... what has that boy gotten himself into this time?"

"Jason would not hurt Donetta," Amy stated, tears in her eyes. "Nathan Dunham, maybe."

Peg hugged Amy's shaking shoulders as Margaret reached over and patted her daughter's hand. "It will be a few hours before they decide on bail. Jason needs an attorney."

The front door opened, startling the group at first, then Bayard's laughter sounded as he walked in the door. Melvyn followed, chuckling, and Ayden stepped inside, closing the door behind him.

Ayden's gaze found Margaret, and his smile faded. "What's happened?"

Margaret quickly brought the three newcomers up to date. "But Bayard should have already known." She spread her arms between Bernard and Bayard.

Bernard flushed. "I blocked Bay earlier and forgot to open back up."

Amy, Alyse, and Jimmy Leigh exchanged glances.

Peg released Amy's shoulders, waved her hand, and the lamps on the mantle lit. They cast a gentle, comforting light into the darkening dining room. "Since we have time before we can see Jason, I'll fix us something to eat."

"There are too many for you to cook for, Peg," Margaret replied as she counted familiar faces.

"Enough to form a coven," Lis said.

"And if you include Garrett, that would be eleven skilled." Margaret nodded. "Isn't that your father's greatest fear?"

"Hmm, yes. The James and MacKenna witches. A rival to his coven, or a war to end the city."

Bernard and Ayden shared a hard, angry look but remained silent.

"There are plenty of leftovers in the icebox. I'll heat what needs to be heated, and we can fill our plates and sit wherever we can." Peg snapped her fingers as she rounded the table. "Full bellies will allow us to make good decisions."

"I'll help." Lis stood and followed Peg into the kitchen.

Ayden and Mel brought in chairs from the sitting room, and everyone took a seat in the dining room.

"Jason has an attorney friend—Keith Hall," Amy said. She held her handkerchief under her nose, her eyes still red. "They were partners when we first married. They still correspond, but I don't know where he's living now."

Margaret nodded. "We should contact Garrett Brown. I'm sure he could help."

"And he may also know how to contact Keith, who is a Barrister. If we can stop this nonsense before it goes to court, Jason won't need a Barrister." Amy sat straight, a glimmer of hope in her eyes.

"Rehm said they can't find Donetta, body or otherwise." Alyse glanced around the table. "Too bad we don't have Hunter to find her."

"Hunter?" Melvyn asked.

Alyse nodded. "Nichole, Jason's cousin, knows him. He helped us immensely in Colorado. Hunter has such strong *spirit-magic* that he could speak with the dead, and they would help him track missing people. I'm certain he could find Donetta, dead or alive."

"I know a *spirit-skilled* woman who speaks with the dead. She's here in Boston." Ayden sat forward, hands on his knees.

Alyse held up a restraining hand. "Hunter required the blood of the missing or a close family member, as I recall," Alyse warned.

Margaret's chin came up, her eyes wide. "I have some."

"Some what?" Amy prodded.

"I have some of Donetta's blood. Remember?" Margaret rose and hurried to the stairs, calling back over her shoulder, "It was on your hairpin. I only need to find it."

Amy groaned. "You kept that, all this time?"

"Some things keep themselves," Margaret called over her shoulder in a softer tone. "That day changed everything." She reappeared carrying the hair ornament wrapped in linen. She carefully folded back the cloth and put the stained barrette on the table in front of Amy. "Remember this?"

"I remember. It is why all this is happening." Amy's voice wavered with frustration.

"Can you contact your friend, Ayden?" Margaret asked.

With a swift nod, Ayden rose and stood before the mantle and stared silently into the lamp's flame.

Margaret's chest tightened as she studied his profile reflected in the warm light.

Thank Goddess, he is here.

Ayden turned and caught her soft smile. "Miera's at her niece's, not far from the Commons. She said she'd come immediately to Margaret's and try to help."

Alyse looked from the pin to her sister. "How is it you have Donetta's blood?"

"It happened before Jason and I married," Amy explained. "A group of young Brahmin men trapped me in a house they had altered to *view* unbecoming acts against young women. They intended to molest me, but Jason burst through the front door and rescued me just in time."

Lisbeth leaned into the dining room from the kitchen, wearing an apron similar to Peg's. "I remember that."

"You were there?" Amy's eyes widened.

"I was posted to watch your house that afternoon. I saw you leave with Nathan, and I followed. When I saw where he took you, I understood what those boys planned to do. I ran, found Jason, and told him you needed help." Lis shrugged her shoulders and disappeared back into the kitchen.

Amy blinked in astonishment. "I never knew any of that." She shook her head, then continued her story. "Donetta was there too, with her brother and the other men. After Jason arrived, she became furious and tried to attack me. I pulled the barrette from my hair and swiped at her with the pin. The sharp end scratched her face." Amy's lips curled with satisfaction. "She backed off after that, the whole group did, then Jason and I ran."

"Did Jason have his sword?" Ayden asks.

"Amy nodded. "Yes, he did."

Peg leaned in from the kitchen. "I saw Donetta today with Otis Pierce. She bears that scar to this day."

Alyse plucked at her skirt. "She accused Jason of cutting her with his blade at the market."

"No, I cut her with this pin, in self-defense. I haven't seen her since." Amy raised her head, but Peg had already vanished into the kitchen. "Otis Pierce was with Donetta?" She called toward the empty doorway.

Peg looked in, wiping her hands, and nodded. "I spoke to them both."

Amy shook her head. "I find *that* odd. Otis Pierce is a low-down, bottom-feeding, loan shark. He nearly ruined Jason. How would the pampered daughter of one of the Boston Brahmin elite, Donetta Dunham, even know someone like him?"

Peg's eyes widened. "You know Otis Pierce?"

"Yes. He used to be Jason's friend. The last time we saw him was in Colorado. He threatened us and maintained it was Jason's fault P&P Investments was near ruin. But it wasn't Jason, it was Otis and his father. Otis Senior sold all those worthless railroad bonds and had their thug, Pearson, rough up anyone who dared complain."

Peg paled and returned to the kitchen without saying more.

A soft knock sounded at the front door, and Ayden answered.

An elderly, olive-skinned lady stepped inside, a colorful scarf draped around her shoulders. A much younger woman, tall and elegant, followed her in and nodded to the dining room occupants as they paused in the entry.

"Everyone," Ayden said as he held out his arm for Miera and the young woman to precede him into the dining room. "May I present Miera Barbaneagra."

"Ve came as soon as ve received the summons," Miera smiled and bobbed her head at the occupants. "Please, no names. There are too many of you and I vill never remember." She touched her companion on the shoulder. "This is my dear niece, Fiona Popescu. She is also *spirit-skilled* and offers to help."

Margaret stood and angled her seat at the end of the table toward Miera.

"I thank you."

Miera settled in the seat as Fiona held the chair, then Fiona stood protectively behind her aunt.

Margaret moved the covered barrette from Amy to Miera and folded the cloth back. "This is the missing woman's blood. Will it work?"

"Yes. It should." Miera touched the decorative hairpin and nodded. "We must dissolve the essence in a small amount of water."

Lisbeth brought in a shot glass half-filled with water and set it carefully on the table.

Miera dipped the stained pin into the glass. Crimson streaks spiraled like smoke, curling through the water in slow, ominous tendrils. The water slowly turned pink, then red. Miera nodded with satisfaction.

"Hunter needed a map and a pendulum to find the missing person," Amy noted.

"Yes. Those would be helpful, but unnecessary if they are not available." Miera shrugged, her eyes still on the darkening water.

Fiona removed her necklace and held it out to her aunt. "This can be the pendulum. You made it for me."

"Ah, yes." Miera took the necklace and gave a soft pat to the back of Fiona's hand. "Thank you, dear." Miera shifted her gaze to Amy. "You have a worthy pendant, as well. I remember I blessed the moonstone when your husband bought it as a gift for the *lovely young woman* he wanted to marry."

Amy's eyes widened in amazement as she moved to unclasp the moonstone locket from her neck.

Miera held her hand up to wait, and her gaze shifted to Ayden. "Your pendant, *Pyromancer,* may be the most powerful item I have ever seen. Tied to ancient *fire-magic* and capable of vonders never dreamed." She nodded and held up one finger. "There is a roll for that pendant, but not yet."

Miera shifted her attention back to Amy.

Amy had remained motionless, listening, her fingers on the clasp behind her neck.

Miera wiggled her fingers impatiently. "Yours vill work best for this."

Amy removed the necklace and reclasped it before she placed the hinged locket in Miera's open palm. The chain piled onto the moonstone locket with a metallic sound.

"Yes. This vill do nicely." Miera brushed her fingers toward Fiona's necklace.

Her niece quickly retrieved the jewelry from the table and returned it to her neck.

"And I think I have the last ingredient." Margaret hurried to the entryway and returned with a map of Boston. She set it on the table before Miera. "Will this work?"

Miera touched the map and nodded. "If the one ve seek is within this area, it should. I require a single candle, please."

Margaret grabbed a small silver candleholder from the kitchen table. She set the unlit candle beside the map. "Dinner is smelling good in there. I think supper may be about ready."

Miera stared at the cold wick and sighed softly. "Vould you light the candle?"

Four *fire-skilled* witches shifted their gaze to the wick, and a tall flame ignited.

Miera leaned back and laughed with surprise. "A small flame is best. Also, this must be the only flame in room, please."

The candle flame lowered, as the lamps snuffed out, darkening the dining room. The single flame wavered, reflecting dimly on the objects before Miera, yet sparkled in her dark amused eyes. "I can see how this *fire-skill* vould be handy." Miera chuckled. "Yes, indeed."

Miera pressed the map of Boston flat on the table before her and smoothed the creases. Lined hands relaxed on either side of the map, she closed her eyes momentarily, nodded once, then opened her dark eyes and stared into the flame.

"Blood seeks blood. Who vill come now to help us find a daughter of this house?" Her eyes fluttered closed, and she tipped her head as if she were listening to whispers in the silence.

Fiona placed her hands on Miera's shoulders. Her pupils widened, then dimmed, as if her gaze tunneled beyond the room. A breeze not born of any open window stirred her hair. "She's here."

A subdued gasp sounded from the kitchen but was quickly silenced.

"Spirit of the mother," Miera intoned. "By your daughter's essence, guide us to her."

Miera's eyes remained closed, but Fiona's darted, searching the room's dark corners. "Bethany agrees to help us." Fiona's eyes followed the invisible specter around the table. "She now stands beside us."

Miera dipped the tip of her finger into the discolored water, dabbed it on all four corners of the map, then dipped again and caressed Amy's locket. She lifted the necklace by the chain, dangling it an inch above the center of the map. "Show us where to find your daughter, Bethany, ve beseech you."

"She reaches for the pendant," Fiona whispered.

The pendant swung, one way, then the next. The candle flickered, then steadied. The chain whispered faintly as it moved above the paper, each pass of the locket above the map like a heartbeat in the silence. It moved in an ever-expanding circle. Miera adjusted the pendant toward one corner, and the circle increased. When she moved the pendant over the northern part of the city, the circle became smaller. Finally, in the far north area of town, the pendant halted. Miera lowered the edge of the moonstone locket to the paper. "She is there."

Fiona's lips moved; her eyes rolled back in her head. Air-cooled vapor expanded and hovered near her shoulders. Her eyelids fluttered as if caught in a dream, her lips parted just enough to release hoarse, chilling words. "Here you will find my living daughter. Help her if you can." Fiona inhaled sharply and opened her eyes. "The mother has departed."

Margaret tore her gaze from Fiona's face, surprised to find Amy and Alyse had moved in the semi-darkness to stand beside the woman. Each daughter rested a hand on Fiona's shoulder, then held the other hand out. Alyse to Bayard and Bernard. Amy to Ayden.

Amy looked down at her hand, resting on Ayden's wrist, then up, into his eyes. "Did you see Bethany?"

Ayden nodded, his gaze watery and soft as he looked into his daughter's eyes, reaching for understanding and forgiveness.

Amy smiled and entangled her fingers with his.

He lifted her hand to his lips and kissed her soft knuckles, reverent. A single tear slid down his cheek.

Margaret brushed a tear from her face. *Maybe this family won't shatter like glass after all.*

"Have you marked the location?" Miera asked, studying the map.

Bernard and Lisbeth leaned close to the lined paper. "The north side of the city." Lisbeth looked up. "There are many empty buildings, squatters, and criminals there." She shook her head. "Not a good area."

"Both Keith Hall and Otis Pierce lived near there once." Amy looked closer at the map.

"My guess is she's at whatever is left of P&P Investments."

"Then let's go get her." Alyse straightened.

"Wait!" Ayden stared hard at the single flame still dancing in the darkened room. "There are no skilled, of any kind, where Donetta hides. In good conscience, we cannot go armed with only magic."

"He's right," Margaret agreed. "We go with the police first and say we had an anonymous tip on Donnetta's whereabouts. Demand they look into the tip. Let them use their non-magical force, but we will be there." Margaret rose from her chair but halted as Peg spoke with authority.

"You will eat before you leave this house. Even witches can't track on an empty stomach." The chandelier and mantle lit brightly as Peg and Lisbeth carried a stack of dinner dishes and utensils to the table. "Potluck style. The food is ready, and there is more than enough for everyone here. Help yourself."

Dinner passed in a blur of clinking forks and anxious glances. No one lingered. Plates scraped clean in silence. Peg and Lisbeth cleared the table, stacking dishes, wiping crumbs, letting the others think.

Margaret rose first. "Not all of us need to go to the police. The rest will wait here."

She looked at Miera and Fiona. "Can you remain receptive to Ayden? If anything changes, he can reach you through flame."

Miera nodded. "We vill stay."

Margaret turned to Bernard and Lisbeth. "You two, can you seek out Garrett Brown? Bernard, if Bay stays here, can you still reach him?"

Bernard touched his temple. "Easily."

Arguments sparked.

Amy wanted to go.

Alyse insisted she should be the one to explain everything to the police.

Jimmy Leigh volunteered to guard the house while Mel made a case to guard the carriage.

Through it all, Peg slowly untied her apron and tossed it on the dining room table. "I'm going."

Margaret gave her a long look. Peg didn't flinch.

Ultimately, Wrigley took Peg, Margaret, and Ayden in the carriage. Superintendent Rehm met them at the station. Once briefed on the new lead, he agreed to a quiet investigation. Rehm and his officers assembled at their police wagon, and the two vehicles departed.

North Boston at dusk looked worse than Margaret remembered. The buildings hunched low and mean, their corners sagging under soot. Bits of trash filled the gutters down the empty street outside P&P Investments. The windows shuttered, and the paint peeling in strips like old skin.

Rehm knocked. No reply.

One of his officers stepped forward with a weighted pole he used as a battering ram and forced the door with a crack of splintered wood. Rehm entered first, followed by two officers.

Peg stepped in behind them, her boots crunched on broken glass.

Margaret followed her namesake inside, surprised at Peg's avid interest on Donetta.

The air inside smelled like dust, unwashed clothes, and something gone bad—wine perhaps.

They moved through the first floor, past a front office littered with empty ledgers. A low groan creaked above them.

"Upstairs," Rehm said.

The creaking resolved into footsteps and the soft hush of bedding.

One of the policemen opened the bedroom door.

A directed lantern—glass-bodied and wick-fed—illuminated the room.

Otis Pierce sat up, shirtless, eyes squinting. Donetta lay beside him, her nightdress rumpled and belly round beneath the covers. She blinked at the light.

Rehm didn't speak. He just waited.

Donetta swallowed hard. "I'm not missing."

"Too late," Rehm said. "You've already been reported. Get dressed. We'll speak at the station."

Peg turned and walked out.

Worried, Margaret followed her down and out into the night air.

The officers escorted Otis, Donetta and Nathan Dunham out of P&P without handcuffs or shouting this time, heads hung low in shame.

Rhem released Jason within an hour. He returned to Margaret's looking tired and sore but whole.

Amy rushed into his arms, and he sank into her embrace like a man freed from water.

That evening, Margaret and Ayden spoke with Amy and Jason in the dining room when Peg walked by.

"Are you alright?" Jason asked, touching her hand.

Peg looked at them and said, "Otis used me to get back at you and Amy. I realize it now." She smiled briefly. "I'll be fine."

Jason nodded and let go of her hand.

Peg rounded the table and dropped into an empty chair. Her chin propped in her hands.

Margaret smiled fondly at Peg, folded the paper with Jason's dropped charges, and gave it to him. She quietly said, "The Brahmin and your father will learn what Donetta did."

"Let everyone know how far her lies went," Ayden added.

Chapter 31

News from the Sea

Margaret Prescott

Late summer sunlight spilled golden streams across her polished floorboards from the east-facing windows. Margaret stood in the entryway arranging cut peonies in a tall vase, their scent sweet and heavy.

Peg flitted between the dining room and parlor with smaller bundles—zinnias, snapdragons, and trailing vines for the mantle. "Too much?" Peg asked, holding a spray of blue delphinium toward the sideboard.

"Not if we want to portray a cheerful house," Margaret replied, her tone dry but fond.

A sharp knock sounded at the door.

Peg set down her flowers and crossed the entry to answer it.

"If that's Mrs. Barrington with more tomatoes," Margaret muttered, adjusting a stem, "tell her we can simply take no more."

Peg chuckled as she pulled open the door.

"Good afternoon, Miss." The uniformed courier said briskly. "Telegram for Mrs. Margaret Prescott."

Margaret paused, her hand stilled above the flowers. A tiny pulse of dread hammered at her brow.

Peg thanked the courier, closed the door, then turned and extended the narrow envelope to Margaret. "No return name. Just Glasgow."

Margaret noted the concern in Peg's eyes as she took the telegram. She opened it with care as she walked to the dining room table. Her eyes swept the page, once, twice—then stopped. Her hand drifted to the table's edge as the world shifted beneath her feet. She sank heavily onto the nearby chair, the note trembling in her fingers, her mouth bone dry.

"Missus?" Peg stepped closer. "What is it?"

A cold pressure climbed from Margaret's chest to her throat, thickening her swallow as tears stung her eyes. "The *Atlantia*..." her voice broke and she cleared her throat. "They've found the ship run aground in the Outer Hebrides."

Peg lowered herself into the chair beside Margaret. "Gods."

"They confirmed it is Robert's ship, and although they've recovered quite a few bodies—" Margaret shook her head and swallowed hard in order to continue. "—Robert wasn't there. His body wasn't found." She closed her eyes as tears streamed down her cheeks. "Robert is listed, along with the remaining crew, as lost at sea and feared dead."

For a moment, neither woman spoke. The sunlight shifted, falling softer now. The summer warmth could not reach them here.

Margaret placed the telegram on the table as if it might catch fire. Her hands rose to her face, covering her mouth. A tremor ran through her shoulders. "I didn't think... I didn't know it would end this way," she whispered, her voice breaking. "No body, no closure. Just—lost."

Oh Robert! The name cracked inside her like a dropped glass.

Peg's hand settled gently over hers. "But we don't *know* that he's dead."

The warmth of Peg's hand was her undoing. A sob escaped and she covered her eyes with her other hand as she wept.

Peg grasped the floral cloth that lined the empty fruit bowl and pressed it into Margaret's hand.

Margaret inhaled shakily and wiped her face as she struggled for control. A memory filled her mind.

Robert at five, hair full of hay, laughing as their dolls toppled from the fence.

She pushed the memory aside.

I can't think of that right now. She folded the memory away like a fragile and precious scrap of paper. *There are things that must be done.*

She cleared her throat and nodded to Peg. "What you say is true." Margaret's lips quivered. "But we don't know if he's alive either. And honestly, with what they've found, the odds are not in Robert's favor."

Peg looked at her with tear-filled eyes. "Do you want me to cancel your luncheon plans?"

"No." Margaret wiped the tears from her face and shook her head. "I'll keep my plans. I need to tell them—" Her voice faded as she stood, slowly, gathering the fragments of herself like scattered pebbles. "My girls should hear this terrible news from me."

Peg nodded. "And Ayden?"

Margaret closed her eyes for a moment.

He'll feel too much and show too little.

"Of course, I must inform Ayden." She dabbed once more at her eyes, then tossed the linen into the empty fruit bowl. "It's not like we haven't expected this moment." She straightened her shoulders. "Tell Wrigley I'll need the carriage in an hour. And... Peg?" Margaret caught her arm. "Please accompany me."

Peg gave a soft smile. "Of course."

"Please send a note to Revere's. I want Ayden to join us at luncheon. Tell him we finally have news of Robert."

They met at Winthrop's Tea Room near Tremont Street, a favorite of Amy's for its long windows and honey cakes. Margaret and Peg arrived early and secured a large corner table for all of them. The afternoon sun pooled across the tables. The beams looked too bright for the news she carried.

The girls arrived first—Amy laughing at something Alyse said. As they passed the sunlit windows, their auburn hair reflected threads of gold.

The sight tugged at Margaret's chest.

My beautiful girls. And I'm about to break Amy's heart.

Jason and Jimmy Leigh followed a few moments later, flushed from the walk, and were visibly pleased to find the girls already seated.

Their ease only sharpened the guilt twisting low in Margaret's stomach.

Ayden arrived last, looking as though he'd run all the way from Revere's, his shirt sleeves rolled up, and a shimmer of sweat tracing the line of his throat. A sign he'd rushed—and worried.

He knows. Or he suspects.

Peg handed out menus, filling the silence Margaret couldn't seem to break, then took her seat under the waitress's steady stare.

Margaret barely saw the words on the page—tea names blurred together, her pulse thudding behind her eyes.

She waited until everyone had ordered—tea for the women, coffee for the men, and water for Ayden, who hadn't touched the glass since sitting down.

He's bracing himself.

Margaret felt it in the air between them, the tautness of a held breath. She reached into her reticule, removed the telegram, and laid it on the table. Even that small motion felt unbearably loud. Her fingers trembled despite her effort to still them.

Amy blinked. "Mother?"

Margaret folded her hands. "I received word this morning the *Atlantia* has been found, run aground on the Outer Hebrides, off the coast of Scotland. The description of the wreckage is...quite devastating. And although they have recovered many of the poor crew's bodies, Robert's was not among them. He is now listed as missing and presumed dead. The authorities have called off the search."

The silence at their table was immediate and dense, almost physical. It pressed against Margaret's ribs.

Amy stared. "Not... among them?" Her fingertips brushed the telegram as though touching something poisonous.

Margaret shook her head, her voice softened. "No. I'm sorry, sweetheart." Her throat tightened. *How many times can a mother watch her child break?*

Amy's lips parted, but no sound came. Then she leaned into Jason's shoulder, and he pulled her close, wrapping one arm around her.

Alyse's voice remained steady, but her expression was difficult to read. "I never got the chance to meet him." Her troubled gaze lifted from her gloved hands, resting placidly on the table, to her mother's.

Margaret nodded in understanding. Alyse's grief was thin and unfamiliar, a grief for a relationship imagined, not lived, and colored by empathy for her sister.

A small blessing in this turbulent sea of guilt.

Jimmy Leigh's hand found Alyse's. "We were going to ask for his blessing to marry."

Everyone's attention lifted to Ayden.

Margaret's breath caught again. *Please don't fold into yourself, Ayden. Not now.*

Ayden met their stares, one by one. "You certainly don't need *my* blessing," he said gently. "But were I in the position to give it, I certainly would."

Margaret let out a slow, controlled breath. For a flicker of a moment, pride nudged through her sorrow. Her gaze circled the table. She could read the shapes of grief as easily as handwriting—Amy's collapse, Alyse's quiet distance, Ayden's internal storm.

Truth is a blade, she reminded herself. *But sometimes it's also the way through.*

"He may be gone," Margaret said quietly, "but he loved you, Amy. Fiercely. That will never disappear."

Jason brushed a lock of hair from Amy's brow. "And you carry that with you every day."

Peg took the tray from the waitress, cleared her throat, and set a plate of lemon scones before of the twins. "You should eat something."

"I can't," Amy murmured. "Not yet."

Margaret reached across the table and took Amy's free hand. Her daughter's fingers trembled against her own. "I know."

No one spoke for a while.

Outside, the awnings fluttered as if the wind couldn't decide on direction. Inside, grief finally took its seat at their table.

Alyse squeezed Amy's arm. "Do you want to go outside? Get some air?"

Amy shook her head once, then stood anyway. "I just... need a moment."

Jason rose with her and guided her gently through the tables and out the door. The bell jingled behind them, too cheerful for the weight they carried.

The remaining five sat in the quiet she left behind.

Alyse watched the doorway long after her sister had vanished through it. "She adored him," she murmured. Not envy this time—understanding.

"Yes," Margaret said. "And he adored her." The words scraped on their way out.

Alyse blinked once, then whispered, "I think I'll check on her."

Jim followed her without question.

And then it was just Margaret, Peg, and Ayden.

Peg—merciful, perceptive—stood. "I'll see if they need anything." She left before Margaret could thank her.

Ayden remained, his head down, eyes shadowed.

The clink of a spoon, a distant burst of laughter from another table, everything felt muffled, as though the room were wrapped in wool.

Finally, Ayden leaned forward, his forearms rested on the white linen tablecloth. "Margaret." Her name in his voice always carried warmth—soft and weighted. Today it carried something else, too—regret...or longing. She wasn't sure she could tell the difference. It unsettled something deep in her ribs.

She swallowed. "I should have been stronger for them."

"You were strong, my dear." His voice was low, steady. "You always are."

She focused her attention out the window instead of at him. If she looked at him too long, she might unravel. "I wasn't prepared to say it aloud apparently," she murmured. "Not yet. Telling the girls made it real."

Ayden's hand hovered over hers on the tabletop—not touching, just there, an offered warmth. "You don't have to carry this alone."

Her breath stilled.

He had said something like that once—twenty-five years ago, in their secret place just before dawn, when they were young and foolish enough to believe the world would bend to their desires.

A promise that never had the chance to be kept.

She blinked hard and looked down. "I can't do this here," her voice a harsh whisper. The room suddenly felt too small, the walls too close, the grief too raw.

Ayden withdrew his hand slowly, respectfully. "Then we won't," he said. "Not now."

Not now.

Not *never*.

Margaret let out a breath she hadn't known she was holding. The room slowly returned to itself—the clatter of cups, the smell of tea, the breeze's soft sway of the awning.

But something had shifted. Grief had carved new edges inside her, and Ayden—quiet, patient Ayden—saw every one of them. Saw her. And chose to stay.

Chapter 32

Cold Inheritance

Ayden MacKenna

The Harrises rarely received guests in the green parlor, and for good reason. The cold, lacquered room felt more suited to the portraits of dead relatives than the warmth of living conversation.

Jason stood at the hearth, arms crossed, while Ayden sat with his back ramrod straight on the floral settee. Across from them, Spencer Harris leaned one elbow on the carved lion of his armrest, his expression unreadable. Rose reclined with casual disdain beside him, thumbing through a contract she neither understood nor cared about.

"You're certain it was lost?" Spencer asked. "*The Atlantia.*"

"Another vessel discovered the wreckage a few weeks ago," Jason said. "Robert's name was on the cargo manifest, but he wasn't among the bodies."

"How convenient," Rose muttered.

Ayden ignored her. "We're here to discuss *the Amylia.*"

Jason nodded. "The ship remains in Glasgow for now. She was to sail for China, but that plan changed after Robert's death."

"*You* changed those plans," Spencer snapped. "That ship was a long-term investment for me. You're deliberately keeping it idle while my capital earns nothing."

Jason's jaw clenched. He exhaled slowly through his nose. "It won't be idle," he replied, voice even. "It's just not sailing to China."

Spencer's face darkened. "I invested with the expectation of returns. Now your wife's family is interfering, and you expect me to take a loss? Typical. You marry beneath your station, drag my name through scandal, and now this."

Ayden glanced at Jason, noting the restraint in his clenched fist. Jason wasn't the same hot-headed boy from years past, but the long-held resentment still raged.

Jason's shoulders shifted forward, but Ayden's calm, soft voice cut through and halted Jason's motion before he could act.

"We are prepared to offer you the full amount of your original investment. Nothing more."

"Nothing more? You take advantage of me!" Spencer came to his feet, eyes blazing. "You think just because you've surrounded yourself with Margaret Prescott and her ever-growing family of strays, you can cheat me?"

His gaze landed on Jason's bladed cane. "You still carrying a ridiculous swordstick? Will you never grow up? What's it for—cutting more defenseless young women? Or do you just impregnate them and leave others to clean your mess?"

"Spencer, dear, watch your language," Rose scolded, then snickered.

Jason glanced at his mother. Her contempt, once disguised as concern, showed openly—and for once, he didn't flinch from it. He stepped forward, his voice cold. "For the record, Donetta's lies were uncovered by the police. Otis Pierce is the father of her unborn child. And I don't care what you or your precious banking friends think of me."

Spencer's nostrils flared. "How dare you speak to me in such a tone! You shame this family."

"No," Jason replied, "If there is shame, you brought it on yourself." He glanced from his father to his mother, then smiled proudly at Ayden. "I've found a much better family I can finally take pride in."

Spencer blinked, visibly thrown.

Ayden almost smiled, then stood. "The Prescott name holds weight in Boston, Spencer. Your peers already whisper, and you know how quickly speculation can harden into rumor and a poor reputation. I'd advise against adding to the narrative. Especially in banking, gossip is as dangerous as debt." Ayden nudged his *mind-skill* toward Spencer. *This is the best possible outcome for you, Spencer. You'd best take it before the offer is off the table.*

A heavy silence followed. The mantle clock ticked evenly, counting the moments.

Spencer rubbed a spot on his forehead. "You'll have the papers by week's end," he said tightly.

Jason nodded once. "Thank you."

Rose didn't rise as they left. "You're still a disappointment, Jason."

Jason paused at the threshold. "It may surprise you, mother, but I no longer care how you feel."

He shut the door behind them without looking back.

In the hallway, Jason paused, one hand still gripping the knob like it might swing back open. His shoulders rose, breath tight in his chest—then dropped with a long, shaking exhale. Anger flashed across his face, but he held it and his pain in check. Finally, he straightened as though something uncurled inside him, and he smiled.

"That was the last time," Jason said quietly, almost to himself. "The last time I let them make me feel small."

Ayden watched him from a step away. He didn't speak but nodded in understanding.

Jason glanced at the bladed cane in his hand, then gave a cynical laugh. "He's always hated this thing. He said it made me look like a boy pretending to be a man."

Ayden arched a brow. "It suits you. And I'd say the boy I knew has grown into a man to be proud of."

Jason's mouth twitched. "It used to hurt, you know. That look on his face. Like I was always one mistake away from being disowned."

"And now?"

Jason gave a short nod. "I'm finished with his opinion of me." He met Ayden's gaze. "Our family is the only one that matters to me from now on."

Ayden placed a hand on his shoulder. "Good. You're your own man, Jason. No one can take that from you—not even your father."

For a long beat, Jason said nothing. Then he blew out another breath and straightened.

"Let's get out of here," he said. "I'd rather be anywhere else."

Ayden smiled faintly. "That, we agree on."

Behind them, the Harrises' fine home remained still and silent, its walls as polished and cold as ever.

Jason didn't look back.

Chapter 33

What Slips Away

Isaac Coleman

Isaac sat alone in the west study of his Beacon Hill home, the room silent except for the soft clink of ice against crystal. His hand rested on a folded letter. The edges softened from re-reading. Lisbeth's handwriting curled like her mother's. The words within were polite, careful—even loving—but each stroke carried a message more piercing than a dagger.

She was gone.

Gone to Margaret Prescott's home, or anywhere except beside her father. Gone to align herself with the witches, Isaac had spent years scrutinizing and scorning.

The door creaked open, and Helena Coleman crept in, drawing a warm draft into the chilled room. "You're still contemplating her letter, I see." She shook her head. "Lis made her choice, Isaac, and she gave her reasons. But she's still your daughter."

"She never wanted that path," Isaac said softly.

"She walked the only path you gave her," Helena said. She placed a hand on the letter. "Encourage her to find a new one. I know you love her. That hasn't changed. If you want her back, make peace with the James family, not war."

Isaac remained silent, pondering his wife's words. *How can I make peace?* Garrett must have resumed his role as coven leader, Ayden's influence continued to grow, and Margaret's household had become a center of power and danger with her brother's return.

A knock pulled his attention.

Gordon Carmichael stepped inside, followed by Milton Kohler. The men wore dark wool, cloaked in the smugness of men steeped in their power.

"Well?" Isaac asked.

Gordon dipped his head. "Our coven watches the James and MacKenna witches as requested. But they've noticed our efforts and have doubled their protections."

"Let them," Isaac murmured. His throat tightened—not with anger, but with the sick, hollow beat of inadequacy he'd spent decades burying. One by one, his fears had materialized.

Ayden built a new coven, despite his denials, and despite my warnings.

My own daughter has run and now hides with them from me.

My power, once unchallenged, now slips through my hands like sand, quiet, slow, and inevitable.

Milton stepped forward. "Their coven has nearly a dozen members now, and Ayden's skill safeguards them all. Not to mention, Garrett has returned."

"Then stay on them," Isaac said, his jaw tightening as heat crept up his neck. "I want to know the moment they slip."

"*Tsk.*" Helena expressed her disapproval from across the room.

Isaac opened a drawer and pulled out a folded map of Boston, with fresh markings in charcoal. "They believe I'm distracted. But we're watching them. Every move."

Outside the window, a small sparrow landed on the sill. It tapped the glass once. Twice.

Isaac frowned.

Chapter 34

The Net Tightens

Ayden MacKenna

Ayden sat in the small upstairs office at Revere's, bent over the ledger book. Columns of numbers marched across the page—orders, expenditures, receipts—but his focus kept slipping. The ink blotched where he'd pressed too hard. He exhaled through his nose and leaned back.

Outside the window, the street bustled with the noise of carts and barkers, but something off in the rhythm caught his eye. Beside the fishmonger's awning, half-hidden by a display of salted cod, a man stood still as stone. A well-shaped hat shadowed his face, but Ayden recognized the stiff posture, the pinched shoulders, the boots scuffed and salt-worn.

Milton.

Ayden's hand moved reflexively toward the ledgers, closing the book with quiet precision. He tied it shut with the leather strap, then locked it in the cabinet beneath the desk. Milton watching Revere's meant only one thing: the scrutiny of them was growing.

Downstairs, a quiet calm filled the tavern after the breakfast rush. A few regulars hunched over coffee and bread. Nothing alarming.

Harry looked up from polishing glasses and grinned. "Morning, Mac. You look like you've seen a ghost."

"Not a ghost," Ayden said. "But something just as pale." The sight of Milton struck a cold place inside him. Milton knew Ayden's strength and yet he loitered on the street outside Revere's anyway. *And Milton is a coward, so what has changed?*

Harry raised a brow. "Want a drink?"

Ayden gave a faint smile. "Not quite yet."

The tavern door opened, and Alyse stepped inside, her arms full of brown paper parcels. She scanned the room and spotted him at the bar.

Ayden straightened. A sudden jolt of concern stabbed his chest.

He met her halfway across the tavern, relieved her of the packages, and walked with her to the counter. "Is everything all right?"

She didn't answer right away. Her fingers rubbed her neck like she was trying to lose a cramp —or a memory.

"I could use some water," she said softly.

Harry slid a glass toward her. She drank half of it before setting it down with a clink.

"I think...no. *I know*." She looked up at Ayden and clenched her jaw. "Someone followed me from the booksellers."

Ayden's expression sharpened. "Describe him."

"Tallish. Short brown hair. Round face. He wore a nice hat, but his coat and boots were worn out."

Ayden's hand curled against the bar. "Gordon," he said grimly.

Her eyes widened. "From the Coleman Cov—" She stopped herself. "One of Coleman's men?"

Ayden nodded slowly. "His friend, Milton, is outside this building right now."

They are watching us. Not discreetly, like before. Boldly.

Ayden touched her hand. "Let me walk you to your hotel," he offered.

Alyse shook her head. "I'm heading to Margaret's, I mean, my mother's." She rolled her eyes at her slip. "I'm to meet Amy, Jason and Jim there."

Ayden smiled at his daughter. "Then allow me to wave down a cab and I'll accompany you."

Bayard, Bernard and Lisbeth were already at Margaret's, deep in conversation, when Ayden and Alyse arrived. Moments later, Jason, Jimmy Leigh, and Amy came in.

Amy averted her gaze from Ayden's, until he told everyone about Milton loitering outside Revere's.

"The Coleman Coven is watching us," Ayden stated flatly. "Not just here and Revere's. They're following you—us—across the city." Ayden glanced at the concerned faces. "One of Isaac's lieutenants followed Alyse today," he added grimly, "A man named Gordon who Margaret and I both know. He tailed Alyse through the bookstore, to Revere's, and Gods knows where else."

Jimmy Leigh's fists curled. "This crosses a line."

Ayden raised his hand. "Lisbeth, would you, Bernard and Bayard warn Garrett this afternoon, then ward the windowsills and door frames at Revere's? I'm done allowing them access. Ask Mel to assist you, he needs to learn this. No one goes anywhere alone. From now on, we travel in pairs."

The heightened awareness of Coleman's threatening interest in them lasted well into the next week, but no one else was followed, then the watchers withdrew.

The following Saturday morning, Ayden, Mel, and Jimmy Leigh returned to Margaret's to help Wrigley inspect what he feared was a cracked axle on the carriage. The scent of varnish, grease, and horses filled the yard as the men repaired the rear axle.

Later in the day, Peg called from the porch, voice light and teasing. "Amy, I'll come with you."

Ayden glanced up from the wagon in time to see Amy and Peg chat merrily on the porch steps before they stepped inside.

When the men finished and returned inside late in the afternoon, Peg, pale and anxious, paced the kitchen. "She wouldn't wait," she said, near tears. "She said she'd return before the kettle boiled. I asked her to wait while I retrieved my bonnet, but she left before I could get back downstairs."

"Perhaps Margaret accompanied her," Jimmy Leigh suggested.

"No." Peg shook her head. "Miss Margaret and Alyse walked to the Commons to hire a Hansom earlier this afternoon. They should be back from the market anytime now."

Ayden checked the clock. "How long ago did Amy leave?"

"At least an hour ago, for what should have been a ten-minute walk."

Jason opened the front door, dust on his coat, his face pinched and tired. "I went to the insurance office." He paused in the entry and removed his jacket. "They've confirmed the *Atlantia*'s manifest, and Robert's name listed therein. However, salvage would not be worth the cost or the effort. The description of the wreck—"

"Amy's missing," Peg interrupted.

Jason froze. "What?"

"She left alone," Ayden said quietly. "To buy ribbons."

Jason's eyes filled with disbelief. "Why would she—Why would you let her—" He cut himself off. "Never mind. I'll find her."

After Jason stormed out, Ayden sought solitude in the east facing morning room. He stood at the window and watched the late afternoon sky darken from blue to indigo.

Had Milton or Gordon abducted Amy? They were the likeliest villains, but to what end?

Anxiety tangled his gut and he turned from the window. Plucking the decorative glass lantern from the mantle, he set it on the low table in front of the sofa and took a seat. Carefully, he removed the hand painted glass chimney and brought a flame to the burner with a thought.

"Amy," he whispered, and willed the flame to show him his daughter.

Images coalesced and faded.

Amy laughing. Amy angry.

Amy in every possible scenario except where he could find her now.

At his chest, the amulet beat a warm staccato against his skin. He pulled the polished stone from beneath his shirt and murmured, "Come."

The spark beneath the smooth surface jumped from the stone to his finger, and the tiny flame danced up to his wrist.

"I see you are worried too, my friend."

Talking to your tiny companion again? Miera's voice reached him through the flickering light.

Indeed I am. He's affected by my concern. Amy, Margaret's daughter, is missing.

Silence for a heartbeat.

You were looking for her in the fire?

I was, but I can't see her. You and Fiona should be on your guard. Someone means us harm.

Thank you for the warning.

Ayden waited for a moment, but Miera had severed their connection.

By early evening, Jason had searched all the businesses near Amy's destination, then returned to walk the length of the dining room a hundred times.

Margaret and Alyse returned with their purchases from the market, but after learning of Amy's disappearance, neither felt like cooking.

Ayden stayed silent until the hour grew too dark for denial.

"We know she didn't just vanish," he said quietly, from his place near the hearth. "Someone has taken her."

Jason stopped pacing and turned to Ayden. "We've had no word, no ransom demand."

Ayden's eyes found Alyse, sitting upright in a dining chair, hands folded tight in her lap. She'd been quiet since she learned her sister was missing. Eyes distant, head tilted slightly, she listened across a bond only she and her twin shared.

"Ayden's right. It's the only thing that makes sense. Amy's alive," Alyse said. Her voice was hollow, edged in steel. "She's trying not to panic. But something's wrong. It's as though she's caught in a memory from when we first twyned."

Ayden leaned forward, studying her face. "Can she tell where she is?"

"No," Alyse shook her head. "She can only see darkness, but she hears birds—wings flutter around her—and a woman's voice."

Jason's hands curled at his sides. "Jim, can you sense her?"

Jimmy Leigh shook his head. "I can only sense direction when their life is in danger." He turned from Jason to Ayden. "Whoever has her means her no mortal harm."

"One small mercy at least." Ayden looked at Lisbeth. She stood apart from the others, arms folded tight. He didn't have to ask.

"It's my father," she whispered, then her voice grew stronger. "Once he had her, he would have taken her to the horse ranch." Lisbeth's expression didn't change—but her pulse hammered visibly at her throat.

Ayden nodded once, then turned toward the windows where the first light of the full moon filtered through the glass. He didn't speak again. He didn't need to.

The storm has begun.

Chapter 35

Under Glass and Feathers

Amy Harris

Amy stirred, trapped in hooded darkness, her wrists bound behind her back. She tried to swallow, to calm herself, but the darkness reminded her of the wardrobe. *Blackwell Jones.* Terror crawled higher in her throat.

Jason will come. He has to.

The filthy black bag over her head smelled of mud and tasted like dirt. She couldn't see, could barely breathe, but she could hear.

Where are you? Alyse insisted through their *twyne* over and over. The panic shared between them hampered them both.

I don't know.

Who took you?

I don't know. I never saw them.

What do you know?

I hear birds.

First one. Then many.

They whisper. She didn't know how she knew they whispered, only that the sound stroked her nerves raw.

They watch me.

A woman's voice. Sweet. Familiar somehow, but strange, spoke in the distance, words she couldn't make out.

She speaks with authority.

Who does? Alyse demanded.

I don't know. I don't know. I don't know.

Panic seized her by the throat, and she sobbed as her shoulders shook.

Somewhere above her, a sharp beak tapped rhythmically against a pane of glass.

Chapter 36

Ash and fury

Ayden MacKenna

They left within the hour.

Margaret's dining room erupted into purposeful chaos—chairs shoved aside, weapons checked, coats snatched from hooks.

A swell of emotion moved across Ayden's chest, like a release valve finally twisting open.

At last, I'm moving toward Amy.

Relief washed through him, sharp enough to sting—but it tangled instantly with something heavier. He looked at Margaret's sure stride, Peg's determined jaw, Alyse's steady hands igniting with purpose, and anxiety curled tight in his chest.

But I'm leading them into danger.

And yet his conviction held—a solid, burning core. This was the only path left. He pushed the door open and stepped into the night, carrying all of it: fear, hope, and the fierce resolve that nothing would keep him from his daughter.

Wrigley drove the carriage hard; wheels rattled over cobblestone in the late summer darkness.

Lisbeth sat beside him, posture rigid, one hand fixed on the edge of the bench as she directed them toward her father's home.

Above them, the full Sturgeon Moon hung heavy in the clear night sky, drowning the stars with its light.

Ayden glanced from the moon to Lisbeth's profile—a statue carved from dread.

Lisbeth touched Wrigley's arm and the carriage pulled to the side of the street. "Wait here. I want to be sure they have indeed left for the ranch."

Margaret pushed back the curtains in the carriage. "Why have we stopped?"

Ayden leaned down from his gelding and spoke softly, "Lis is checking the house to make sure her father has gone."

Margaret, Peg, and Alyse nodded as one and the curtain swung closed.

When he looked up, Lisbeth hurried back to the vehicle and climbed onto the bench.

"They left before sunset," she whispered, her breath thin and sharp as she glanced at the full moon. "They will have the coven with them."

No one spoke during the ride out of the city. The men followed the carriage on horseback.

Ayden rode directly behind the carriage. Hooves struck sparks in the growing dark. He kept scanning the horizon—*old habit, older instinct*—waiting for trouble to show its face.

As they passed beyond the city's edge, the night wind kicked up the scent of manure and pine. The air near the Coleman ranch tasted like old magic and something worse—scorched cloth and cracked stone.

This stench isn't fresh. It's been simmering.

When the carriage slowed, Lisbeth's boots hit the dirt before the wheels stopped turning. Attired in men's leather chaps and a long, split riding coat, her platinum braids gleamed silver in the moonlight. Without her glamour, she looked both young and fierce. She touched the iron-posted gate—wards shimmered, faltered, and snapped.

"My parents are here," she whispered. Not with relief, but with dread.

"Leave the horses," Ayden stated softly as he dismounted.

They crossed the yard like a single shadow. The barn rose ahead, hulking, dark, and quiet.

Alyse's arm snapped out, barring Ayden's chest. "Someone's inside." Her whisper trembled with warning.

Ayden felt fire coil through his fingers, eager. *Good. Let them try me.* His amulet throbbed against his chest as he stepped forward and kicked the barn door. It groaned as it swung open.

A messy line of salt lay scattered across the threshold—a ward set in panic. Beyond that, a flickering light pulsed in the dark—small, like a guttering candle flame, it grew and spiraled out, illuminating the hands that nurtured it.

Milton and Gordon stood at the far end, flanked by other members of Isaac's coven—men and women armed with magic, braced, and waiting.

"You shouldn't have come," Milton murmured, his eyes glinted with disdain and fear.

Ayden stepped inside, flame simmering along his knuckles. "We've come for Amy. We're not leaving without her."

Surprise reflected in Gordon's eyes as his sneer cut through the shadows. "She's not here. And *you're* not leaving." His hand shot up—fire blasted from his palm. The barn shuddered.

Bernard threw up a shield and shoved Lisbeth behind him.

Margaret flung a glowing rune overhead.

Bayard and Alyse surged forward like twin lightning strikes.

Chaos erupted.

Fire and force collided with ribbons of light and thunder. Spells cracked across timber, wind shrieked between beams, firelight and lightning strobed over startled faces.

Peg hurled a wild wave of wind upward, knocking a witch from the loft.

Then a stone, hurled by Gordon, struck Alyse's temple. She crumpled to the ground and lay still.

Jim's roar of anger and anguish rang out above the fray as he charged across the barn to Alyse's side.

The sight of his daughter lying still on the ground while sparks rained down tore something deep inside Ayden's chest.

The amulet at his chest pulsed violently, beating with his racing heart. Fear sharpened into one terrible need: *Protect her. At any cost.*

Beyond caution or care, he tore the amulet from his neck and lifted the pulsing stone high above his head near the center of the barn. "Caz," he bellowed, "Aid Alyse."

The stone erupted.

Liquid fire burst from the gem and slithered down his arm like lava. It hit the ground and coalesced into a shape of smoke and ember. A figure stood, sprite-like at first, small like a burnt wick, then furious it grew. And grew.

Ten feet. Fifteen. The air warped with heat. Caz's eyes opened—two blazing coals full of confusion... and fury.

The entire barn froze.

Milton stumbled back; terror etched across his face.

Ayden's breath hitched. He'd seen full elementals in India—towering creatures of living flame—but never imagined the small Caz capable of becoming *this*. He'd only thought the tiny elemental would defend and bolster Alyse and her uncles' *fire-magic*.

Caz shrieked—a roar of flame and anger—then suddenly lashed out.

The barn convulsed.

A beam cracked and fell; Melvyn dragged Peg out from under it, rolling hard into the dirt.

"Are you alright?" he asked, panting.

Peg coughed smoke. "Yes. Look out!"

Fire leapt to the loft. Hay ignited. Screams echoed as witches broke and ran. Horses screamed in the nearby stables.

Margaret, Bernard, and Bayard moved fast, *fire-skilled* hands shaped barriers and redirected the blaze.

Peg conjured water with frantic gestures, dashing it over spreading tongues of fire.

From just outside the barn doors, Lisbeth screamed, "Ayden! The stables—they're catching!"

Smoke billowed toward the sky from the adjacent stable.

Ayden looked at Alyse—Jim cradled her in his arms. Bayard and Bernard guarded them both.

She stirred faintly.

She's alive! Relief punched him, sharp enough to hurt.

He shouted to the men, "Keep her safe!"

"We will." *Twyned* for battle, the brothers responded in unison as Jim enfolded Alyse in his embrace.

Ayden turned and ran.

He vaulted the fence, hit the ground running, and reached for the earth's pulse as he neared the livery. Stable doors swung open at his command.

Inside, hooves crashed against their stall gates with panic. Flames already licked at the dry straw.

Using his *Earth-sense*, Ayden snapped opened the stall doors and nudged the frightened animals to flee. One by one, they burst into the field beyond and fled into the night.

By the time he returned, the air in the barn was thick and choking.

Alyse knelt beside Jim, conscious, pale, her hands glowed faintly as she worked her fire.

Bayard and Bernard flanked the couple, steady, focused. Together, the group faced the giant elemental.

And Caz—Caz trembled. Flames guttered along its limbs. It looked not monstrous but lost—like a giant child, unsure what it had done.

Ayden approached slowly. "Caz," His voice softened, weighted with gratitude and guilt. "You came because I called. You protected Alyse. You did everything right."

Caz's head tilted toward him; its blazing body flickered with uncertainty.

Ayden lifted the amulet. "You did nothing wrong. Come home now. It's time to rest."

The elemental seemed to sigh. Its embers dimmed as it folded inward—smoke collapsing into ember, ember into spark—and vanished into the stone.

Smoke curled around them as silence settled over the wreckage.

Then— "Father!" Lisbeth's shouted. She ran to the collapsed rear wall.

Ayden followed, his boots crunched on the blackened, smoldering straw.

Isaac Coleman lay beneath a scorched rafter, blood at his temple, his breath shallow.

Helena rushed past Ayden and sank to her knees beside her husband. "Dear Goddess have mercy—Isaac—*Isaac!*"

Smoke-stained and shaken, Lisbeth pressed her hand to his chest.

Isaac groaned.

Ayden crouched, jaw tight. "Where is Amy?"

Isaac's eyes opened—pain-glazed but clear. His voice rasped, hoarse from smoke and pain. "I don't know. I haven't seen her."

Ayden's voice dropped to iron. "Don't lie to me."

Isaac's lips barely moved. "I would never take one of yours." His gaze flicked to Lisbeth, and something profound, unguarded, passed between them. He blinked and his stare returned to Ayden. "I know what it is... to lose someone you love."

Ayden looked into his eyes a moment longer, searching. Finally—he nodded. "I believe you." He stepped back. "See to him."

"I'm here," Lisbeth whispered, and gripped his hand. "It's over, Papa. We don't have to fight anymore."

"I didn't mean..." His breath rattled. "I wanted to protect you."

"You tried to control me." Her voice cracked. "But I still love you."

His fingers curled weakly around hers. "I was wrong... about them. About Margaret. Ayden. About you."

A tear slid down Lisbeth's cheek. She gulped back her emotions. "I know." She patted his hand and smiled at her mother. "Just rest now. Let us take care of you for once."

Isaac's gaze flicked to Helena, then back to Lisbeth. "I'm proud of you, daughter. So proud."

She bent low and kissed his temple. "We'll talk more when you wake."

"I'd like that," he whispered—and then his eyes closed, too heavy to keep open.

Helena touched Lisbeth's shoulder gently. "You brought him back."

"But without Amy," Lisbeth whispered, "we have no healer."

"We have other means." Alyse pressed a bloody handkerchief to her forehead. "Let's get him inside."

Peg pulled a tin of salve from her pocket. "Amy's special blend. It'll help—but he'll sleep for hours."

Helena accepted it immediately.

Bayard, Bernard, and Ayden lifted the beam. The women carried Isaac into the house.

Alyse and Helena cleaned Isaac's wounds as Lisbeth held his hand and murmured encouraging words. "You never wanted this," she whispered. "You were just afraid."

"And now?" Helena asked quietly.

"I hope he knows better."

Ayden and Margaret found Milton and Gordon, broken and burned, near the paddock. Their blackened skin beyond even a healer's help.

"Do you remember that day on Garrett's farm when Gordon and Milton bullied you?"

Ayden pulled Margaret into his arms, and she collapsed against him, resting her head against his shoulder. "I do. They were mean children that grew into angry men, but they didn't deserve to die like this."

"Nobody does," Margaret whispered.

Neither Milton nor Gordon survived the hour.

As they returned to the ranch-house, Ayden surveyed what remained. The ranch smoldered. Smoke drifted across the fields. Behind him, voices murmured as the others prepared to leave.

Peg, exhausted, sat on a log until Melvyn helped her to her feet.

"Are you sure you weren't hurt?" he asked.

She looked at him, a smile breaking past the soot-streaked face. "You saved my life in there."

"You're not easy to keep track of."

"I'm not meant to be." She took his hand.

With Isaac's wounds tended, Helena and Lisbeth settled in to watch over him. "I'll stay until he wakes," Lisbeth told Bernard.

Bernard leaned down and kissed her temple. "And then you'll come back?"

"I will."

Ayden's group returned to Margaret's house, exhausted, ash-covered, and empty-handed.

Amy was still missing.

They gathered at the dining table, drained, waiting for something—*anything*—to point the way.

Two sleek black cats padded in from the kitchen, weaving between skirts, boots, and chair legs. They stopped before Alyse, sitting in perfect unison.

Ayden arched a brow. "Friends of yours?"

Alyse blinked. "Sabine? Anaïs? How did you—"

The cats shimmered. Their bodies dissolved into twin sparks of light as they spun upward, dancing over Alyse's lap.

Her hands flew to her mouth. Tears welled. "They can help find Amy." Her voice caught. "They can find her."

Chapter 37

Bonds and Whispers

Amy Harris

The darkness pressed in, smothering.

The bag cinched tight across her face, but even if it hadn't, the air was too thick, too wrong to breathe easily. The damp chill in the room curled around Amy's skin like fingers, and somewhere above, a floorboard creaked under the weight of someone pacing.

But it was the birds that captured her attention. Not the flutter of wings, the whispers.

They murmured nonsense at first, the rustle of feathers blended with snatches of old prayers and twisted lullabies. Words that didn't make sense.

Twins... wings... burn her clean...

A woman's voice broke through the muttering.

"You were always my special one," the voice cooed. "Always the one with the dark hair and the dark eyes. I saw it. I saw it in Colorado. You don't remember me yet, do you? We were such close friends."

Amy's heart slammed against her ribs.

The voice cracked into laughter—high, brittle, broken. The birds echoed it with flutters and clicks, as if they agreed.

"My sweet Miss Amy," the voice continued, syrup-sweet and sickening, "I scrubbed your boots and washed your linens. I took care of you. I loved you like a daughter, you know."

Amy's inhale hitched. "June," she whispered.

The name summoned the face—bland and round, but eyes like glittering glass beads. June McKay, the housekeeper. The woman Jason fired for her hatefulness toward Nichole. Amy had forgotten her voice, but not the feeling. Not the way it had slithered beneath pleasantries just before she left.

"You're mine now, aren't you my darling," June cooed, as if responding to one of the birds. "The colorful sweet things who used to visit are all gone. Did you send them away? It doesn't matter. New ones found me. They bring messages and tell me the truth. The birds see everything," she whispered.

Amy flinched as something soft and feathery brushed her arm.

Birds?

They circled her now. Not caged. Not distant. Crowding her. Alert.

Is this a remnant of the Demon Morago? Amy shook her head. *How would that be possible? We destroyed him.*

But a nagging horror remained.

What if some part of the Demon latched onto June's shattered mind?

Not a fully realized demon, more a lingering hunger wearing June's thoughts like a skin. It didn't speak in commands, just urges—obsessions twisted with her own divine ideas. Whatever evil this was had found a home in June.

She already danced along the edge of sanity and obsession.

Now the craving clung to her with claws and feathers and shadow.

Amy's skin prickled. She reached across the bond.

Alyse? Alyse wake up!

Her twin's presence flickered—dim, distant—then solidified slowly as Alyse woke.

I know who has me. Amy poured her fear and recognition into the link.

It's June McKay. Jason will remember her.

The birds began to chant—words not meant for human tongues. Amy shivered, then continued.

I still don't know where I am, she sent silently to her sister. *They won't let me see. They only let me listen.*

Then, just above her ear, a voice not June's, not human, not whole, rasped from every bird's throat at once, layered and shrill:

She tells her... Tells the other... Fire and Air... Tells the Ssissterr.

The air thickened with the weight of the whispered message.

Tell her she is right. The trap cracked, and a snake slipped through.

Amy's pulse stuttered.

We are now the hollow wing of Pure Fire. We are the eyes that see, the ears that listen.

The whisper flared into something harsher—louder—then dropped again to an ominous snake-like hiss.

Tell them we are watching. And we are hungry.

Chapter 38

A Name from the Past

Alyse James

Alyse jerked awake, a gasp half-formed in her throat. The room was dim, cloaked in the hush of pre-dawn blue. The fire burned low, only glowing coals now, and silence wrapped the space except for the occasional creak of the house settling.

Margaret sat in a wingback chair, her eyes closed, knitting needles still in her hands.

Jimmy Leigh and Ayden spoke quietly near the door.

Jason leaned against the far wall, arms folded, his eyes closed but not asleep.

Sabine and Anaïs—fluffy, black, and warm—dozed on Alyse's lap as she reclined on the settee. But it wasn't their weight that woke her.

Alyse, wake up! I know who has me, Amy whispered through the *twyne*, urgent and raw. *It's June McKay.*

Alyse's heart slammed at her sister's voice. She sat up fully, sending the cats tumbling to the floor.

"Jason!"

He startled upright. "What is it?"

Alyse stood, breath quick. "Amy spoke to me. She says it's June McKay."

Jason's face went sheet-white. "June McKay? From the Highlands ranch?"

"Wasn't she Amy's housekeeper?" Margaret asked. She dropped the knitting needles into the basket near her feet.

"The one you dismissed for being hateful to Nichole," Alyse clarified, meeting Jason's eyes.

Jason ran a hand through his hair. "She disappeared after Timothy Caine took her to Denver. As far as I know, no one's seen her since."

Ayden rose from the chair. "June McKay... you mean *Mother McKay*? The Pure Fire cult leader?"

"I don't know." Alyse shook her head. "Amy didn't say that. But maybe. She says June talks to birds—listens to them. *Dozens of them.* She thinks it's some leftover part of the demon. Not entirely him... just a sliver. A remnant. Like something poisonous buried in her mind."

On the rug, Sabine stirred. Then Anaïs. Their golden eyes blinked open in perfect synchrony.

Alyse dropped to one knee. "Please find Amy. You've done this before. Once you find her, one of you come back and lead us to her. The other should stay with her. Keep her safe. Will you do this for me?"

With one last lick of her paw, Sabine shimmered, her form blurred. A spark darted above Anaïs, who blinked solemnly at the light. After a dramatic yawn and stretch, Anaïs joined her twin. They danced to the window and slipped through the narrow gap beneath the sill.

Outside, in the gray, pre-dawn light, two red-tailed hawks took flight—wings wide and silent—heading east.

Ayden exhaled. "Let's get ready to go."

"Morago again," Jason muttered. "This is bad."

Jimmy Leigh stood beside Ayden. "Ayden, Jason, and I should go. If this is some remnant of Morago, he may still want the twins. They shouldn't be there together."

Alyse wanted to argue but stopped herself. She nodded. "You're right."

Melvyn spoke from the doorway. "We'll hold things here. Peg, Wrigley, and I—unless you need us."

"No. Jim's right." Ayden clapped Jimmy Leigh's shoulder. "We ride before dawn."

Jimmy nodded. "Mel could help ready the horses. We'll want to pack light, saddles and weapons."

Chapter 39

The House of Watching Wings

Ayden MacKenna

At the livery stable, Jim handed Ayden an ammunition belt as they prepared their mounts. "I never told you the whole story. About the curse. How I find Alyse when she needs me, and how I lose her over and over…" His voice faded.

Ayden tucked the belt in the saddlebag and tightened a strap. "I can't imagine."

Jimmy Leigh cleared his throat. "A few thousand years ago…"

"A few *thousand*?" Ayden paused and stared at Jim.

Jim nodded. "My father was the clan chief, and we traveled one year to a neighboring tribe so I could marry their Shaman Priestess. Well, Alyse, or who Alyse was in that life, and I got it wrong. She didn't know about the agreement, and I didn't know she wasn't the priestess. One thing led to another, and we were caught."

Jason lifted a saddle over the back of the livery gelding he'd chosen to ride. He slipped his sword cane through the rifle loop and continued to work the straps while Jim and Ayden talked.

Jim adjusted his saddle strap, then leaned one elbow on the leather. "The real Priestess cursed me with life eternal, to love only Alyse forever. To know when she is in mortal danger, giving me only the direction I must travel to find her." He reset his Stetson and crossed his arms. "In some lives, I reach her in time and save her. Some I don't, and then I wait again for the call. If I find her and save her, we will have the chance to fall in love again. I watch her grow old. Bury her. Mourn her. Eventually, I feel the burning compass on my forehead pointing the way to her once again. If I can reach her in time."

"Dear Goddess, Jim." Ayden gripped Jim's shoulder. "I don't know what to say." He shook his head, picked up a long rifle, and slid it into the saddle loop. "Pyromancy is the bane of my life, and the joy. Sometimes, it feels like it will consume everything I touch, everything I hold dear."

Jim tightened a strap on his mount. "You ever feel like you're meant to burn it all down?"

"I used to." Ayden smiled sadly. "Now I know I'm meant to protect what's left."

"We both are." Jim nodded. "This time we protect Amy and bring her home."

Melvyn gathered the horses' reins and led them to the stable yard.

Jason, Ayden, and Jimmy Leigh mounted.

A single spark zipped across the sky and hovered at the edge of the yard.

"I think that may be your guide," Melvyn said, watching it with wide eyes.

The three men nudged their mounts forward, and the spark darted toward the harbor.

They followed the faerie spark into the growing predawn light.

It danced ahead of them—bright, sure, bobbing over cobblestones like a living lantern. The quiet rhythm of hooves echoed off shuttered shops and slumbering inns. Still wrapped in their early morning hush, suspended between night and day.

Then, with a flick of light, the spark dropped low.

Ayden pulled his horse to a slow trot.

The spark touched ground, shimmered, and transformed—its light expanding into a large, black wolf.

Jason let out a low breath. "Sabine."

"You can tell them apart?" Ayden marveled.

"Only sometimes," Jason admitted.

The wolf looked back once, its golden eyes sharp with recognition, then turned and loped ahead. They followed.

Down toward the harbor they rode, the wolf their silent scout. The road curved north past Revere's, then past the blackened bones of Harbor's Delight. Ayden glanced at the ruin, shadows and soot clung to the skeleton of what once stood proud and bawdy.

The harbor road veered north, and the wolf slowed, turning inland. Its paws moved cautiously across uneven flagstones. Trash littered the curbs. Doors sagged. Windows stared back, black and broken.

Here, the buildings were ghosts—long-closed shops, row houses left to rot—a neighborhood forgotten by downtown revitalization.

Then the wolf stopped.

Ahead, a crooked mansion rose from the grime and broken fences, cloaked in shadows and filth, exposed by the breaking daylight. The wood siding had long since darkened with neglect. Half the windows were boarded; the other half shattered or sagged open like mouths caught in a silent cry.

And atop the neglected mansion, hundreds of birds. *Thousands.*

Perched along the gables and ridgelines, they lined the rooftop like sentries, unmoving, waiting.

Jason drew a slow breath. "She's in there."

Ayden didn't answer. He felt it too.

The wolf turned, met Ayden's eyes, and became a spark that streaked into the mansion through one of the open windows.

Only the house remained.

And the birds.

Chapter 40

Fire and Feathers

Amy Harris

A chill settled on Amy's skin and seeped through her summer gown. Her wrists, tied behind her back, burned and chafed against their bindings. The birds no longer murmured nonsense but spoke in shuddering unison, repeating phrases Amy couldn't bear to hear again: *burn her clean, twin-born, soul-torn, the other will break.*

Someone—*probably June*—paced above her, boots thudding in an erratic, unsteady rhythm. Amy anchored herself to the frayed edge of the *twyne*, drawing in Alyse's steadiness. It kept her from screaming.

Jason, she thought. *Find me. Please.*

A screech from above caused the birds to scatter with a rush of wings.

Something is happening.

"Jason!" she shouted, her voice raw beneath the mask.

Boots pounded down the stairs, and a taloned grip yanked Amy up by her arm. "Enough of that. Your precious Jason won't get here in time to save you."

She choked as the scent of kerosene rose from her bodice and soaked to her skin through her skirt. Amy jerked away from June's grip and stumbled against a sharp edge.

The birds squawked in unison: *burn the witch... cleanse her soul... make them pay.*

The cloth bag ripped from her head and Amy blinked, coughed at the strong scent, then looked up into June's madness.

June's once dark hair, now streaked with white, escaped a bun wound tight at the nape of her neck. Wild white hair made a frenzied halo around June's pale and angry face. She held a glowing lantern in one hand and a metal tin of kerosene in the other. Her lip pulled back in a snarl, exposing yellowed teeth as she hurled the tin at Amy's head. "He will never take you from me, do you hear me?" With her empty hand she yanked Amy to her feet with surprising strength and pushed her across the stone lined cellar toward narrow wooden stairs. "Up!"

"June stop! Why are you doing this?" Amy demanded. She gulped fresh but dusty air as they emerged from the cellar. *Where is Jason?*

Amy, what's happening? Alyse insisted through their *twyne.*

June has lost her mind. She's threatening to set me on fire.

The iron grip pushed Amy across a wide hallway toward a dilapidated staircase.

"You'll want to be careful," June directed as she shoved Amy up the first few steps. "The handrail is gone, and the wood on your left is rotted through. That's it. Stay near the wall. If you start to fall, I will let you."

Frantic, Alyse barked instructions into Amy's mind.

Set her on fire!

You know I have no fire-skill.

Use mine. You don't have time to think, just trust me.

But I'm covered in kerosene.

You could—

Enough sister! I'm trying not to fall.

June barked orders to a half dozen men on the second floor. "This witch's servants will try to rescue her. Kill them quick, then attend me."

The men wore dark, tattered coats and stovepipe hats. They had the beards and demeanor of the religious sect Amy had seen preaching prohibition and warning of sin around Boston. In single file, they hurried down the staircase. Three had shotguns, two carried hand pistols, and one held a worn and worried bible.

"Amy—I'm coming!" Jason voice echoed from somewhere below.

"Jas—" June's fist struck the side of Amy's head, knocking her against the wall.

The madwoman yanked Amy up, close enough for her to smell June's fetid breath.

"Make another sound and I will burn you right here. I don't care if I burn as well, it would be righteous for us to die together." Her eyes shone with terrible certainty. She dug her torn fingernails into the flesh of Amy's arm and shoved her toward another staircase.

These stairs were in even worse shape than the previous, with treads broken, and in several places missing altogether.

Amy stumbled once and June yanked her to her feet and thrust her through an opening at the top of the stairs and onto a large west facing balcony.

Amy fell to her knees and onto her side, her arms still bound behind her back, unable to break her fall.

Below, the sharp explosion of gunfire erupted. A man's shout ended in a scream of agony.

"Here you die," June laughed and knocked the glass chimney from the lamp. The covering shattered as it struck the deck. "I want all of Boston to watch you burn."

Chapter 41

The Fall and The Rise

Jason Harris

The house leaned like it wanted to fall. The porch sagged and its shutters swung loose in the morning breeze. A second spark—*Anaïs*—hovered briefly before vanishing inside through a crack near the roof.

Jason dismounted, already moving.

Ayden and Jimmy Leigh flanked him.

"I see two men on our left," Jimmy Leigh whispered. "They're armed."

"I'll take this side," Ayden instructed. "Go."

Jason didn't wait to see what happened and pushed through the warped front door. The stench of mold and candle smoke hit him like a slap.

The first fanatic charged, swinging a rusted knife. Jason ducked, drove a fist into the man's gut, then swept his legs. The man dropped to his back and Jason finished him with his *épée* blade.

Another man burst from the hallway.

Jimmy Leigh, who had followed Jason inside, intercepted him. The men crashed into the wall, scattering old photos and trash on a nearby table.

Jason hurtled down the hallway. "Amy—I'm coming!" Past a broken staircase, he raced into a room, blade in hand, but the room was empty.

At a howl of pain, Jason spun on his heel.

Ayden stood inside the broken front door and gaped at Jimmy Leigh's tall frame.

Jim leaned against the peeling wallpaper in the hall, a pained grimace distorted his features as he scrubbed his forehead with his knuckles. Slowly, he opened watering eyes, looked at Jason, then turned his gaze toward the staircase. "She's above us," he uttered. "And we have to hurry."

Heart pounding, Jason charged for the stairs and up, conscious of the missing handrail and creaking treads.

Ayden followed close on his heels.

Above them men filed down the staircase. In the dim light, the first man raised a long gun.

"Watch out," Jason yelled as the weapon fired. Inches above Jason's head the wall splintered, sending debris into the three men. Pain lanced across Jason's brow as a shard of wood found his forehead.

Ayden pushed Jason against the wall and motioned with his free arm just as another gun sounded. Two men screamed and tumbled from the broken staircase to the floor below.

"No fire, Ayden," Jim called as he mounted the steps. "I smell kerosene."

Ayden made a fist and growled as the fiery glow around his hand diminished. "Damn."

Jason blinked blood from his eyes and wiped his arm across his face.

Ayden threw out his other hand toward the group above them.

The next three men grabbed their throats as Ayden motioned, tossing them off the stairs while they choked.

Ayden chuckled.

The remaining man waved his bible above his stovepipe hat. "Mother McKay will call the vengeance of the Lord down upon your demon heads." He turned and ran up the stairs, disappearing into the shadowed hallway.

"Go." Ayden released Jason.

Jason took the remaining steps two at a time then stopped. There was no one in sight. No indication which way he should go to find Amy.

Ayden and Jim followed through the opening.

Jim pointed to the right. "That way." And took the lead.

Jason raced up another flight of stairs behind Jimmy Leigh.

Jim paused and looked back at Ayden and Jason. "There are some treads missing. Slow down and be careful." With that, he raced ahead.

Jason struggled with impatience and hurried forward, taking care to step over the missing steps. He burst into the cloudy morning light with Ayden immediately behind him.

Across the wide balcony, June stood, a glowing lantern in one hand, the other gripped Amy's hair at the back of her head.

June has changed.

Gaunt where she had once been well rounded, disheveled, where she'd once kept herself overly prim and tidy, the former housekeeper practically reeked of madness.

And Amy...

On her knees, her hands bound behind her back. The smell of lantern oil radiated from her dress. Tears raced down her cheeks as she begged her former friend and confidant to let her go.

But June was beyond redemption, as far as Jason was concerned.

He took a step forward, but June lifted the lamp even higher and her eyes sparkled. "I want you to see this, Jason. I want you to see what you have done to this once lovely woman, a daughter to me."

"Mother McKay?" Ayden inquired. "This is the day you die."

The fanatic that had raced from the stairs suddenly emerged from the staircase opening. Shaking his tattered bible and brandishing a handgun, he pointed the weapon at Jim. "Get back!" he yelled and pulled the trigger.

Jim stepped in front of Ayden and grinned as the weapon misfired, exploding in the man's hand. He screamed in pain, holding his bloody limb.

Ayden flicked his wrist and the man sailed over the edge of the deck.

Two sparks of light bounded through the doorway and moved with purpose toward June. One changed into a hawk, talons extended, the other growled in anger as it became an enraged black wolf.

"Demons!" June screamed, smashing the lantern to the deck at Amy's knees.

Flames engulfed both women but were quelled immediately by Ayden.

Both animals struck June, talons to her face, canine incisors to her gut.

June staggered back, her hand tangled Amy's hair.

Amy, unharmed by the flames, screamed as June toppled from the edge, pulling her along.

Jason dove for Amy, grabbing her dress, her legs, and sliding to the edge as Amy followed June off the balcony.

"No!" Ayden shouted.

Half over the edge, Jason looked down. June lay at the foot of the mansion broken and torn. But Amy floated upward, two bright lights danced around her as she sobbed.

"How?" Jason tore his gaze from his wife and looked at Ayden.

Ayden stood on the edge of the balcony, jaw clenched with strain, his hand extended, the magic coiled and steady beneath Amy. He lifted her over the edge and sat her gently on the deck beside Jason.

"I've got you," Jason whispered, and pulled the knotted twine at her wrists loose. "You're safe now."

"June?" Amy rasped. "Did she fall? Oh Goddess, the birds—"

The sky shifted and darkened. Above them, thousands of birds screamed a raucous chorus. They beat their wings one by one, rising in a panicked spiral, scattering to the wind.

A dark mist—a last sliver of evil—peeled from the house, thinned and vanished into the rising light as the clouds broke and sunshine bathed the city below.

They watched the birds, tightly packed in a murmuration, spin and twist, slowly separating and dissolving into the distance.

"Jim, if you would lead us out of this place." Ayden asked as he helped Jason and Amy to their feet.

"Gladly."

Outside, Ayden helped Amy mount in front of Jason and two large black wolves escorted the group safely back to Beacon Hill.

Chapter 42

The Shape of Return

Margaret Prescott

The tea was over-steeped, but Peg didn't say a word, which was unlike her. She'd been unusually quiet since arranging the summer blossoms in the vases that morning.

Margaret sat across from Peg in the sitting room, a crisp linen cloth spread across the low settee table, the scent of lemon scones mingling with lavender from the garden.

"Is everything all right, my dear?" Margaret inquired.

Peg shrugged both shoulders and made a face as she took a quick sip of the tea. "I'm still worried about Amy. She just isn't herself."

As if summoned by their thoughts, the twins breezed through the front door and into the sitting room, right on time.

Alyse, overly bright and smiling, untied her sun hat, and slid into the settee beside Peg. "Is it terribly wrong to plan a wedding with everything that has happened?" The grin across her face spoke of excitement.

Amy, still pale from last week's ordeal with her former housekeeper moved slower, each step deliberate as she entered the room.

"Yes," Margaret said. Her worried glance moved from Amy to her other daughter, and she winked at Alyse. "Which is why we're going to do it anyway."

"I agree." Amy removed her bonnet and gloves, then took the chair beside Margaret and poured herself a cup. "You could have the ceremony at the same chapel where Jason and I were married." She sipped the brew, hesitated, then returned the cup to the table.

Alyse shook her head. "No. No churches. Not after what we've seen. I want something real. Honest. Not bound by anyone else's traditions."

"Then where?" Margaret inquired and forced another sip of the bitter brew.

"Someplace that means something. Not just to Jim and me, but to all of us."

"What about Revere's?" Amy offered. "It's familiar."

Alyse grimaced. "No. That doesn't seem right."

Margaret said nothing for a long moment. She looked around the room—the table filled with sunlight and tea leaves and the faint aroma of late summer wildflowers drifting in from the garden.

An ounce of new joy would push back the shadows that still haunt this house.

"I think you should be married here."

Alyse blinked. "Here?"

"Yes, here." Margaret nodded. "In the garden among the early autumn leaves and late roses in your sister's old garden. It's not a chapel or a temple, but it's familiar and well-loved."

Peg gave a small, happy sigh. "I think it's perfect."

"I don't have an altar," Margaret added, with a shrug. "But we can improvise. You'll want Garrett to officiate, I assume?"

Alyse's voice softened. "He already said he would, we just didn't know where."

"Thank you." Amy reached across the table and squeezed her mother's hand. "But it will be a lot of work, having it here. We could always have it at the hotel."

Margaret's smile deepened. "It's really up to Alyse and Jim, but here would be perfect for a small ceremony, with mostly family as guests."

Before anyone could reply, a firm knock sounded at the front door.

"Now, who could that be?" Margaret wondered aloud.

"I'll get it." Peg brushed at her skirt as she rose and hurried to the front door. She returned with a sealed parchment. "It was a delivery boy from the harbor. He said this note is from a foreign ship that arrive this morning."

Margaret rose to her feet, dread pricked along her scalp.

Not more bad news, please.

She held out her hand and took the note from Peg. "The seal says Rakesh." Her gaze rose from the letter and she scanned the anxious faces around her. "Why is that name familiar?" Then her heart gave a sharp jolt.

It can't be.

Her fingers trembling as she broke the wax.

Amy came to her side without saying a word.

Margaret began to read aloud; her voice shook with emotion.

"To Mrs. Margaret Prescott and Mr. Ayden MacKenna,"

She quickly scanned the remainder of letter and gasped. Her numb fingers let the letter fall to the table.

Dear Goddess, how can this be?

Amy wrapped her arm around her shoulders.

Quickly, Alyse picked up the missive and continued to read to the room.

"My ship recently made port in Boston from Bombay. There are two men in my care you will wish to see. One, you will remember as Robert, though few would recognize him. The other man you will know as Halstead.

Please come to my ship if you wish. You will be received in peace.

Forever your servant,

Magi Aamir Rakesh Kapoor"

Alyse's gaze rose to Margaret. "Who is this, mother?"

Margaret looked up and took a gulp of air, her voice barely above a whisper. "Rakesh is a terrible man, but if we can believe him, Robert and Hal are alive."

Peg shook her head. "The Lady preserve us..."

Amy released Margaret and stepped back with a gasp. "Father..."

The kitchen door crashed open, and angry footsteps pounded down the hall. Ayden strode in with Wrigley just behind him. The carriage driver held his cap in one hand, his eyes wide with unease. But Ayden—Ayden looked carved from storm clouds and stone.

"I think he's here, Margaret," Ayden said flatly. "Rakesh has come for me."

How did he find out? He must have come from Revere's and seen the ship in the harbor.

"We know he's here." Margaret's voice shook as she picked up the letter and offered it to Ayden. "He sent word."

"To you?" Ayden's jaw clenched and he ground out, "When did you receive this?"

"Just now. I couldn't place the name right away..."

Ayden took the paper offered and scanned the letter.

Amy stepped forward. "He has news of my father... of Robert."

Margaret whispered, "We can't ignore this, Ayden. Not if what he says is true." She placed her hand on his forearm, offering what strength she could muster between the joy and guilt of Robert's potential return.

Ayden's gaze lifted from the letter to Margaret. He exhaled through pressed lips and shook his head from side to side.

This has to be agony for him.

Ayden dropped the letter onto the table and turned away. He paced to the window; his back turned to the room. His shoulders rose and fell as he struggled to contain his emotions. "You know that man held me in servitude for twenty years, bound by blood and magic." His voice grew louder as he spoke. When he turned, his jaw clenched tight and his eyes glimmered with angry tears. "When it ended—when I finally escaped—he sent one of his *Earth-elementals* to kill me." He took several deep inhalations. His stare locked with Margaret's.

Margaret's voice was low. "Then you must be there when we speak with him. That letter is addressed to you as well, after all."

Ayden straightened, and for a moment, something vulnerable flickered in his eyes. Then he nodded. "I'll want Jim and Jason to accompany us."

Wrigley, who had stayed respectfully near the door, nodded. "I'll get the carriage."

"Now?" Alyse uttered as she grabbed her bonnet. "Do you need to change?"

"Why would I need to change?" Amy retorted with more spirit than she'd shown all week.

"I'll wait here," Peg moved the half empty cups of tea onto the tray.

"You both look fine," Margaret ushered her daughters out of the room. "Thank you, Peg." She followed Wrigley and Ayden through the dining room and kitchen and out the back door.

"Jason is at the hotel with Jimmy Leigh," Amy called to Wrigley as they hurried across the small yard.

"I figured as much." Wrigley stopped and looked at the women. He lifted his derby with the back of his hand and scratched his balding head. "I still have to hitch up the carriage, ladies. Turn yourselves around and I'll pick you up out front, like always."

"My horse is in the alley. I'll follow Wrigley." Ayden proceeded through the gate.

Margaret heaved a heavy sigh. She followed her twins back through the house, past Peg, who only grinned, and out the front door to wait for Wrigley.

Margaret pushed back the window curtain as Wrigley pulled out of traffic and came to a stop. The unpleasant but familiar scent of the harbor filled the carriage. She opened the door and found Ayden waiting, his gelding already tied to the back of the rig.

"I find my stomach tied in knots," she admitted as Ayden helped her from the carriage.

"That would make two of us," he replied. "At least." His gaze slid to the twins exiting the carriage.

Jason helped both girls alight from the carriage as Jimmy Leigh stepped down from the bench beside Wrigley.

The ship waiting in the harbor was sleek and foreign. Her flag was red with the British Union Jack in the corner. An unusual star emblem graced the center with a majestic crown floating above it.

Magi Rakesh met the three couples on the gangplank. His thin black hair carried a good deal of gray at the temples, and his visage was careworn, but proud. He smiled, carved from charisma — but his eyes lingered a beat too long on Ayden, measuring, weighing, as though counting something long overdue.

"Come aboard," The Magi said, opening his arms as he bowed low. "We have much to discuss and many pleasant surprises."

The captain's cabin was quiet and comfortable. It smelled faintly of exotic spices and salt.

Ayden's expression darkened. "You have some nerve, Rakesh. Twenty years under magical bondage, and when I left, you sent a damned *Earth-elemental* to kill me. Then you have the gall to act like I wouldn't kill you on sight."

"I never wanted you dead, my son," he said as he turned to face Ayden. He bowed his head. "I wanted to wish you farewell with thanks for your many years of service, and to give you your share."

Ayden stared at his former captor, fire skipping across his knuckles as distrust and confusion rippled across his face.

Margaret squeezed his arm. *Be steady my love.*

"You were like my child or younger brother," Rakesh added more quietly. "And you ran when the bond unexpectedly released—without even a good-bye. I admit, I was... furious with you and filled with grief that you would flee like you did. But I never wanted you dead." He pulled an envelope from his coat. It was thick. "Your earnings from twenty years, along with my gratitude." He held it out. "This is yours. Take it."

Margaret released his arm as Ayden stepped forward.

He weighed the envelope's heft without opening it. Uncertainty clashed with anger, hesitation haunted eyes. "What if I would rather have those twenty years back?"

"That, I am not able to give. Besides, you were not the only one bound by *blood magic*." Hooded eyes challenged Ayden's. "I would have given us both our freedom, but I could not, any more than you could." The Magi stepped back and bowed. "All I can offer is my regret at not confiding this to you while you were still with me, my sincere gratitude for your years of service, and your share, earned from our partnership."

When Ayden made no response, the man nodded toward the back of the room. "There are others here who wish to speak with you."

The curtain separating the sleeping quarters moved, and a barefoot, tanned, long-haired pirate entered. A scar ravaged the left side of his face and neck and extended to his shoulder on that side. "Don't all rush to greet me at once." Then the pirate smiled.

Margaret's world shifted and she gasped. Immediately, her gaze turned to Ayden.

What will he say?

Amy drew her attention as she staggered, her hand to her mouth. "Papa?"

Robert caught her as she flew into his arms.

Amy clung to him, tears spilled freely as she laughed and cried. "You're alive. I thought you were gone."

Robert held her tight, his voice rough with emotion. "We nearly were. But Hal and I survived the wreck. A merchant vessel found us adrift near the Hebrides. Rather than return to Glasgow, their vessel continued to the Far East." He looked up from Amy to Margaret. "While at sea, the ship's doctor tended to us and saved our lives. Once we docked in Bombay, we ran into Magi Rakesh in a port tavern. Upon further conversation, it seems we had an acquaintance in common."

Jason stood frozen beside the table. His voice was barely a whisper. "This is unbelievable."

Ayden crossed his arms, still tense. "Why didn't you send word?"

"By the time we *could* send word," Robert continued, "we were half a world away." He stepped back from Amy and addressed them all. "We were barely alive, and the crew didn't know our names. When we recovered and heard the news of *Atlantia's* loss, we were already presumed dead. I was shocked—and freed in a way I'd never known." Robert's gaze begged Margaret to understand. "In truth, I wanted to stay dead."

His gaze swept the room, then landed on Alyse. He stared, startled. "What is this?"

Alyse stepping forward with a soft smile. "I'm Alyse. Amy's twin."

Robert blinked. "We have *two* daughters?" He looked from Margaret to Amy, stunned. "Why didn't I know?"

Amy shrugged with a tearful laugh. "We came to Boston to tell you, but you had already set sail."

Margaret pulled a handkerchief from her bag and pressed it to her mouth as a bittersweet sob escaped her throat.

Robert looked between the two girls, still trying to grasp what he was seeing. "Identical. My God..."

Jimmy Leigh stepped beside Alyse, offering Robert a polite nod. "We've never met, sir. I'm Jimmy Leigh. Alyse and I—we're engaged to be married."

Robert blinked again, slowly nodding. "Congratulations, son. Seems I've missed quite a lot."

Margaret advanced, anger and guilt tightened her chest. "Robert, we mourned you. Do you have any idea what your death did to me? To your daughter?"

"I couldn't have helped that." Robert lowered his head. "And in all honesty, all that was Robert Prescott before the shipwreck *is* dead."

Margaret's throat tightened so hard she couldn't speak.

Hal joined Robert, taking his hand. "And we don't have to hide anymore."

Amy wiped her eyes and looked from her father to her mother. "What does that mean?"

Margaret swallowed hard. *Oh, my sweet, innocent daughter, that will be a hard conversation.*

Robert addressed Margaret, his voice sincere and soft. "I'm not staying in Boston, Margaret. I'm not even going to get off the ship. I can't. My life is out there, and yours is here." He tipped his head at Ayden. "You know, this is for the best."

Margaret blinked slowly. "But you're still my husband."

"No. Not anymore," Robert said gently. "The authorities have declared Robert Prescott dead. You have the papers. Consider that declaration the truth, bury him and get on with your life." His somber demeanor lightened and he smiled, "But if you ever want to write..." His grin widened as he pulled a card from his coat pocket and pressed it into her hand. "Address your correspondence to Bob Devi. Hal and I have a bungalow just outside of Bombay."

Hal's hand never left Robert's, fingers curled there like an anchor, as though letting go might send them both back to the sea.

Margaret gulped and blinked. A deep steady sadness filled her heart, but it held room for future happiness.

Perhaps this is best—for both of us.

Margaret stared at the card, then at him, then let out a long breath she hadn't realized she'd been holding. Her chest eased even as tears streamed down her face.

Her lips trembled. "Then I guess this really is goodbye, my dear Rob. I shall always miss you."

He gave her a sad smile. "Goodbye, Margaret. Bob Devi hopes you will write and come visit."

Robert stepped forward and enfolded Margaret in his embrace.

She kissed the side of his face, then stepped back into the solid protection that was Ayden.

"But I don't want you to leave." Amy gripped her father's hand. "You must stay."

"I cannot, my sweet child. Anyway, you will return to your beautiful Colorado ranch with your husband. You know I love you." He hugged Amy one last time, then returned her to Jason's side.

Together, Robert and Hal stepped into the corridor, the cabin door swinging shut behind them with a quiet click.

Silence in the room held for several moments, then Rakesh bowed again, opened the door, and preceded them from the cabin. "We will remain in port for a few weeks. However, I do have passenger cabins available if any would like to return with me to India when we depart." He stopped at the gangway. "And I am still in need of either a partner or an apprentice. Perhaps both." He bowed a last time and held out his hand to Ayden. "Again, you have my humble thanks for your time in my service."

Ayden took his hand, but the Magi pulled him close and hugged him. "I have missed you these years, my son. I am glad you found your Margaret."

Ayden stepped back after they embraced and glanced at Margaret. "As am I. Go in peace, Rakesh."

"And you as well, my young prodigy."

Chapter 43

The Garden Vow

Alyse James

The house brimmed with the scents of lavender and lemon balm. Decorative linens trimmed the armchairs, and a crisp lace-edged tea cloth covered the dining room table. Wildflowers—cut just that morning—spilled from stone urns near the door.

Peg and Margaret had spent hours arranging petals down the short path to the garden. The new trellis, decked in ivy and soft white ribbon, framed a flower-bedecked altar. Everything gleamed in the late afternoon sun.

Inside, guests gathered with a hush that wasn't silence but reverence.

Alyse waited in her gown at the top of the stairs, pale white silk pooling like cream around her feet. Peg had twisted her auburn hair into delicate braids, pinning them with sprigs of rosemary and rosebuds. A single sapphire shimmered at her throat, and atop her head rested the silver and pearl tiara Amy had worn as a bride—its matching earrings catching the light with every breath. She smiled at her uncle.

Bayard offered his arm with a proud smile. "Ready?"

She took it, squeezing once. "Now I am."

Uncle Bay used to play tea party with me when I was little.

They descended the stairs together.

At the bottom, Bernard waited in the entryway. He smiled—gentle and wide—and bowed slightly when Bayard placed Alyse's hand in his.

"My turn," Bernard said.

Alyse laughed softly through the emotion that tightened her chest.

Uncle Bern taught me the fundamentals of fire-magic.

Together, she and Bernard crossed the dining room and entered the back garden through the kitchen door. Bayard followed a step behind, silent and beaming.

On the porch, Ayden waited. He took Alyse's hand from Bernard without a word, and for a moment, his eyes glistened. He didn't speak, but his silence brimmed with pride.

He's the father I found, and despite the years lost, a bond has taken root between us.

Ayden smiled, kissed her forehead, and tucked her arm into his. "You've chosen a good man."

"I know I have—father." Alyse swallowed a sudden tightening in her throat as their gazes met.

The guests gathered in a wide crescent beneath the old hawthorn tree, awaiting her arrival.

Jimmy Leigh stood before the trellis in a black coat and open-collared shirt, his dark hair caught by the breeze.

Garrett Brown waited at his side; the judge's black robes draped in seasonal flora.

Ayden walked Alyse the final steps, then placed her hand into Jim's hand with quiet ceremony.

"Take care of her," Ayden said, voice steady but thick with feeling.

"I always have," Jim murmured, never looking away from Alyse. "And I always will."

Garrett's deep voice carried across the garden: "Rings have been given as promises and sureties since early times. Magical and never-ending, a ring has no beginning and no end. Like the ring, true love itself is infinite. It goes on, defying boundaries and restrictions. It flourishes and blooms both in the light and in the dark.

"Love is a gift freely given to each other and to the deepest parts of ourselves—a sacred trust offered with heart and soul.

"Today, we ask the infinite light of our Lord and Lady to shine upon this union and allow me to bless this ceremony and the rings I hold."

He raised his hand, palm up. The two rings gleamed like stars.

From across the yard, two sparks of light flew over the guests' heads. Dancing joyously, they cavorted momentarily before dropping down to touch each ring in Garrett's hand. Blessing bestowed, then floated to the ground near the base of the alter, becoming two black cats, content to watch the night's events unfold.

Garrett smiled at the faerie felines and then continued. "Bless this marriage with the gifts of the East. Bring this couple a lifetime of bright beginnings that renew each day with the sun's rising. Grant them communication of the heart, mind, body, and soul.

"Bless this marriage with the gifts of the South. Provide them with richness in their souls, a light in their hearts, the heat of passion, and the warmth and comfort of a loving home.

"Bless this marriage with the gifts of the West. Show them the soft and pure cleansing of a rainstorm, the rushing excitement of a river, and a commitment as deep as the ocean itself.

"Bless this marriage with the gifts of the North. Allow them to build a solid foundation for their lives, the abundance and growth of their home, and the steadiness of holding one another at the end of each day."

A hush fell across the garden. The air itself seemed to hold its breath.

Garrett nodded to Jimmy Leigh. "Take the ring you chose for Alyse."

Jim took the silver band from Garrett's hand. "Alyse," he said, "I promise you my honor and fidelity. I will share your laughter and your joy. I will support you in times of need and stand beside you when darkness comes. I will dream with you, hope with you, and love you more with every passing day."

He slipped the ring onto her finger.

Garrett turned to her. "Alyse, please take the ring you chose for Jim."

Alyse lifted the gold band in trembling fingers. "I promise to walk with you in light and in shadow. I'll hold your hopes, your burdens, and your joy. I'll stand beside you in times of trouble and hold your hand in peace. I'll love you fiercely, every day more than the last."

She slid the ring onto his hand.

"Your vows are spoken. Your promises made," Garrett said. "Now, if you would take each other's left hands, holding your rings close. Over your left hands, take each other's right hand."

From beside the trellis, Peg stepped forward and offered the long white ribbon she'd saved from Alyse's bouquet.

Garrett took it and gently wrapped their joined wrists, tying a loose knot.

"This ribbon is a symbol of your life, your love, and the eternal connection you have made. The true bond is not in this ribbon or this knot—but in your words and your hearts, now bound together as one.

"By the power of your love and commitment, and the blessings of those gathered here, I now pronounce you husband and wife."

Jimmy Leigh leaned down and kissed Alyse—a soft, steady kiss that deepened as the garden broke into applause.

Garrett unwound the ribbon without untying the knot and raised his hands.

"May I present Mr. and Mrs. Leigh!"

When Alyse stepped back to smile at the guests, she caught Amy's eye across the garden. Her sister was crying openly now, smiling through it, and for a moment the noise of the guests faded until there was only that look—shared history, shared survival, shared joy.

The final notes of the celebration's music drifted in the warm fall air, laughter trailing behind the guests as they gathered in the garden once more. Alyse stood near the trellis, her gown glowing in the candlelight, bouquet in hand.

"Alright," she called, smiling at the small group behind her. "Are you ready?"

Peg, Margaret, and Lisbeth stood in a loose cluster, hands at their sides, and their eyes half-rolled in good humor.

"No cheating," Alyse warned, giving the bouquet a practiced spin.

She turned and tossed it high over her shoulder.

The silence in the garden thickened as the spray of white roses and rosemary arced through the air—and landed neatly in Lisbeth's hands.

Everyone gasped and laughed. Peg clapped. Amy whooped.

Lisbeth blinked down at the bouquet, startled. "I didn't even reach for it."

"That means it was meant for you," Margaret said gently, her voice warm with meaning.

Lisbeth's smile flickered, then settled into something softer, something hopeful.

Chapter 44

With Quiet Promise

Ayden MacKenna

From beside the trellis, Ayden listened to the laughter ripple through the garden.

I discovered my daughter, only to give her away.

Ironically, the thought made him smile. He lifted his gaze to his loved ones enjoying themselves in Margaret's back yard.

The soft glow of lanterns danced across familiar faces—Peg and Melvyn seated on the steps, Amy leaning into Jason, Jimmy Leigh with one arm snug around Alyse's waist.

But it was Lisbeth who drew his gaze now. Her silver braid shimmered in the candlelight; the bouquet pressed awkwardly to her chest as Bernard drifted to her side. The moment hung with quiet promise.

Garrett's voice broke the silence beside him. "She'll make a fine leader someday."

Ayden nodded slowly, hands tucked behind his back. "She already does."

Isaac joined them near the edge of the garden, his arm still in a sling. Though gaunt from his injuries, the fire in his eyes hadn't dimmed. "Some from my former circle are asking for guidance," he said. "Some wonder who will lead now that I've stepped away."

Garrett exhaled. "It won't be me. I've served my time, and I've no wish to shape another generation."

"We've no place large enough to gather," Ayden began, then stopped when Margaret cleared her throat.

"I bought the farm, Ayden. Garrett's old place. Years ago, when it first went up for sale. I've kept it up. The land's still strong."

He turned to her slowly, something caught between disbelief and admiration rising in his chest. "Of course you did," he murmured.

Margaret smiled. "I couldn't let it go. It holds so many of my most precious memories."

Ayden was about to respond when he noticed Bernard stepping toward Isaac, the bouquet still in Lisbeth's arms like a silent herald of what was coming.

"Mr. Coleman," Bernard said, his voice low and steady. "I would ask your blessing—if you'll give it—to marry your daughter."

Ayden could feel the hush fall like dew over the garden. Isaac studied Bernard for a long moment, his expression unreadable, then glanced at Lisbeth. Her cheeks were pink, but her chin lifted in that proud, defiant way that reminded Ayden of Margaret.

"You would make her happy?" Isaac asked.

Bernard didn't hesitate. "Every day, sir. Or die trying."

Isaac's mouth twitched—not quite a smile, not quite forgiveness. But close. "Then you have my blessing. You had it the moment she smiled like that." Isaac shook his head and chuckled. "Who would have guessed my daughter would marry one of the infamous James twins. Ha! I need a drink."

"Beverages are in the dining room," Margaret laughed.

Ayden let out a quiet breath and turned toward Margaret.

She caught his glance and arched a brow again. "Don't look at me like that."

"Like what?"

"Like you just remembered you love me."

"Oh that." Ayden took her hand and lifted it to his lips. "I never forget that." *I've carried that torch since I was no more than a child.*

Before Margaret could reply, Wrigley cleared his throat from the edge of the garden path. He leaned on a new cane, eyes twinkling, hat tucked respectfully beneath one arm.

"Well now," Wrigley remarked with a wink at Margaret, "weddings blooming everywhere you look. I can't help but wonder when *Mrs. Prescott* might find herself walking down the aisle again."

Margaret arched one brow. "Is that so?"

Ayden felt every eye in the garden shift toward him. He met Wrigley's gaze first, then looked at Margaret.

Her expression was amused—but there was something hopeful behind it. Something unspoken that had waited too long.

Ayden stepped forward, heart thudding. "I suppose now's the time," he said softly. He reached into his coat pocket and withdrew a small band of silver—nothing ornate, just a perfect, simple circle.

Margaret stared as he sank to one knee on the flagstones, the same stones where they'd shared coffee and love in all its strange, stubborn forms. The stone was solid and cool beneath his knee.

"Margaret Prescott," he said, steady now, steady in the only way that mattered. "Will you do me the honor of becoming my wife?"

She didn't answer right away; she just looked at him and through him, as if seeing every year they had lost and every year they still had. "Yes," she said finally. "Of course I will."

Cheers erupted around the garden.

Garrett stepped forward, his voice calm but resolute. "Then let's not waste good moonlight."

He raised both hands. "If the bride and groom will come forward."

Laughter rippled through the group as Margaret took Ayden's hand and pulled him to his feet.

They faced Garrett with hands joined; lanterns swayed gently above them. He didn't ask for rings. He didn't need to read any vows aloud. When he spoke, his voice carried everything that mattered. "By the light of the moon and the strength of your bond—this union is made sacred. This is not a beginning but a continuation. A reunion of two hearts long intertwined."

He touched their joined hands with a folded ribbon pulled from his coat pocket, the same type of pale ribbon used in handfasting—and tied a single knot.

"Let no shadow fall between you," Garrett said. "Only light."

Then he stepped back.

Margaret smiled. "Well?"

Ayden grinned. "With pleasure."

Their kiss was soft but sure. The kind of kiss meant to seal something not just in spirit but in stone.

Around them, the garden hummed. Laughter sparked like fireflies.

Alyse clapped, Amy wiped her eyes, and Wrigley tipped his hat toward the stars. "About damned time I say."

Margaret leaned into Ayden's side and whispered, "Now everything is accounted for."

Ayden smiled as he breathed in the scent of her hair. "At last."

Chapter 45

Loose Ends

Ayden MacKenna

Ayden unfolded the note, smoothing the parchment with his thumb as he read it for the tenth time.

Ayden—

I'd like to meet you tonight. I'll come to Revere's by eight.

I hope you don't mind if I bring Bayard.

—Bernard

He folded the message with care and slipped it into his breast pocket.

The sun had long since dipped below the rooftops, and Revere's Tavern pulsed with low, warm light and the hum of conversation.

Ayden chose a table near the bar with a clear view of the front door. Not out of caution—there were no more watchers, no dark-eyed figures loitering across the street—but his old habits seemed to die hard.

Their absence comforts me more than it should.

The tavern's main room smelled of bread, beer, and hearthstone. Behind the bar, Harry and Melvyn poured drinks and wiped down polished counters, working in tandem.

Glenda wove through the crowd, her tray steady and her smile sharp.

The door opened with a gust of cool evening air. Bernard and Bayard stepped inside, dressed like proper Brahmins out for an evening in Boston. Pressed waistcoats, cravats, polished shoes—no hint of their past as frontiersmen or witches.

Ayden stood as they approached. "Bernard, Bayard," he greeted them, clasping each man's hand in turn. "You look like you're headed for the opera."

Bayard grinned. "We came to make you nervous."

"It's working," Ayden said dryly as they took their seats.

Bernard leaned forward, folding his hands on the table. "Apologies for the cryptic message. I wanted to speak with both of you at the same time."

Ayden tilted his head. "Couldn't Bay have just read your mind on the way here?"

"No." Bayard snorted. "Bernard's blocked our bond. He only allows it when absolutely necessary."

Bernard gave a sheepish shrug. "It wouldn't be fair to Lisbeth. Not anymore. She deserves someone who's wholly present, not sharing thoughts with his twin in the background."

Bayard nodded. "Understandable."

Ayden raised a brow. "So what's this about?"

Bernard's gaze settled on Ayden, then flicked to Bayard. "I wanted to tell you both that I've decided to sail with Rakesh when he returns to India."

Ayden blinked. *I never saw this in the fire.*

Bayard sat straighter. "What? What about Lisbeth?"

"She's anxious to go," Bernard said, smiling faintly. "We've spoken at length. I've agreed to serve as Rakesh's apprentice and partner for two years. It's a written contract—not a blood-bond like Chantal used on Ayden."

Bayard exhaled slowly. "Well. This is a surprise."

Bernard looked at his twin. "And you? Do you plan to return to Colorado?"

"Not yet." Bayard shook his head. "Furniture can wait. I've decided to head north. I'll take the train to Toronto and see what's left of our old homestead. Maybe put up a headstone for mother or rebuild the woodshop there instead."

Ayden smiled. "I believe Chantal would like that."

A quiet moment passed with the three of them surrounded by Revere's familiar clink and chatter.

"I suppose my news pales in comparison," Ayden said finally. "Harry's given his notice. He finally took that job aboard a merchant ship."

"When will he leave?" Bay asked.

"He sails to London in two weeks."

Behind the bar, Harry laughed at something Glenda said as he topped off a frothy pint. Melvyn worked beside him, focused, steady.

"Mel's agreed to train with him until he leaves," Ayden added. "He'll take over as bartender once Harry's gone."

Bayard raised his glass. "Then to new journeys."

Bernard followed suit. "And bright horizons."

Ayden clinked his glass to theirs, and for the first time in weeks, he allowed himself to feel a flicker of peace.

"Bernard," he said, turning slightly toward him, "since you're headed to India, I need to ask a favor."

"Of course." Bernard set down his glass. "What do you need?"

Ayden lowered his voice. "The *fire-elemental* I carry—Caz—I've been trying to explain to him that I believe he'd be happier if he were released in his home desert." He hesitated. "As far as I can tell, he agrees."

Bernard's brows rose. "And you'd like me to release him?"

"I would," Ayden said. "Somewhere far inland, where the air burns and other *elementals* roam. A place where he won't be feared or bound."

"I see." Bernard nodded slowly. "How do I release him?"

"I'm not quite sure," Ayden admitted. "I'll ask Miera. She may know more than I do. I'll find out before you sail."

Bernard's expression turned thoughtful. "We depart at high tide, at the end of the week. I'll do it, Ayden. I'll set Caz free."

"I appreciate your help," Ayden said quietly.

They sat for a moment longer, three brothers bound by spilled blood, choice, and a woman they all love.

Ayden opened the door to the apartment above Revere's. Melvyn had officially taken over and was busy turning the space into something between a laboratory and a storage closet. Ayden didn't mind—he liked knowing someone was there, someone curious and kind and sharp around the edges. He walked through the small residence one last time and closed the door, not bothering to set a ward, and headed downstairs. He waved to Melvyn behind the bar as he passed and stepped outside to hail a cab.

Tonight, he returned to Margaret's home for good.

My home.

On Beacon Hill, Ayden stepped into the dining room and paused, listening to the stillness. The faint scent of rosemary and hearth ash lingered from the afternoon tea. Outside, the wind rustled the hawthorn hedges and scattered leaves. Inside, the only sound was the soft creak of the floor beneath his boots.

Ayden lit a candle on the mantle with a thought. The flame curled to life, small and golden.

"Miera," he said quietly. "I could use your counsel."

The air shifted. The candle's flame bowed to one side, then stilled. A warmth stirred in his chest—Miera's magic, her presence. He closed his eyes.

I am here, Ayden. What can I help you vith?

"I want to release Caz," Ayden said, moving the candle to the table and taking a seat. "He's not meant to be mine forever. Not like this."

I see. A silent pause as Miera considered—then: *First, you must ask him if that is what he wants. Then, after your elemental friend is freed, you must smash the amulet to break ze binding spell.*

"Thank you, Miera," Ayden replied, and Miera ended the communication.

Ayden pulled the sunstone amulet from his shirt. It pulsed faintly in his palm. "Caz," he whispered, "come if you're willing."

The stone flared. A spark spilled from the surface, then grew into a flickering, ember-bodied figure no taller than Ayden's hand. The little elemental, all wick and flame, blinked up at him with eyes like polished coal.

Ayden leaned forward. "I want to set you free. In the desert. In your home. Do you understand?"

Caz spun in a slow, joyful circle on the table. The fire on his head crackled like laughter. Then he nodded, his glowing face serious, and bowed once.

"Good," Ayden said softly. "Soon. Bernard will carry you there and release you."

Caz tilted his head in understanding, then tucked his flickering arms inward.

Ayden held out the amulet, and the little flame-being folded into it, vanishing with a spark and a breath of heat.

The room dimmed again. Ayden exhaled and held the stone against his chest for a moment. "Thank you," he whispered.

The docks were bright with the morning sun. Salt air mixed with the scent of pitch and fish. Gulls cried overhead, but the water was calm and golden-tipped.

Rakesh's ship rocked gently in the tide, freshly scrubbed and flying no colors today but his own.

Ayden stood with Margaret beside him. Amy and Jason and Alyse and Jim flanked them. Wrigley leaned on his cane nearby. Peg's arm hooked through Melvyn's. Helena and Isaac lingered slightly apart, their hands barely touching.

Lisbeth paused as she looked over the group gathered to bid farewell. She wore tailored pantaloons of pale cotton beneath a long, fitted tunic and short traveling jacket. Low-heeled boots scuffed from real use, her unadorned silver braid hung down her back.

Bernard beamed with pride as he stood beside her in his gray wool traveling suit and bowler.

Lis approached Margaret first. For a moment, she didn't speak. She simply studied her—really looked at her—as if committing her to memory. The sunlight off the waves caught the silver in Lisbeth's braid, but her gaze was steady, unguarded.

"You saved me from burning when you believed no one else would. You didn't need to do that. And later, after I revealed my true face, you never asked me to be smaller," Lisbeth said quietly. "Or quieter. Or easier. Or different."

Margaret's breath caught, just slightly.

"You allowed me to remain in your home when it would have been simpler, perhaps even safer to send me away," Lisbeth continued. She flashed a wry smile at Bernard. "You taught me to have faith in unlikely alliances, and to trust my heart."

Margaret reached for her hand, but Lisbeth caught it first and squeezed.

"You didn't try to change me," Lisbeth said. "You just gave me space to decide who I was going to be." Her voice softened. "That mattered more than you know."

Margaret swallowed. "It mattered to me too."

Lisbeth nodded, accepting that without ceremony. Then she leaned in and embraced her—firm, brief, and real.

Margaret brushed her thumb across Lisbeth's knuckles. "Then go," she said gently. "Give yourself the opportunity to explore the entire world, with love by your side."

Lisbeth smiled at that—small, genuine—and turned to the others.

To Jason, she inclined her head, a spark of old mischief flashing briefly in her eyes. "Try not to underestimate the quiet ones," she said. "They tend to notice everything."

"Or the big ones." Jason huffed a soft laugh. "I learned that lesson the hard way."

To Amy, Lisbeth stepped closer, lowering her voice. "You were never weak," she said simply. "Not once. Don't forget that."

Amy's throat tightened. She nodded, unable to answer.

Ayden met Lisbeth's gaze last. There was no need for many words between them.

"You stood beside me when others would have watched me die," he said.

"You offered me shelter, when others would have turned me away," Lis replied. Then after a beat. "Take care of them."

"I will," Ayden said. And meant it.

Finally, Lisbeth moved to Isaac and Helena. Her father stepped forward, the lines of pain and pride etched deep into his face.

"I thought I'd never get to say goodbye to you properly," Isaac said. "I never dreamed it would be like this." He tipped his head toward the ship.

"I know. And I wasn't sure I wanted to," Lisbeth admitted, her voice wavering. "But I do. I love you, Papa. I always have."

Isaac's voice cracked. "And I love you. I failed you in so many ways, but I never stopped being proud of you."

"You did your best with what you knew," Lisbeth said gently. "Listen to my mother. She has your best interests at heart."

Both Isaac and Helena laughed.

Helena embraced her, wordless and firm, a quiet anchor in the tide of emotion.

"We'll write," Lisbeth promised as she pulled back. "From every port."

"And we'll be here," Helena said. "Every time."

Bernard appeared at Lisbeth's side and offered his hand. She took it and together they stepped toward the gangplank.

Ayden walked forward and placed the amulet around Bernard's neck.

The flicker of light within the stone fluttered and changed its beat, then settled.

"Find the right place for him. A wild, free place. Somewhere he can burn without fear. Once he's free, Miera says to smash the stone."

Bernard nodded solemnly. "I will."

Bayard stepped forward, hugged Bernard hard, and then tipped his hat to Lisbeth. "Write me from wherever you land. Toronto gets lonely, too."

Rakesh approached last, his long coat catching the breeze. He bowed to the group but looked at Ayden. "One final time—I am sorry. I meant never to betray you."

Ayden extended his hand. "We were both bound. We're free now."

They shook hands—firm, brief—no additional words needed.

After another round of embraces, final words, and misty smiles, Bernard helped Lisbeth up the gangplank. Rakesh boarded behind them. A crewman called commands, and the sails began to fill.

The foreign ship creaked as it shifted away from the dock.

Margaret stood rooted beside Ayden, her hand wrapped in his, watching her brother sail away.

Ayden exhaled. "Well. I suppose that's everything settled."

"Almost," Margaret said.

Ayden turned toward her with a curious look.

She gave him a sheepish smile. "You've been wondering who owns Revere's Tavern."

"I have. No one has notified me about that at all."

She cleared her throat. "That's because I bought it from Marion. Quietly. Months ago."

Ayden blinked, surprised. "You bought Revere's?"

"I forgot to tell you." Margaret shrugged with an impish grin.

He laughed softly. "You didn't forget. You waited for the right moment."

"I did," she said. "And this feels right."

Ayden turned to face her fully. The harbor breeze tugged at her hair, and he brushed it back gently.

This is everything I've ever wanted.

Then he kissed her.

From the docks, with sails shrinking into the sunrise, they watched their family move into a new chapter—while behind them, the door to Revere's stood open, the hearth waiting, and the future unfolding like sunlight over the sea.

Sneak Peek at Aubrielle's Call

If you enjoyed the world of the *Soul of the Witch Saga*, continue J.L.'s journey in

— • —

Aubrielle's Call
A full-length novel in *J.L.'s Timeless Quest Series*.
Additional Timeless Quest stories explore J.L.'s earlier adventures through a collection of short fiction.

— • —

In 1939 Europe rushed toward war.
Consumed with grief over the death of his soulmate, immortal John Larson trades his spurs for the scent of the sea and the life of a merchant sailor.
Condemned by an ancient curse, he must wait for her rebirth, the threat to her life, and the magical summons that calls him to her side.
In the heart of Paris, Aubrielle Cohen struggles to survive. Resolved to support her dying father, she sells flowers from a horse-drawn cart to tourists now fleeing the approaching war.
Beneath the Eiffel Tower, she learns a hard lesson about trust and meets a stranger whose presence evokes a yearning she cannot explain.
As the Nazi war machine prepares to invade France, John must gain Aubrielle's trust, defend her life, and rekindle the passion he hopes still stirs deep within her heart.

Also by

Soul of the Witch Saga

Prodigy — Book 1

Pyromancer — Book 2

Passage — Book 3

Prophecy — Book 4

Paradox — Book 5

Patriarch — Book 6

—

J.L.'s Timeless Quest

Aubrielle's Call

The Corsair's Tempest

Hawthorn and Mistletoe

—

The Hunter Chronicles

Hunter's Gamble

Hunter and Lily Graham

The Kid in Black

Penelope's Heart

All of these stories take place within the same shared universe.

About the Author

C. (Connie) Marie Bowen writes paranormal romance and historical fantasy set within a richly layered, persistent universe. Her award-winning novel *Passage* launched the *Soul of the Witch* series, introducing a world where magic, loyalty, and sacrifice intertwine.

Bowen's stories span multiple series, with characters crossing paths and timelines within the shared universe of the Soul of the Witch Saga. Figures such as Hunter from *The Hunter Chronicles* and J.L. from *The Timeless Quest* play meaningful roles within this interconnected world.

Born in Denver, Colorado, Bowen grew up with a love of ghost stories and storytelling. She now lives in the greater Chicagoland area with her husband and two rescue pets, Abigail and Rousseaux.

Visit https://www.cmariebowen.com to explore her connected series and learn more.